Seasons o'Steeas

by

Mike Silkstone

UNDEAD TREE

Undead Tree Publications
9 Normanby Terrace, Whitby, North Yorkshire, YO21 3ES, England.
http://www.undeadtree.com

ISBN 978-1-898728-20-7

2   3   4   5   6   7   8   9

Set in Garamond by Undead Tree Publications.

Printed and distributed worldwide by Lulu.com

Contents

To Trevor, Ivan and Poll-Doll.

Part I   1901

There is a tide in the affairs of men
Which, taken at the flood, leads on to fortune:
Omitted, all the voyage of their life
Is bound in shallows and in miseries.
On such a full sea are we now afloat,
And we must take the current when it serves,
Or lose our ventures.

Julius Caesar, Act IV, scene 3.

Chapter 1

Sketchbook in hand, she stood at the edge of the quay watching the boats being launched on the evening tide. The sun behind the fossil-packed cliffs gilded the cloudy-red mackerel sky, casting deep-toned shadows of blues and mauves across the staithe where figures moved as only sea-booted, sou'westered fishermen could. A rolling gait, restless as their cruel master, now rocking and reflecting cobalt and indigo in the summer light.

A man with blackish, already-baited lines passed her, another with oars and floats looking like big balloons slung across his shoulder. Children and dogs darted here and there, while women, strong-armed, helped slide the cobles over the timbers. Then, when they were launched, would cry "she's afloat"—and the skipper-husband would stop pushing and fling himself over the stern.

Onlookers watched the sails unfurl, making a flash of contrasting colour against the sea and sky. Mainsail, mizzen and jib a daub of venetian on the water, till the coble disappeared round Penny Nab. Then came another, flaunting a mainsail of white and ochre that was suddenly bathed in beams of mustard as it sailed into them across the evening sun. Laura made colour notes at the side of her sketch: she must have things accurate.

When the last boat was launched and on open water, the wives, after a day of cooking, cleaning, caring for children and baiting lines with flithers (limpets) they had collected at first light, for relaxation—and as though by magic—produced knitting needles holding garments in various stages of completion. Guernseys done in the "Steeas" (Staithes) pattern—for each fishing village had its own—or stockings. Every item of clothing bore the owner's initials, should only part of the body be found following an accident at sea.

Laura had shuddered on first hearing this, but three years of living amongst the fishing community had given her some insight into their way of life. She had also been surprised to learn that very few of the fishermen could swim, for they believed that to be able to do that only took longer to drown—a logic particular to these fisherfolk.

A young girl walking past offered a shy "evenin' Miss Johnson."

Laura smiled, "It's Evelyn, isn't it?"

She nodded in reply, then Laura asked, "Is your dad out tonight?"

"And Adam. He says they'll be back with a net full. It's the 'errin' season."

"Mmm." Laura gave a knowing nod of acknowledgement. Both herself and Rosie, who she shared a house with, had lived on them for the past two weeks. Still, she consoled herself, it made a change from porridge, which often had to be the main part of their diet.

Evelyn had beautiful bone structure, and a confident deportment in one so young. Laura had on several occasions noted her carrying fish-nets as though she were a model, or on the quay, deftly gutting fish with sequin-scaled fingers. If her paintings sold at their forthcoming exhibition she would certainly ask Evelyn to pose for her—for she would be able to pay her.

Green emeralds of spume specked with topaz were splashing over the slipway, women were clicking messages on knitting needles, rounding a heel on the turn of the tide as Laura meandered from the staithe and into the High Street. The seductive evening shadows sidled, mounted then made love to the village to a mewling of gulls and the "kyowing" of the birds that gave Jackdaw Well its name. They were preening their feathers, parading—bowing their hooded heads as a prelude to their elaborate courting gavotte.

Outside the Cod & Lobster, old men smelling of rough shag and mermaids sucked on, or swore through, clay pipes, removing them only to spit black tar. A woman came from the shadows round and fruitful, while Old Rall, standing at her door collecting gossip greeted her with "now then."

The woman in shawl and bonnet stroked her belly. "If there's anoth-er, I'll droon misel'."

"Nea."

"Ah will, an' all. Men 'ave their way, then leeave t'women to bring 'em oop."

"Nea."

"'Usbands mun work, for theirs is easy. It's woman mun weep."

The matriarchal head shook in sympathy then, as Laura approached, Rall gave a discreet cough to signify that confidential business not for the ears of "coomers-in" was being discussed. She carried on past Bakehouse Yard where a pet monkey slept in a cot, the mongol child in its cage, then Barber Row, where the woman lived who drank laudanum. Laura had seen her only the once, but would not forget the red eyes and sallow face. On her left was Joseph Verrill's, a shop with a window full of sweets, and where treacle was sold straight from the barrel.

He sold everything. Oil-skins, ships chandlery, tallow and twine, wines and spirits, and also household provisions. He'd had a busy month, for during the days running up to "fair week," every housewife in the village (so it seemed to Laura) had made a dash to his shop for last-minute ingredients for their baking.

The air was already one delicious smell of spice cake, and there would also be gingerbread (made according to jealously guarded family recipes) curd tart, and—and just thinking about it made Laura's mouth water— blacklock pie. Made from prunes steeped in brandy and covered with an open latticed top. She'd never known such things before coming to Staithes.

She paused, remembering that afternoon three summers ago when, with Aunt West, her sister Sissie, friend Rosie, and Harold, a friend of the family whom she'd known from their Nottingham Art College days, the party arrived for their month's holiday to a village where houses clung like limpets to the cliff, before seeming to tumble into the sea, and where artists were already working. There were Isa and Robert Jobling. Isa, a striking figure of a woman who, at fifty, had already made a name for herself, and like her husband, had had works accepted by the Royal Academy. They had now forsaken Cullercoats, favouring this stretch of coast for their summer painting. And Hannah Hoyle, Fred Mayor and Richard Bagshawe were also names to be counted among other already established painters.

Since their leaving Art School, Harold had furthered his studies in Paris, at the *Academie Julien*, and was now an accomplished painter, whilst she (and she readily accepted this) was still "learning". After their month's holiday the girls returned to Nottingham, but Harold stayed, taking lodgings in Gun-Gutter with artists Arthur Friedenson, a Russian from St. Petersburg, and Fred Mayor. The following summer she'd returned with her friend (and now pupil) Rosie, and the two of them shared a "studio" on the quay, eventually installing themselves in a cottage at the top of the hill.

They had come to know this closely-knit inbred community. Been accepted by them: possibly through economic necessity on the part of the villagers. A sudden influx of artists renting near-derelict buildings as studios, needing models (fully clothed) and board and lodgings could augment the uncertain income derived from the precarious "living off the sea", and some of the group were now sufficiently established painters to be able to buy properties in the area. Henry Hopwood had built a house in nearby Hinderwell, William Booth had recently built a studio in the garden of his Scarborough home, while Richard Bagshawe was rumoured to be looking for a house in nearby Whitby, and these (the more success-ful painters) had connections with potential patrons. The prosperity of the late Victorian era had, in the Industrial North—for several of the group came from Yorkshire—created wealthy mill-owners and industrialists who were keen to buy pictures to grace their homes.

Paintings that reflected life as it was then.

Laura hoped such patrons would be at their forthcoming exhibition at the Fishermen's Institute, the first to be held by the newly-formed Staithes Art Club. Some of the members had previously exhibited with the Yorkshire Union of Artists, of which the Staithes Exhibition was a breakaway group, and Laura so hoped that she and Harold would sell their work. It was to be held later in the summer, after the Fair Week. Harold's pictures were finished, two of hers needed varnishing and framing.

Thinking about her canvases, and her painting of the wooden bridge that spanned the beck, Laura lingered, being only yards away from her subject. She'd heard tales… that on Friday nights the men stood at the bridge selling their wives for weekend beer money. Then, perturbed by such thoughts, Laura continued along the High Street. Past the Black Lion, the Wesleyan Chapel, then the Bethel, and almost opposite Bells Bank, there was yet another place of worship. Then there were the Primitive Methodists, where (because there was no organ) one of the locals led the singing. He'd stand, hand cupped over his ear to help him "Git 'pitch" and make various sounds till he hit on what he considered to be the correct note, and that the congregation must follow. Near the staithe was the Mission Church of St Peter the Fisherman, while at the top of the bank was the Catholic Church of Our Lady Star of the Sea. Laura marvelled that such a small community could support so many different faiths, and that among this seafaring people the Lord's Day was strictly observed. Even painting had to stop on Sundays, as some of the group had discovered to their cost, having had fish heads hurled at them for defiling the Sabbath. Neither her nor Harold had incurred such wrath, however, and as Laura began the steep ascent up the High Street, her thoughts moved from the fishermen who could be near the bridge hoping to do business, and to the young man in her life, Harold Knight.

He scraped his palate, cleaned his brushes, stood back and took a critical look at his work. The glazes he'd painstakingly applied had really brought the painting to life. They were crashing waves that were coming over the boat, not simply "water" and the Prussian green, albeit transparent, had given a depth and power to the picture. Glazes dried quickly. It would be ready in time for the exhibition. It might even sell.

Harold Knight was the son of an amateur painter, and on befriending Laura Johnson in their Nottingham student days, he discovered that not only did they share a love for painting, but that she also had an artist for a parent. Charlotte Johnson had studied in Paris, yet despite her revelations of that city, its artistic climate had little effect on him, for he was more drawn to the Johnsons as a family than by maternal artistic achievements.

Disregarding Charlotte's tales, he did study in Paris, only to return to Nottingham penniless, where he tried, not very successfully, to set up as a painter. Yet after six months of living in Staithes with two fellow artists, his work took on a different dimension. His painting *The Last Coble* had been accepted by the Royal Academy. He was becoming known and recognised. His work had sold at major exhibitions, and he supposed that one day soon... he would ask Laura to marry him.

Thinking of her, he hoped she wouldn't understand the double meanings in the song that he and Arthur were to sing at the show the artists were to perform for the Fair weekend. Fellow artist Frank Mason had written and was producing the show, sketches had been specially penned, favourite poems learned, songs rehearsed, the words slightly altered to make them topical and, although his own lines were bawdy toward the end, Frank had assured both men that it would "go down a treat."

Singing wasn't really Harold's forte: he preferred painting.

Reluctant to leave the staithe, Evelyn Dacre watched the last of the cobles disappear before slowly making her way toward High Barrass. She lingered by the Cod & Lobster, drawn by the lights and laughter, a world away from her own thoughts and memories. Then, suddenly feeling guilty at indulging in such self pity, she quickened her step and tried to put on a cheerful face. Hannah and David would be waiting for her, and there were still things to do, despite her elder sister having so successfully taken over the household chores. Perhaps Hannah was too busy to mention it, or was purposely avoided the subject, but it was twelve months to the day since mam had died.

Some days, Evelyn refused to accept her death, and she'd return to an empty house and tell herself that mam was with a neighbour, or in the outhouse, boiling crabs. Baiting lines, flither gathering on the rocks, helping dad put to sea, anything, save... dead! But there was no pretence tonight. As she'd watched dad and her brother Adam launch their coble, Evelyn was acutely reminded that "someone" was missing, and she again felt the loss of her mother just as painfully as she had the day of her funeral. It was easy, she told herself, for Hannah, for she worked relentlessly, looking after dad, Adam, herself, and David, their younger brother and now the baby of the family.

There had been other brothers. The twins, Mathew and Simon who had both died of cholera when they were infants. She remembered the two small coffins, and her aunt Bridie bossing everybody about and constantly reminding mam and dad that she was "payin' fer everythin'— even t'flowers". When mam died, they'd managed without aunt Bridie. Bridie had her hair scraped into a bun, wore heavy gold ear-rings that turned the pierced holes into slits and had, reputedly, chamber-pots full of sovereigns under her bed. Hannah said she'd also a spiteful tongue, and because her sister was twenty-three and looked after the house, she could say more or less what she wanted. Adam, her aunt's favourite, tall as a tree and with a copper mane was two years younger, and helped dad with the boat. He was sweet on their cousin Polly, and come Christmas, they were to be "promised".

She was next in the family, but at sixteen, had no thoughts about young men. Besides, when the time was right one of her uncles and dad (or perhaps Hannah) would arrange things. Hannah herself was… well, she was friendly with Capt Danvers-Griffiths, retired. While mam was still alive, Hannah would twice a week call at his villa at the top of the bank and scrub the house from top to bottom then bring home a bundle of dirty washing which would be returned spotless and starched on her next visit. When Evelyn had joked to Hannah that Capt Danvers-Griffiths was sweet on her, her sister had replied, "Eee, doy, that'd suit me lovely. For I'd rather be an old man's darlin' than a young man's slave any day."

Hannah had been busy all week in preparation for the fair, tidying the house for the influx of visitors, both friends and family. Fair Week was special, for it was a time when family grievances were put aside, or buried, and when the house needed to look its best. There were new antimacassars to put on the chairs, white nets for the windows, and a tab rug for in front of the hearth. Brass candlesticks and copper kettles had been given an extra good clean, oil lamps were fettled and their wicks trimmed, and the most important thing, the big black sweet cake had been baked. Too important to be trusted to the kitchen range, it had, (as had the others in the village) been mixed then rushed to the bake-house. Hannah had also baked gingerbread, which needed to be made in advance for it to "come again". Then, nearer the day itself there would be shortcake, curd tarts, sponge cakes, tea-breads and all the other things that mam used to bake. Earlier that evening they'd sat down to another of mam's specialities, ling pie. Made with hard boiled eggs, and rashers of streaky bacon laid on top before putting the crust on.

Also bubbling in the copper used for boiling crabs was a whole ham, a yearly present from uncle Reuben who had an allotment at the side of the beck and always killed a "Grecian" for the fair. He collected their scraps to feed the animal on, and the ham was a "thank you". Neither of the sisters cared much for uncle Reuben. He had roaming eyes and, according to Hannah, straying hands. Uncle Reuben had married his cousin, Hephzibah Merrill, a woman with a hawk-like profile and tired eyes under tired tulip-petal eyelids. She was meek and sallow, and had the beginnings of a moustache to suit her black plaited head of hair. Their marriage had been blessed with two daughters, Patience and Prudence, and there was a son, Jonas, who, according to village gossip had been sired by Hephzibah's brother. Near Hannah's age, and uncle Reuben was not only looking to find him a wife, but was looking in Hannah's direction. Overtures had been made, but, thankfully for Hannah, her father, claiming that she was indispensable to the smooth-running of his family had turned down the proposal. The two sisters had laughed as they watched their uncle walk away disappointed, for they were so relieved.

To have to marry Jonas Dacre!

"Inbreedin' keeps t'brass in t'family," Adam had commented, "but nature charges a terrible price." Yet in Staithes, to marry one's cousin was the accepted thing. There were also other customs to be strictly observed by this fishing community. A fisherman must never launch, or put new gear onto a boat on a Friday, must never put to sea if on his way to his boat he were to meet a woman, don't wear white (or whistle) at sea, never mention the work "pig"—it was "a Grecian"—and most important for the womenfolk, one must never wind wool after dark, as this would wind fishermen to their graves.

They had another belief. A man who is not afraid of the sea will soon be drowned—in Staithes that had been proved correct on more than one occasion.

The Fair Week gave way to autumn and misty mornings, when sea and sky merged into one, becoming a haloed vision of infinite remoteness. The now grey waters lethargically swelled the beck and licked the boats moored to the wooden struts of the bridge. In it's more energetic moods the sea, like a bad tempered monster foaming at the mouth would hiss, and spit driftwood onto the staithe, to be dragged above the waterline for winter fuel. The days grew shorter, and angry breakers like frothy yeast raced and spewed over the slipway and up Church Street. Then it was Christmas, culminating in a special New Year's Eve celebration for the "promising" of Adam and Polly. He was now twenty-two and had a part-share in his father's boat. Polly, in a family of two sisters and eight brothers all of whom were unmarried, was seventeen, pink cheeks and blonde ringlets, and constantly giggling.

Her brothers were regarded as "troublemakers", and this was a branch of the Dacre family tree that the villagers tried to avoid. Her sister, Lucy, to be free of them, had married a man twice her age who, when he was drunk, would beat her face to squashed plums, till Nathaniel and Josh, her two elder brothers taught him a lesson. Lucy now had a cripple to care for. But, she consoled herself, a docile one who'd never again raise a hand against her.

The soon-to-be brothers-in-law viewed Adam Dacre not so much with "respect" as with caution. He had the strength of ten men, yet with their sister was as gentle as would be a puppy. Nor was he ever seen around the village parading battle scars from some earlier misunderstanding. He was a "quaire 'un, and no mistake"—and not one to cross.

Nevertheless, the brothers held themselves in readiness.

A few minutes before midnight as the men went outside to "let in the New Year" Nathaniel, blaming drink for his sudden stumble (at the same time pushing against Adam), made the opening move in the rift that was to come between them. Adam ignored him. Nathaniel Dacre was not a man to be disregarded.

The "first-footer", chosen for his dark hair, carried with him the traditional piece of coal and silver coin. After saying the words "may your hearth never grow cold" the coal was placed on the red embers of the fire and Hannah, who had taken her mother's place, presented him with the silver sixpence. He was then invited to cut the special New Year Cake, which was eaten with Wensleydale cheese, and good luck was assured for the household for the next twelve months. The following morning, boys going round the village "first-footing", some carrying tiny bags of salt or bread and sprigs of holly were invited in, their gifts signifying that the recipients were "the salt of the earth", and the bread was to ensure the household would never go hungry, and the holly "to keep friendship forever green".

The New Year saw swollen seas and screaming winds, and at night a full moon wild inside its nest of stars, the sky pierced with pin-points of light, restless as the sea's skin which at times seemed about to burst.

Hannah would pull her shawl close to her shoulders as she'd stand on the staithe, and deep in thought, stare first into the heavens, then at the distorted moons reflected in the water. A fisherman would shuffle past, giving the customary "now then" and the mood would be broken. It was difficult to be alone in Staithes, there was always somebody about, and she would hurry along the High Street then over the Bridge, past the herring houses and salting sheds, and if she were particularly energetic, to the fulling mill some half mile up-stream. Returning home she would pass Granary Yard, and the boat-builders, and the buildings where processed fish produced cod liver oil, then make her way to High Barrass by way of the Ropery, storing her problems up for another day.

February and March were Sunday School Anniversaries, when the cruel winter finally gave way to spring and it was the start of the crab and lobster season.

The best catches were to be made on the rocky sea bed several miles north of the village as far south as Runswick Bay. Dad and Adam with their upwards of fifty pots were landing good catches with sometimes as many as fifteen crabs to a creel. Hannah was busy spring cleaning at both her own home and also at Capt Danvers-Griffiths, and Evelyn seemed to be getting as near as could be called "regular work" especially if one considered the fickle fortunes of the artists who were paying her to pose for them.

Laura Johnson was all right. A proper lady. Hannah had made it quite clear among the men that there was to be no "funny business" like asking her sister to pose without clothes—not that Evelyn would, but Hannah had to lay down certain rules. She'd heard one of the group had bought a house in some fancy foreign country. Tangiers, wherever that was, and he'd even persuaded some of the artists to spend the winter months with him. Well, Evelyn wouldn't have gone, even if he'd asked her.

The weeks flew by. It was Easter, and the presentation of Sunday School prizes, then Chapel Anniversary celebrations—soon it would be the week of the Fair!

And for those talented painters, the summer was also a busy time. They were to hold their second exhibition, again, at the Fishermen's Institute, with the private viewing on the 1st of August, and works on display ranging from pastels by Fred Mayor at two guineas to *Moonlight on the Bay* by Charles Mackie, A.R.S.A., priced at sixty pounds. Laura Johnson's *Mother and Child* and *And Women must Weep* at five and eighteen guineas respectively. Four paintings by Harold Knight, a similar number by

Henry Silkstone Hopwood and Richard Bagshawe and, also works by John Bowman, Arthur Friedenson, Isa and Robert Jobling, Thomas Barrett and Frederic Jackson.

After the private viewing, the general public were admitted for an entry fee of two pence, the proceeds to be donated to the Fishermen's Institute. Anxious to see herself on canvas, Evelyn was one of the first of the Staithes locals to part with her money, closely followed by Old Rall and her crony Sair-Anne, who studied the prices more than the actual paintings.

Pausing in front of a work by Isa Jobling, Sair-Anne shook her head in disbelief. "Four guineas fer a vase o' roses!"

"Nea! Sair-Anne, we could walk oop Cowbar an' pick a bunch o' flahs fer nowt."

Following their exhibition, the artists hoped the critic from the Whitby Gazette would be more favourable than some of the villagers. They were on the staithe listening to Frank Mason singing what he assured them was the "latest song" when, with several newspapers under his arm, Arthur Friedenson put a temporary end to his fellow artist's vocalising. "Here it is in black and white—what we've all been waiting for," and he began to distribute the copies among them.

"Listen to this," Richard Bagshawe read aloud, "Charles Mackie's *Moonlight on the Bay* is "a dreamy rendering of the Bay of Runswick when bathed in soft toned light of a summer moon.""

"And what about your *Staithes Beach?*" Charles replied. "It's 'a carefully painted piece of shore work with cobles in an angry sea, the colour and sentiment of which is thoroughly Stathian.' And yours, Robert," he read on, "*The Orchard* by Robert Jobling, a very fine, sunny picture, delightful in treatment and interesting in subject: a young woman, with a child in her arms, feeding some hens."

"And your work's mentioned, Laura," another of the group broke in. "Your figure subjects are 'cleverly painted, and add considerably to the success of the exhibition'."

"That's good, isn't it?" Charles, as ever, was being kind to her.

"Mmm, it's very good," Arthur agreed.

" '...And of Harold Knight's four paintings' " Laura read, " 'we were particularly struck with *Launching Cobles*, the colour being good, though the figures were a bit lacking in substance.' " She turned to him and assured him, "I thought they were all right, Harold."

"Of course they were," Arthur agreed with her. "And we should all be proud. We exhibited some powerful work. One day we'll be rich—every one of us."

Chapter 2

The scrim of earlier sea mist had now burned off, revealing a sky shot with wild streaks of topaz which teased and contrasted among the elder-flower umbrellas rocking on the far horizon.

Rounding the headland, Hannah rested her burden, signalling Evelyn to do likewise. The two of them had been up since first light, engaged in the most laborious of tasks: flither gathering. Some days this could involve miles of walking over the flat scaurs of rocks, beyond Skinningrove and as far north as Saltburn, or, on occasions, travelling by train to Redcar, and picking and walking part of the way back. Winters were particularly cruel, and even as a summer occupation, it had little to commend it.

"Skaning", using a razor-sharp knife to remove the flithers from their shells, required dexterity and was not without danger, nor was the next process, the baiting of the barbed hooks. This was traditionally woman's work—as was carrying nets, helping to launch the boats, holding a family together and being strong, both physically and emotionally. Men had it easy: it was the women who had to work.

The two sisters took deep breaths before balancing their skips on their heads. A couple of hundred yards, and the village would be in sight. Above the screams of the gulls they could hear the crowd on the staithe, and anxious to miss nothing, this gave them a final impetus. They moved toward the scurrying helpers in khaki smock-coats and bowler hats, locals with deadpan expressions revealing nothing of the morning's fish prices, be they good or bad. Woman stood at a respectful distance, taking all in but saying nothing, children and dogs darted about, seabirds hovered and screamed, the sea unobtrusively crept up to steal the land, and seeming oblivious to all of this, the local auctioneer played to his audience.

"Coom on, gen'lmen. One an thrup'nce, one an' thrup'nce." His voice rose above the sudden raucous jackdaws as he strove to maintain the attention of both buyers and sellers. "One an' thrup'nce. One an' six? Coom on, fill 'er oop. Who'll gi'e me two shillin' ?"

Since the coming of the railway had attracted buyers from further afield, and the three regular weekly fish trains to Middlesbrough, prices had risen. Crabs could make as much as five shillings for a box of twenty, and in a good year when shoals were plentiful, the man with the gavel could coax buyers to pay over ten shillings a score for choice cod and ling. There were some in the village who disliked the local auctioneer, referring to him as "nowt but a coomer-in" because his family were from Cornwall, yet the man was likeable and agreeable, and in Hannah's book, even courteous—certainly by Staithes standards. He turned to his next lot. " 'Alibut, an' she's a beauty. Two pund? Coom on, who'll start me off at two pund?" He looked in the direction of Sally Hicks, a regular fish buyer who arrived for the sales in her pony and trap. "One pund then? I 'ave one pund bid," and he waved his hand in the direction of the cautious lady speculator.

Evelyn looked around her. A man with mutton-chop whiskers and jacket open to reveal a gold watch chain across his waistcoat. Beside him a local, a man with trousers consisting of patches and more patches. There were women in bonnets and billowing aprons, and a baby sucking on a linen bag of sugar, men with "sea-boils" on their wrists, and poverty on their faces. Another young woman was surveying, and also recording the scene. Laura Johnson, sketch book in her hand. Whenever there was any activity in the village, one of the group of artists would be there to record it on their canvas of time, their easels littering up the staithe and tucked away in alleyways with half completed paintings, stools, brushes and paints. The sea, clouds, funerals, anything and everything they would capture, even the lines of salted rows of black-jacks hung out to dry for winter, and fish fields at Cowbar. Nothing was overlooked, or considered to be of no consequence.

Hannah Dacre stood on the cliff edge overlooking the cluttered rooftops that clung either side of the steep ravine. Above her, grey smoke emitted from cracked chimney-pots drooped like a shawl of chenille, and on the far horizon an amethyst sea fret fused two elements into one.

She looked around her, seeing and sensing a finality, even though the year had two months to run, despite all being (in the Dacre household anyway) "safely gathered in".

Fish had been salted and dried for winter use, and recent weeks of making preserves had now come to an end. Apple trees had been stripped, their fruit individually wrapped and stored, or turned into chutney. She and Evelyn had picked baskets of blackberries, elderberries had been made into cordial, a remedy for winter colds, while the ripe rowans had produced a clear, tart jelly, an ideal accompaniment for pork or the Christmas goose.

Chapel Harvest Festivals, with balconies draped with nets and an abundance of not only the sea-harvest of crabs and lobsters but also of all manner of fruit and vegetables, had now taken place, the harvest hymns already sung and forgotten till the following year:

All good gifts around us are sent from Heaven above;
Then thank the Lord, oh thank the Lord, for all his love!

Hannah questioned the words, as she stared toward houses where there was not enough food on the table and too many mouths to feed. At women, old before their time; men trapped by poverty, or drink, one condition worsening the other. At "respectability" and the high price it demanded … and her own life: ended before it had begun.

At twenty-four she'd a father, sister and two brothers to care for. And then there was Polly who, for all her sweetness, was still someone else she must take under her wing. There were the fishing chores to see to daily, and the house to run. She'd two houses to oversee, for there was also Capt Danvers-Griffiths's villa at the top of the bank, and if she were not keeping his home spick-and-span, then she was at her own home doing his laundry. The weekly wage gave her an independence—but for what?

What could she do with her life, except care for her family?

Dad was getting older, his hands now crippled with arthritis. If it were not for Adam helping him with the boat—and then there was all this silly talk of her brother's that could never amount to anything more than that—just daft roguery. And each time he raised the topic it ended up in arguments and bouts of sulking. Besides, his place was here helping dad instead of talking about "goin' to sea proper".

But hopefully, when he and Polly were wed he'd forget such silly notions—and well, Polly was little more than a child herself. Instead of caring for a husband, she'd need Hannah to look after her till she was older. The bairn seemed to be spending every spare minute she had under their roof, and if she were not mooning over Adam, then she'd be sat staring at her dad as would a spaniel hoping for a tasty morsel. But if she were to believe half of what she heard, then Polly's life with her brood of brothers was hell—absolute hell!

She pulled her shawl closer to her thin frame, and because they were down Ridge Lane and out of sight from prying eyes, Polly allowed Adam to snuggle up to her.

His own body seemed unusually warm, his arms strong, and unlike her army of brothers, Adam didn't smell. Leastways, not of stale sweat and the previous night's beer. There was something gentle about Adam. Even the way he was now curling her ringlets. Her brothers would have tugged and brought her close to tears, whereas Adam was coaxing the blonde hair round his finger. She looked up at him as would a grateful child.

"You warm enough, doy?"

She nodded.

"It's not far, now," and Adam Dacre sounded confident, "and we'll find lots of holly so's you an' Evelyn can make t'best garland in all o' Steeas."

"And ivy," she reminded him, "we'll need long trails to make it look pretty."

"What about mistletoe?" he asked, as he fumbled beneath his jacket then produced a sprig of distinctive green with two near transparent berries. " 'Suppose to be lucky, kissin' under mistletoe," and he held the twig above them in one hand, the other circling her.

"I'd... kiss you without," she blurted out, surprising herself at her sudden boldness.

"Aye?"

"I do love you, Adam."

"An' I love you, an' that's why I'm thinkin' about, " and he suddenly struggled for the right words. "Look Polly, when we're married—"

"Yes?"

"Well, I want us to be a 'proper' 'usband an wife'—wi' a place of our own."

She stared. "Not sharing?" She seemed surprised. "But I thought we'd be livin' wi'—"

"My family? That'd be no problem, for they all love you, but aunt Bridie's promised us Ring o' Bells for our weddin' present. We'll 'ave a place of our own."

"Adam—that'll be wonderful."

"Aye. We'll be able ter love one another without anybody listenin'."

He could feel her body suddenly tense. "What d'you mean, Adam?"

"An' I want it to be perfect, Polly. That's why I don't try any funny business when we're alone. An' I don't take you under the bridge an' behave like other men do wi' their sweethearts. When you give yourself to me... I want it to be beautiful—it's got to be special."

"But... our own house," and she seemed more taken aback by such extravagance than anything else he could be implying.

"That's why... I'm thinking' o' signin' oop wi' some ship in Whitby. Just the one trip to Greenland, or wherever, so's I can make some real money for us. What d'you say?"

"But Adam," and a fear had seized her, "s'posin' somethin' 'appened to the ship, an' all 'ands were lost?"

"No, doy," he was quick to assure her, "besides, fishermen 'ave bin drowned in t'waters round Steeas, despite t'Jonathan Scott bein' launched to rescue 'em. Pot o' Steel 'as dragged many a man under. But don't think

on that. I'll come back in one piece, never fear, so long as I know you'll
be waitin' for me."

"What does Hannah say?"

Adam pulled a face. "Shu's none too pleased. But I do know what I'm
about. An' it'll be for us. You an' me. What d'you say?"

"But... Greenland?"

"Well," and he now sounded unsure, "it could be. Or Iceland.
Norway. It all depends on which ship's takin' on extra 'ands, an' where
they're bound for."

"You won't get into any fights, will you?"

"No, Polly. You know me. I'm not like your brothers."

"That's what worries me. Nathaniel can more than care for himself."

"He's a bully! You surely wouldn't want me to be like him?"

"No Adam," and now Polly was all anxious to please. "I wouldn't
change you for... oh, a 'undred pounds."

"Or all the tea in China?"

"That an' all."

"An' if I do—an' I'm only sayin' 'if' then I'll be back for our weddin'
next summer. We'll get Ring o' Bells to our own likin', an' at nights we'll
be tucked up in a big double bed... an' when we... you know, I'll be so
gentle with you, Polly. I do so want to love you."

"An'... I love you too. An' I'll try to be a good wife, 'onest I will."

He held her close, and as his hands sought her body he wanted to take
her—but knew that that was not the right time or place. Besides, they'd
come to collect holly.

The cooking, baking and cleaning were done. The cake iced. Mince pies
that had been made by the dozen were in tins, or on the dresser, a cloth
covering them, as were loaves of bread and ground rice cakes. There was
also Christmas gingerbread and a standby pie. The pudding, made several
weeks prior to the big day, would need steaming from first-light the
following morning, and in the side oven of the kitchen range would be
the goose that Evelyn and Polly had between them carried from the farm
at nearby Roxby, which was now plucked and sat on the drainer beside
the sink.

There was a piece of beef for later on in the festivities, and Hannah
had even gone to the extravagance of buying a bottle of wine from Lizzie
Howarth who had a shop that was open from morning till night and sold
everything at very high prices, and never had things her customers
wanted but made them buy something else. She wore her religion as a

cloak of respectability, and was forever quoting passages in the bible, rather than the actual words, so that one was forced to pick up the book and read the chapter and verse to find out what she was talking about. Lizzie would cut a currant in two before give generous weight, and there were those who claimed under the black skirt and hessian apron, Lizzie "wor bowlegged wi' brass". But Hannah felt she had to be charitable, for after all, it was Christmas.

As she took a rest from her back-breaking day, upstairs in a double bed, Evelyn and Polly, reluctant to go to sleep, were telling each other stories. Polly was giggling, so pleased that she now had a "sister" with whom she could share secrets, while Evelyn was more than happy to have a bedmate. Polly would soon to be part of the family proper, when she and Adam were wed, and she'd just said a most wonderful thing—she'd asked her to be her bridesmaid.

"An' when you get a sweet'eart, Evelyn, an' you... well, I can be your bridesmaid in return."

"Mmm. That'd be nice."

"I do love Adam, you know. An' we might 'ave lots of babies. But we've not—" and the two girls went into fits of laughter. "One day, Evelyn," Polly tried to control her mirth, "you'll be able to visit us for tea, an' bring your young man. You'll 'ave a young man before long."

"I've got one now."

"Evelyn!"

"But it's a secret."

"Who is he, Evelyn? Please, I won't tell a soul."

Her bedmate was silent, then suddenly announced, "It's Tim 'Owarth."

"Oh Evelyn—an' 'is mother tart as an old crab-apple."

"It's Tim I'm sweet on, not 'is mother."

"But they say she's pots o' money," Polly was quick to point out.

"She got 'im under 'er thumb," Evelyn grumbled, "that's why we mun keep it secret. Tim says there'd be a reight to do if she found out."

"She'd race you all round Steeas wi' a besom brush."

"She'd noooan catch me."

"Then... if it's a secret," Polly asked, "an' you can't be seen together, 'ow do you—?"

"Oh, we manage. Old Lizzie's too busy makin' money to notice everythin' that Tim gets up to. An' just as well," she laughed, "or we might be getting' married affore you an' Adam."

"You mean, you an' Tim... ?"

Evelyn smiled to herself. " 'Night, Polly." She knew she'd said more than enough.

"You... 'kiss' one another?"

Evelyn thought about the lad she'd been seeing in secret since Harvest time. Still freckled from the summer sun, blonde hair falling over his forehead, top two buttons of his shirt undone as he slaved behind the counter in his mother's shop. Beneath the striped shirt Tim was tantalisingly hairy.

"Oh yes, Polly, we've certainly done that."

Relaxing after the Christmas activities, the New Year was, for Laura Johnson, a time for both reflection and expectation as she walked toward her magnet. The sea!

Today one would need a palate of flat secondary colours, with ochre merging to pewter for the sky. The subject held a sadness, like lovesick violins.

Such a year had 1902 been, not only for herself but for the other members of the group. Harold's painting *The Last Coble* accepted by the royal Academy two years previously had been purchased by the trustees of the Holbrooke Bequest and presented to the Art Gallery in Nottingham. He also had commissions to do in that town, and a portrait painting of the Mayor of Newark. As a result of their painting exhibition their next one was to be held under the patronage of Sir Charles Palmer, MP, of Grinkle Park. Also, love, that most elusive thing to capture and immortalise, had not only come into bud, but had blossomed shamelessly among the members of the group. Hannah Hoyland, the daughter of a wealthy Sheffield manufacturer, had fallen in love with group member and son of a clergyman Fred Mayor.

Because of Charles Hoyland's refusing to give his permission for them to wed, the couple had eloped. They'd married in London and been taken pity on by Hannah's actress cousin Edith Wynne Mathison, leading lady to Henry Irving. Lending them enough money for their journey, they had set sail for France, and had settled in Montreuil-sur-Mer.

Love had conquered. It was wonderful.

Laura, thinking of her own situation, stared onto a vast expanse of restless green and umber, suddenly shot with mustard from the beams of the late afternoon sun. The colours seemed to symbolise her own forthcoming wedding. No explosive bursts of primaries, not even pale lilacs, or wishy-washy blues. Certainly no dramatic vermilion and royal purple, for her marrying Harold Knight had, from their early Nottingham student days been a foregone conclusion. The bright morning and the dazzling noonday sun had already passed them by, marriage would be as dreary as a November afternoon.

Harold would be "dependable" and, she told herself, if other passions had not already been spent they would have to "lie in wait."

The fire in the kitchen range gave a welcome glow as the two bedraggled, near frozen women stepped over the threshold. "We mun 'ave soom 'ot tea an' a bite to eat affore we do owt else," pronounced Hannah Dacre, blowing on her fingers to try to bring some life into them. "My, but it's a raw day out there, doy."

"Hardly seems worth the effort," and Evelyn surprised even herself by her outspoken opinion, "when there's no boats goin' out. What good's bait? We can't eat flithers."

" 'Appen we can't," Hannah agreed, "but ours not to reason why."

Days of white water and lashing gales had necessitated the boats being moored in the upper harbour or tied to the wooden bridge. With no money coming in, men grew fractious, and more than one woman Hannah had seen with bruises on her face. "Nooan looking where I wor goin' " or "slippin' on t'step". One lie, she supposed, was as good as another, and even though there had been such winters when mam was alive, not once had dad ever so much as laid a finger on her. Although they'd been poor, they'd been rich in love.

The iron kettle started to sing, and Hannah need only take the briefest of glances to confirm that the cupboards were bare. Her uncle Joseph would let her have basics on account, and, she supposed, if things did get desperate she had her nest-egg to help the dwindling family fortunes. A good thing she worked for Danvers-Griffiths: her accumulating wages could be needed any day. Yet if they could remain intact then, when Adam returned, and he and Polly set a date for their wedding, she would be able to give them a good start.

On hearing of Adam's new venture, Capt Danvers-Griffiths had taken a keen interest in his bold decision. Old sea-maps had been brought down from his loft, dusted off, and with great enthusiasm the captain re-lived his seafaring days. "Of course, Hannah, I sailed the China Seas— but nevertheless, with this…" and he unrolled the map across the polish-ed mahogany dining table, "…we can see where Adam should be right now. Six weeks since he left port, he'll be about… here, I shouldn't wonder…" and he pointed to a fishing area marked a different colour from the rest of the sea. "And he should be home…" and he paused for effect as he did yet another calculation, "...early summer. Beginning of June. And no doubt be a rich man as well."

" 'Ee's promised never to do it again."

Danvers-Griffiths smiled and stroked his neat once-black but now-going-grey beard, a faraway longing in his eyes. He was thinking of a young Chinese girl, the mother of his two sons. A different time; a different world.

"And when Adam leaves the nest," and he closed the door to his past life, "you'll have one less to care for. Make an old man happy, Hannah. Say you'll marry me."

"Go on Owen, stop teasin'," she tried to make light of his advances, but there was a look of... not so much hope and expectation as sadness and loneliness in his rheumy eyes.

" 'Can't bring all my family up 'ere, wouldn't be right," she reasoned, "an' I can't leave 'em to look after themselves."

"You leave them. Come on, Hannah, say 'yes' while everything's still ship-shape and in working order. We could have a wonderful—"

The kettle steaming and spluttering into the coals brought her back to reality. What had they to eat? Nothing. Then, suddenly remembering, Hannah rushed upstairs and returned with a bag of humbugs. "Here, mint'll help you breathe better. Warm you up."

"I'd rather have salmon fish-cakes."

"Wouldn't we all, doy."

Dad, along with the other men, would be in the Fishermen's Institute. Some of the hotheads of the village would be in the Cod & Lobster, drinking away what little money they had and, even though there was no necessity to bait the lines for the following morning, there were still other chores to do. Evelyn went on the beach to gather wood for the fire. Hannah, wanting to delay running up credit, took ten shillings of her wages, and was able to fill, albeit temporarily, their store cupboard with basics. She'd bake some bread, there were still some preserves left. With bacon bits, oatmeal and onions something warm and appetising could be made for their evening meal. If she could think up yet another different way with cabbage, then their dinner could even be interesting. And for afters? Dad didn't like milk puddings—but just as well, for there was a shortage of milk. Some sort of cake, perhaps. Plain. It would have to be. Fish was their staple diet—when the boats could put out.

Returning home, she busied herself, cooking potatoes in the skins to make them go further. The bacon was fried then cut up fine before being mixed with oatmeal and onions and bound together with some of the bacon fat, the rest poured over the cabbage. The concoction was shaped into balls then baked in the over to give them a crispy topping.

She lit the lamps, it was coming dark. Scarcely had they finished their meal when there was a persistent banging on the door.

The sight that greeted Hannah was to remain with her for a long time. The tear-stained face, torn clothes and bruises to her neck and arms left her in no doubts as to the nature of the attack. "I've... nowhere to go," she sobbed.

"Coom in, doy." From the winter's night into the light of the kitchen stepped... Polly Dacre.

Chapter 3

As she moved into the welcoming heat of the room, Polly took sudden deep breaths. Then, the ceiling spinning, the walls closing in on her, she swayed into the arms of the head of the family, Jacques Dacre.

"Coom on, doy, let's be 'avin' thee," and he stared at the pitiful sight as he carried her to the settee.

"What's 'appened ter Polly?"

"Nay David, that's what we all want ter know. Though I can guess, looking' at 'er." To Hannah (although not to her young brother) Polly's recent ordeal was obvious.

"She's coomin' rahnd. Nah then, bairn, what's ter do?" and Jacques' kindly eyes looked on the pathetic bundle his son was to marry.

"'Appen I sud go an' get t'doctor," Evelyn offered.

"No, doy. The fewer folk know abaht this the better," and Hannah was already in charge of the situation. "David, get thee ter bed, an' dad, you'd best go ter t'Cod fer a drink, till we get Polly sorted out. 'Ere," and she shoved some bits of change into his hand. He licked his lips appreciatively. "An' dooan't thee rush back. An' say nowt ter nobody."

He looked at his daughter. "Yer'll... sort it, then?"

She nodded. "An' she'll nooan want ter talk in front on a man. But ter me an' Evelyn, she might. When I know what's happened, I'll know what ter do."

"If it what I'm thinkin'—be careful."

"They dooan't frighten me."

"No, I can tell."

Jacques Dacre was the head of the household, but he knew better than to offer advice to his eldest daughter. He shuffled out into the night.

"Now Polly," and Hannah spoke as she would to a small child, "we mun get thee a drink, then get thee cleaned oop. There's soom 'ot water, tha'd best take a bath." Seeing the look of consternation on the girl's face, Hannah went on, "No need ter be shy, an' then, when we've got thee all snug an' warm, we'd best know what's upset thee."

"I can't tell yer. I'm too ashamed. Oh Hannah, what am I ter do?" and she burst into floods of tears. "When... when Adam finds out, he'll—"

"Like as not want to murder the animal that's touched thee. Now coom on, Polly, let's get thee aht o' them clothes. Evelyn mun bring t'tin bath in, an' we'll fill it oop wi' 'ot water."

As Polly slipped out of her garments and into the warm suds, the extent of her injuries became self-evident. Hannah stared. "Polly," she coaxed the pathetic little more than a child, the ringlets now wet and going into rat-tails, "I just need a name, doy. All tha needs ter do is tell me who did this ter thee."

She stared, mute, till Hannah suggested the man responsible for what had occurred.

Polly nodded, and Hannah knew what she must do.

"Nah then," said Hannah suddenly all businesslike, "when tha's all dry we mun find thee one o' Evelyn's nighties, and tuck t'two o' in bed wi' a 'ot brick as we keep in t'oven bottom so's yer can put yer feet on it ter keep 'em warm. An' then?—well, I 'ave things ter do. Yer'll look after 'er, Evelyn."

"Mmm. Like Christmas, when yer stopped wi' us."

Her charges safe, Hannah Dacre strode resolutely along the High Street, the wind in her hair, taste of salt on her lips, justice in her walk. She could hear the sea pounding, as angry as she was herself, but soon she would be able to take revenge out on the man who had brutally assaulted her future sister-in-law. She hurried past the Cod & Lobster, and a few doors further along, Old Rall, collecting and storing gossip as would a pelican with a beak full of fish greeted her with, "Nah then, doy, An' what's ter do?" but was ignored, much to her dismay. Hannah stared at lighted upstairs windows, while below, through small panes oil lamps bathed living rooms in a warm yellow glow and hearths burned bright. There was more noise than usual coming from the Black Lion, but, Hannah reasoned, it was late, and some men the worse for drink. She turned down the yard leading to the bridge, the sulphur sheen of lamp-light on the water in the beck glugging lethargically against the moored boats that bobbed up and down. Ropes creaked, as did the bridge's timbers.

On the other side of the wooden structure, lobster pots were piled up like giant rat cages, while high above her the sky seemed luminously silken, pin-pointed by a shoal of stars. The full moon lit up sea, and cast shadows from the cliffs. Hannah braced herself for what lay ahead. No longer feeling the biting north wind, for she was burning with a desire to see him exposed for what he really was.

She resolutely banged on the door. "Coom on, or yer'll 'ave no paint left. I know yer in there Nathaniel Dacre. I'll nooan go away till I've said me piece, an' if yer doant want all Steeas ter know abaht thee, then tha'd best—" and at that point the door was opened to her.

"Nah then, an' what's ter do?"

She pushed past James Dacre, a wheezing man, old before his time. "Where is 'ee?" she demanded, "that son o' thine as sud 'ave geldin' irons ta'en ter 'im."

The Dacre brood looked at this cousin of theirs with a sudden curiosity. Then a figure dressed in black, her haughty profile a reminder of the Huguenot sailors who (two hundred years previously, after their ship was wrecked, had sought sanctuary and settled in the village) stirred and came toward her. "tha'd best calm thissen," Leonora Dacre tried to assert her authority. "Tha cooms in 'ere sharp as a cracked pittle pot, an—"

"My business is wi' your Nathaniel" she ignored her aunt. "Nah then," and she looked round, "where is 'ee?"

"What can Nathan do as we can't?" a rough voice tried to ridicule her, "ee's no more a man nor me."

She turned to the head of the house. "Well?"

"In bed—unless 'ee's in t'Cod."

"Get him down here. Now."

"But 'ee might be—"

"Then I mun show 'im up in t'pub, in front o'all t'village—but get this, James, thy lad'll answer tonight for what he's done."

"An' what's that?" and from upstairs, and only half dressed, Nathaniel Dacre appeared.

Seeing the determination of Hannah Dacre, and sensing the defiant mood of his son, James Dacre nodded toward the rest of his lads. "There's business ter discuss."

As they reluctantly sidled out into the night, Nathaniel was about to do the same till Hannah barred his way. He tried to push past her. She stood her ground.

"Move," and he spat in her face.

" Dooan't thee try brute strength on me. An' if tha knows what's good for thee then this is one Dacre woman tha'll nooan lay a finger on."

"Who'd want to?"

"But not so wi' thee own sister?"

"Eh?" and as the father looked first at his son, then at his niece.

"I 'ad a visitor earlier. Your Polly. An' in such a state the poor mite wor. Covered wi' bruises… but there's worse ter come. Somebody tried ter rape 'er."

"Oh, she'll say owt," her elder brother blustered, "next she'll be sayin'—"

"As it wor thee, Nathaniel."

"Get out. Get out o' this 'ouse."

"Just a minute, lad. It's my 'ouse, an' I'll say who gets out."

"Shu's here ter cause bother," Leonora spat the words out, quick to defend her son, "An' shu's nowt but a trollop 'ersen. Carryin' wi a man owd enough ter be thee father, tha sud be t'last ter talk."

"Polly's been tryin' it on wi' me for weeks," her son boasted. "Since your Adam went she's been like a bitch on 'eat. Goin' after any feller to get a good stiff—" He reeled as a fist smashed into his face. There was a cry of pain, and a bloodied nose and mouth.

"Tha'll nooan use that sort o talk in front o' thee mother"

" 'True anyway. Shu wor beggin' for it."

"Liar," and Hannah grabbed at the unruly mane, slamming his head against the wall to punctuate her word.

" 'Ere, we'll 'ave less o' that. What does, or doesn't go on under this roof is nooan o' thy business. Away wi' yer."

"But… she's your lass," Hannah tried to reason with her aunt, "are yer not worried abaht what this… 'animal's' tried ter do?" She stared, unable to believe the attitude of the woman. " I knew this side o' family were a law unto themselves, but… anyroad, yer can show me where Polly keeps 'er clothes, for she's livin' under my protection from now on. She say's wi' me till Adam gets back."

"Dad," Nathaniel nagged his father, "dooan't let 'er tell us what ter…"

James Dacre looked at his eldest son. "Get out. An' dooan't thee coom back."

"Nay James, dooan't thee be so silly as ter…"

"It's a pack o' lies," his son strove in vain to assert his innocence, "it's Polly as yer want ter throw aht. She'll be big wi' a bairn any day nah. Yer'll see."

"An' it'll nooan end 'ere," Hannah warned her cousin, "for when Adam gets word o' this…"

"Yer'll nooan see Adam Dacre ageean. D'yer think he'll coom back ter Steeas? No," Nathaniel taunted, "if 'ee's nooan drooned, then 'ee'll want ter see the world. An' a wife'll be t'last thing 'ee wants."

"Tha's got it wrong, Nathaniel. An' when 'ee finds out what tha's tried ter do ternight, it'll be thee as is leavin' Steeas. Nah, do I go oopstairs an' get Polly's things?"

"She mun coom for 'em. Tha'll nooan go rummaging abaht on thee own."

"All reight, aunt Leonora. I'll be back—wi' Polly, first thing in t'mornin'. I'll bid yer 'goodnight'." At the door she turned to her cousin. "An' if me uncle James does throw thee out, don't think tha gettin' off lightly. Adam'll find thee. An' tha'll nooan be comin' ter t'wedding'."

"There'll nooan be one," Nathaniel called after her as she walked along the High Street. As his words rang in her ears Hannah, for the first time, began to have her doubts.

She had a fitful night, rose early, and from the steps of High Barrass saw the sun streak over the horizon like a deranged woman. The short, sharp violent light slashing the morning sky and pouring onto the sea, and Hannah thought yet again about the wrong done to Polly by her brother. She went indoors, as if by magic produced food for a breakfast "of sorts" then after coaxing a hesitant Polly to claim what was hers, and offering her support, the two women strode along the High Street in the direction of the salting premises and curing sheds above the bridge. One frightened, the other, as she was the previous evening, resolute.

"Everythin' ", Hannah instructed, "clothes—an' stuff yer've saved for yer bottom drawer, it's all comin wi' yer this mornin'."

"What if mi mam an' dad won't let me?"

"That's why I'm 'ere, in case o' trouble."

As they neared the bridge, Polly froze. " 'Ee's there, Hannah. Supposing'—?"

"Just 'old yer 'ead 'igh as we walk past. Yer've done nowt wrong. It's Nathaniel as sud skulk away." As they neared her brother, now making derisive comments for the group of fishermen to see how big a man he was, Hannah for one moment feared that Polly would run. But she seemed to draw on some inner strength. "That's it, just rise above 'im," Hannah whispered. " 'Ee daren't touch thee, not when yer wi' me."

"What did me mam say? Wor she cross wi' me?"

"No. I keep telling' yer, doy, yer've done nowt wrong. Now, let's get thee things."

"I couldn't do this without you, 'Annah. Adam said yer wor a special person. Now I know why." Hannah Dacre at that second had a speck of dust... that was bringing a tear to her eye.

Minutes later, Polly's possessions tied up in a shawl, the two women caused a certain speculation among those who saw them returning to High Barrass. Hannah supposed tongues would wag, but Polly moving in with them would be a change from the usual back-biting gossip.

Besides, there was always "something".

Either babies were being born, or the old folk were dying and the bidder was going round the village announcing details of the funeral. Only days before, when Joss Theaker at nearly a hundred and destined to live for ever had been discovered by his nephew, his death had been announced in the manner particular to the village. "Yer's ter coom ter Joss Theaker's funeral," the bidder called out as she made her tour of the alleys, "fer 'ee's bin fund deead. Friday mornin' at eleven o' clock.

'Bearers 'as bin picked, an' 'ymns as yar's ter sing. Will yer coom? Coom ter Joss Theaker's funeral fer 'ee's deead."

Should anyone dare to ask Hannah the reason for Polly being under their roof, she would say… that they were making arrangements for the wedding. It was women's work and not the sort of thing to concern her eight brothers. That should stop any surmising—but Hannah would feel happier when Adam returned.

Laura Johnson would also feel happier when she returned to the village—as Laura Knight.

The 3rd of June, 1903, was so be the date of her wedding. Harold was in Nottingham, her sister Sissie, recently returned from France was helping her to clear the cottage in Staithes, where things were being auctioned off at the doorstep. Antique dealers, feeling cheated at there being nothing of value, cursed their having a wasted day. The sea-fret covered everything and everybody in a fine mist, and Laura felt that even the day itself was in sympathy with her. Still, she consoled herself, she would be returning, and possessions could sometimes be a burden and the money they would bring would be more than useful.

For a few pence Evelyn bought a pile of sketches, including some of herself. Polly invested the two shillings Hannah had given her in a boxful of ornaments and vases.

"For mi bottom drawer," she giggled, as she and Evelyn carried their treasures away with them, returning home to "visitors". Uncle Reuben and cousin Jonas.

Never one to miss an opportunity, his father had had him fitted out in a suit of tweed, and as one might parade a prize bull at a cattle mart Jonas was displayed before Hannah, Evelyn and (because he had heard a whisper that her forthcoming marriage might not materialise) the other young woman living as part of the household, Polly.

"Nah then, Jonas, share thee sweets wi' thee cousins. Let 'em 'ave one o' thee 'umbugs. 'Eee, but 'ee's a grand lad," and the overweight Jonas gave an imbecilic grin, then slowly from his pocket took out a bag of boiled mixtures. "They came thro Lizzie 'Owarth's, they wor reight dear."

The mention of Lizzie Howarth, and the thought of her son, caused Polly and Evelyn to exchange secret glances. Evelyn's eyes twinkled and she gave a bold smile as she asked, "wor Tim in t'shop?"

"An' she doesn't 'alf boss that lad abaht. She's got him under 'er thumb an' reight. Yer wouldn't think a frail body such as Lizzie 'Owarth could be such a forceful woman."

"Not like aunt 'Ephzibah?"

"No," he replied to Hannah's question. "Thee aunt's a quiet sort. She's bin poorly o' late, an' 'ud like nowt better na' seein' Jonas 'ere settled wi' a lovely little wife."

"Well, yer spoiled fer choice. It's plain ter see, Jonas must 'ave all t'young lasses in Steeas fancyin' 'im." Jonas clasped his podgy hands together and the two younger girls wanted to laugh as Hannah kept her serious expression.

"An' ... Polly's... ter wed Adam?" and her uncle seemed to have a doubt in his voice.

"Aye. Coom summer."

"Er... gi'e thee cousin Evelyn another 'umbug."

"Well, I bet there's lot's o' girls sweet on you, Jonas," Evelyn teased. He gave a shrug. "Dunno."

"An' there'll be a lovely 'ouse waitin' for whoever Jonas weds. An' money in t'bank. Whoever marries this lad'll want for nowt." There was a pause for his generosity to register, then as if it were of no importance, her uncle asked, "an' 'ow's Capt Owen Danvers-Griffiths?"

"Nay, but yer mun ask him yersen," Hannah refused to be drawn.

"They do say... as 'ee's sweet on a 'certain' young woman'."

"An' who could that be?"

"It's... just... what folks is sayin'," and he stared into the fire, realising he was on dangerous ground.

"Don't believe all yer 'ear, uncle Reuben," Hannah's warning was friendly, but firm. She'd have to quell any such gossip before it went round the village. The amorous captain didn't need any encouragement, for he was promising marriage twice a week.

"I don't think as 'ee'll be gettin' wed in t'near future. Leastways, 'ee's nooan said owt ter me, an' I think I'd be t'first ter know, don't you?"

"...Oh aye."

"Then we'd better make sure such tales don't go any further. An' we mustn't detain you an' Jonas, for you're busy men... an' we've work to do."

"Aye... Well, we'll be gettin' on... an' 'appen at Polly's weddin'..."

"I reckon as yer'll be gettin' an invite," Hannah cut him short. "An' Jonas might bring 'is intended."

The three woman watched them turn into the High Street before bursting into fits of uncontrollable laughter. It even lightened the cloud that had, of late, descended over the household. All were missing Adam, none more than Polly.

Polly sank further and further into a decline. She said and ate little, but would cry at the slightest provocation, or be silent for hours, staring into nothing. Hannah, fearing that the change that had come about her was because she was carrying Adam's child was somewhat relieved when Polly did finally confide in her the reason for her behaviour.

"I can't sleep night, for I'm that worried... that Adam's ship might come to grief." She spoke through sobs and sighs, then trying to wipe away her tears she struggled without success to find her handkerchief.

"Here, use this," and Hannah lent her hers.

"But they do say," and Polly paused to draw breath, "that fer two an' six, Sair-Anne could call up t'spirits, an' for as much as 'alf a sovereign can work a powerful charm as'll strengthen an' protect—"

"No, doy, we mun steer clear o' that old crone. She'll fill your pretty 'ead wi' rubbish."

"But folk's say—"

"No," Hannah tried to calm her, her thoughts racing. "But if we do want a magic charm... then... we mun go to Beck Meetin's an' ask t'fairies to 'elp us."

Polly dried her eyes and blew her nose. "D'yer think it'd work?"

"We could try," replied Hannah, battling to keep a straight face."

"When? When could we go an' ask t'fairies ter protect Adam?"

"Tomorrow mornin'. We'll need ter take gifts, mind. Some short-bread, a bunch o' flowers an' a bit o' coloured ribbon."

Polly was suddenly much brighter. "Are there really such things as fairies?"

" 'Course there are," Hannah spoke as one having great authority on such matters. "Why, there's fairies at Claymore Well at Kettleness, who wash their clothes then bleach 'em in the moonlight."

"'Ave you ever seen 'em—at Beck Meetin's?"

"But I know somebody who 'as."

The following morning the two of them walked up the steep bank, then reaching the road from Whitby to Loftus they turned down the track that led to the nearby hamlet of Dalehouse collecting celandines and early bluebells as floral gifts. They crossed the bridge, taking the path that led to the ford and the meeting of the two moorland streams.

"An' when we ask the fairy-folk for their 'elp, we mun turn round three times, for that's their magic number."

"You do know some things, 'Annah." Polly spoke in awe at one so wise in fairy power.

"Oh, aye. Now yer'd best give them our flowers now. We'll save the ribbon an' cake till we leave."

Suddenly serious, Polly stood at the edge of the streams, curtseyed then sprinkled the flowers on the surface of the waters, closed her eyes then held her hands together as though in prayer. Hannah could have believed herself, had she not been the one who had devised this ritual. She saw Polly turn the required number of times, then as Hannah looked away to indulge in a secret smile, her charge suddenly called, "I've seen one 'Annah—I've seen a fairy. Look, she's over there."

"Where, doy?"

"In the 'edgerow, behind that fern. Creep up, an' you'll see 'er."

As they move closer something among the fronds moved quickly. Seeing the look of disappointment on the other's face, Hannah was quick to compliment Polly on her keen observation. "That were a clever fairy an' no mistake—ter suddenly change into a baby rabbit."

He was counting the days. Eighteen, and the ship should be in port.

He had stared through ghostly morning mists at infinite remoteness, a strange silence enveloping his world, for all around and below him, was the vast expanse of water. Land was nothing more than a memory. Something in his mind, but no longer real, for he was on this floating world with a will of its own. At times calm, then, like some fickle woman, everything would change. The monster would awake, and he would fear for his life. Polly, and the comfort and comparative calm of the waters round Staithes seeming so very desirable as the ship was lashed by furious gales. Sometimes he would have frost on his eyebrows, lips cracked and finger-ends numb, such were the near arctic conditions.

At other times there would be strange lights in the sky, reminding him of the fires on the staithe to warn the boats and guide them in. He would stare at this phenomenon, his eyes burning with the beauty of the sea. Another eighteen days. The ship was already heading for home, and this was the very last time he would be parted from Polly. Roll on their wedding day.

Bells were also sounding for Laura Johnson and Harold Knight, who after their wedding feast went to London to spend (Laura remembered the description from Staithes) their "honey-money". There were art galleries to visit, including an exhibition of Dutch paintings at the Guildhall, before they returned to Nottingham for Harold to complete his comm- issions, and Laura consider the prospect of now being Laura Knight.

She pondered about her new name. Should she now sign her paintings Knight or Johnson? She would lie awake at night, unable to decide.

Marriage was already presenting problems.

Hannah had baked and iced the cake. New clothes had been bought. Polly had chosen a dress of white with blue forget-me-nots, Evelyn was to wear pale blue, and her dad would look smart in navy blue serge. David had chosen a brown check, his first ever suit that was not one of Adam's hand-me-downs Her own outfit was being made by dressmakers in Whitby, which meant several visits for fittings, but Hannah wanted to do the family proud. She still had matching hat and gloves to buy, but perhaps when she picked the dress up, she'd find just what she wanted. She'd also wear "mum's necklace". Seed pearls, she'd called them, and Hannah neither knew nor cared if they really were—or as valuable as mum had claimed them to be, for they were to be symbolic, not simply an adornment.

Presents were starting to arrive and being stored in Adam's bedroom. There were the invitations to send, which would depend on when Adam returned and there was also the problem of Polly's family. Weddings were to be happy occasions, but when Hannah thought of her soon-to-be in-laws, she could visualise problems. Nathaniel, having left the village and reputedly signed on with some ship, temporarily resolved one prob- lem, yet if Adam should discover the reason for his bride-to-be having to leave her home, then there would be scores still to settle.

Nathaniel and his brothers were scum, they'd probably beat Adam to a pulp between them, for they fought in packs, too cowardly for single combat. She could remember when as children she's seen Nathaniel poke a kitten's eyes out "fer fun"—and the adult was ten times more cruel than the child. Perhaps, if she could talk to Jacqes, and he could some- how control his sons or, at the very least, promise a truce for the wedd- ing, then they could be among the invited guests. Besides, there were appearances to keep up, and a wedding without the bride's family would cause much speculation and surmising. It would be better that the young couple began married life without obvious in-law problems.

The mere mention of weddings once again had Capt Danvers-Griff- iths offering true love and faithfulness and promising a lifetime of devot- ion if only Hannah would say yes to his proposal. She'd earlier managed to decline without sounding ungracious, but now began to take his offer more seriously. On the rare occasions when she dared to think about her own future there seemed to be an absence of eligible young men in the village, certainly none that could care for her as would the retired captain.

Young love was all very well, she supposed, if you were young and in love, but she was neither. And after the early days, and when passions were spent? Well, there would still be the bills to pay. When a woman reached a "certain age" as she herself was fast approaching, then she needed security, and no silly "love" notions. A proposal from a man such as Owen Danvers-Griffiths wasn't to be dismissed lightly.

Earlier in the week he'd put his arms round her, and nodding to the ships on the horizon had cheered her up by saying, "Your Adam could be out there. They're waiting for the tide before they approach the mouth of the Tees."

"Do yer think so? Then he could be home in… a couple o' days?"

"Mmm. The train to Middlesbrough, then the one to Steeas—why, he could be having supper with you tomorrow."

"Let's 'ope so, fer I've fears about this weddin'."

Haunting her was Nathaniel's prediction that Adam would not return to the village, and if that were to happen, then what would become of Polly, who now seemed a fixture under their roof? They couldn't turn the poor lass out, nor would it seem right her lodging with them while her brother was gallivanting about. And supposing he'd changed his mind about marrying her? Supposing. Supposing.

And another thought gripped Hannah. The wedding cake.

She could always keep it for Fair Week, but silver cupids and bells and bows didn't seem altogether appropriate. It was now the end of June, and not a thing had been heard of, or from, Adam. Hannah was beginning to have misgivings about this forthcoming marriage.

But her doubts disappeared when, only days later, a sunburnt, seemingly-taller and slimmer brother stepped over the threshold, his hair now long and bleached with the sun, his upper arms sporting tattoos, his face wreathed in smiles. Polly giggled and kissed him. Hannah wept tears of joy.

The organist hit several uncertain chords, then tackled an ambitious cadenza as uncle Reuben and family were ushered down the aisle. He in stripes, aunt Hephzibah in maroon. But she was a dowdy, insignificant looking woman with a pale complexion and long bony fingers. She'd been old since Hannah could remember, her only saving grace was that she "knew her place" as her uncle pointed out on every possible occasion.

Jonas, her son, stared round. His two ugly sisters wore identical pink to draw attention to themselves as they strutted, defiantly flaunting their near idiocy through inbreeding. They were gawkish, straight haired, plain featured and destined for certain spinsterhood. The pew in front of them accommodated aunt Bridie. In her usual black despite the occasion—for she saw no reason for weddings to be in any way joyous occasions. New finery was, in her book, a waste of money. In the front pew, his mouth suddenly dry was Adam Dacre and his best man, David. " 'Got the ring?" he asked yet again.

His brother nodded, tapping the top of his waistcoat pocket. From the two of them waking up in Capt Danvers-Griffiths's spare room at the top of his house (for Hannah had insisted that Adam didn't see the bride on the day of her wedding until the actual service) Adam had been in a nervous state. He'd stubbed his toe on the bedpost, cut himself shaving, and appeared at breakfast with a face covered in bits of paper, and had felt too sick to eat the greasy bacon and eggs that the captain had insisted was the only meal suitable for a man soon to lose his "freedom".

"Mind you," the captain boasted, "I'd gladly change places with you, if your sister'd say yes."

"Evelyn?" and Adam seemed surprised.

"No, he means Hannah."

"Well… are you…?"

The captain gave a forlorn sigh. "If only, Adam. If only."

But, as Adam reasoned as he tried to calm his thoughts, there was a saying: "one wedding made another"—and who was to say yea or nay? Hannah had been looking after his house (and probably the captain as well) for long enough to know what she'd be taking on if she were to wed him. But Adam had other thoughts on his mind as he, somewhat apprehensively, speculated as to what would be expected of himself that evening when he and Polly were alone together. He knew about "things" but wondered if Polly did. He hoped that Hannah perhaps… ? Still, an unmarried sister should herself be mystified as to how a bride should behave on her wedding night, and be the last to offer advice From there would be no voice of experience, just… but perhaps when they were under the sheets, then things would "happen" without giving the matter any thought.

He glanced over to the sparse congregation to his left, and the front pew reserved for his soon-to-be in-laws. It had been empty for too long, something was wrong. Perhaps Polly had had second thoughts, and was with her parents now, and any minute someone would burst in, have hurried words with the Minister, who would stand in front of the assembled gathering to announce, "I'm sorry, ladies and gentlemen, but there will be no wedding today."

He could just hear the words in his mind, and he began to imagine aunt Bridie marching over the bridge to the Dacres' and demanding an explanation. She'd be hammering on the door, wanting all Staithes to witness her righting this terrible wrong done to her favourite nephew. Aunt Bridie had a loud voice, nor did she choose her words carefully.

The organist had further difficulties. Aunt Bridie looked annoyed. Adam examined his fingernails, and felt as though everyone was looking at him—and it should be the bride who was the centre of attention.

...When she arrived.

"Is owt 'appenin' yet?" he whispered to his younger brother.

David turned his head. "Polly's family are 'ere. Leastways, some on 'em."

The younger sons and their mother trooped into their pew and there was activity inside the porch. Then the organist changed tune as the wedding party walked down the aisle, Adam and David rose to their feet as the bride came to meet them. Adam suddenly wanted to cry—with relief. The wedding would take place, after all.

The celebrations continued throughout the day, and after the wedding breakfast, declared to be "as good as a funeral tea" the guests made suitable "ooh's" and "ah's" of appreciation as they viewed the generous gifts the newly weds had received. There was the only to be expected table and bed linen; an abundance of crockery, vases and ornaments; a tab rug from uncle Reuben and aunt Hephzibah; cutlery from Capt Danvers-Griffiths (chosen by Hannah); fifty pounds from Dad—and from aunt Bridie, who had to outdo everybody, the key to Ring 'o Bells.

Polly spent an afternoon giggling, Adam shook hands of well wishers, kissed young girl cousins and elderly aunts, and laughed and pretended to listen to "good advice" given by uncles and male friends. The elder brothers of the bride were conspicuous by the absence, Polly's parents quick to disappear after the formalities were concluded, which pleased Hannah, who wanted no trouble on this, of all days.

Then suddenly, and now changed into "going away" clothes, the newly-weds were accompanied to the railway station at the top of the bank, where they caught the early evening train to Whitby, as the start of their honeymoon. With confetti stuffed in their pockets and strewn in their hair, that they had been married that day was obvious. The wedding guests watched the train pull out then disappear before returning to continue the celebrations, for there was still food to be eaten, and wine to be drunk.

Hannah was yet again complimented on the lavish spread she had laid on, for this wedding would be a talking point for months to come, and as the guests helped themselves Hannah managed to have a few words with her sister.

"One day, doy, it'll be your wedding."

"Mmm."

"An' we'll put on just as good a do fer you an' yer young man, never fear."

Evelyn wanted to mention Tim, but Hannah, not even pausing to take a breath continued, "an' I mun go 'ome an' put a comfortable pair o' shoes on. These are killin' me. I won't be five minutes."

Wedding finery was all well and good for those who were used to being trussed up like chickens. Every time aunt Bridie had moved her corsets had creaked like ships timbers, and a trim figure was wasted on an old prune such as she had become. But, Hannah reasoned, she had been more than generous, even though a cottage for a wedding present made the rest of the gifts seem insignificant. She walked carefully (and painfully) over the cobbles, she'd need to put a plaster on her heel, then find something to wear that didn't rub. The sun was setting. There was a warm evening breeze. She'd make herself a cup of tea, and perhaps a ham sandwich.

The house would seem quiet with Polly and Adam gone, and now that she thought about it, she supposed that Evelyn might in the not-too-distant future announce that there was some young man wanting to walk her out, or one of her uncles would call on dad to say that he had a son looking to get married, and her sister's fate could be settled. That would leave only David and dad to care for, and unless she gave the captain a favourable answer, she'd end up an old maid. Perhaps he'd settle for a "long engagement" until such times as...

Then she unlatched the door, and stopped supposing.

She gave a long sigh as she kicked off the torturously painful footwear, stretched her toes then gently touched her heels before removing her stockings. The blisters were like raw liver, she'd attend to them while waiting for the kettle to boil. Busying herself, she heard, before she saw the intruder, as, turning toward the sound, Hannah called, " 'That you, dad?"

"No, it's..." and she saw his ungainly frame filling the doorway.

"Why, uncle Reuben. An' what's ter do, then?"

" 'Allo, 'Annah." He stared at the silk stockings thrown over the chair. "Dooan't let me stop thee."

"Yer should be wi' me aunt 'Ephzibah. There's ter be dancing' an'—"

"I'd rather be wi' thee." He lurched toward her. She sidestepped. He touched the stockings. "Nice."

"They cost enough."

"Thee aunt 'Ephzibah wears—"

"I dooan't want ter know."

"Shu's nooan… a 'responsive' woman, if tha gets me drift."

"I do," she snapped, "an that's enough o' that sort o' talk."

"Tha's a good lass, 'Annah, an' ah reckon that retired sea-captain's a lucky man." He tried to stand upright, but had consumed far more alcohol than was good for him. His hand went toward her dress, she roughly pushed him away. He continued staring, licking his lips as would a child on seeing a jar of lollipops. "Captain… still, tha'll be on first name… even 'intimate' terms wi' 'im."

"Yer surmisin'. An' what's between me an t'captain is nowt ter do wi' you—or anybody else in Steeas."

His breathing became more laboured. He was staring at the top of her dress that had become unbuttoned. She tried to sidestep him. He barred her way, his hand on his groin. "Be nice ter me, 'Annah. Fer who's ter know, 'cept thee an' me?"

She stared at him, feeling nauseated. "Yer leet gi'en tup," she finally managed, "yer nooan fit ter be called uncle, be'avin like that. What'd mi aunt 'Ephzibah say if she could 'ere yer?"

"She's a cold fish, that aunt o' thine. Knows nowt abaht a man's needs."

"An' d'yer think I do?"

"Tha could satisfy mine."

"I'll put an end to 'em if yer nooan out o' this 'ouse affore I count ter three. One—"

" 'Annah—"

"Two… three. Nah then, let's be 'avin' thee," and Hannah made a desperate effort to manhandle the twice-her-weight worse-for-drink uncle toward the door. Suddenly, his hand smashed into her face. She reeled, this was not what she had expected. She looked round in desperation. No sense in calling for help, for everyone was still enjoying the wedding celebrations. Her hand went to her cheek. "When dad 'ears abaht this—"

His trousers were undone, he was on top of her. She must struggle, fight with every ounce of strength. But uncle Reuben was a big man, nor was he making allowances for any physical advantage he may have. As they wrestled, her knee came up to his groin. He momentarily drew back.

"Yer dirty old sod," she managed to yell as she looked round the room for something, anything, to keep him away from her. He came at her again. She could feel his weight on her, smell cigar and alcohol, his breath and his stale sweat. He began tearing at her clothes—his hand was up her skirt—and then she saw it!

On the draining board. She reached out and her fingers went round the handle. The battle continued till Hannah grabbed part of his anatomy in one hand, and with the other made a decisive slash with the knife she used for gutting fish.

After she had done the deed there was a moment of sublime calm, then she felt a wetness between her fingers as she hurled something into the fire. Uncle Reuben was suddenly near-angelic—there was an unbelievable look of innocence about him—until he realised what had happened. There was a sizzling and something like chicken skin shrivelling over the coals, and a wetness of blood suggested to him—nay convinced him—that all was not well in his privates' department. There was an agonised scream and a now-slashed and partially-circumcised uncle was rolling on the floor.

Hannah wiped her hands down her dress. She was numb. It had happened... well, it had... just happened.

His continued screams brought her back to reality. She stared into the glowing, spitting embers. What had been part of uncle Reuben was now oozing over the front of the fire grate. "Tha shouldn't 'ave tried owt on wi' me, uncle Reuben, an' I'm truly sorry, really I am. But dooan't thee worry, lots o' little lads, even young men, 'ave it done."

She must get David to run to Hinderwell to fetch the doctor, and then try to explain to aunt Hephzibah that she now had a husband who would not trouble her in the forseeable future when night-time came.

She might even be grateful! Who could tell?

Chapter 4

Seven days after their wedding, the new Mr and Mrs Dacre were seated round the family table enjoying their homecoming meal as they described the wonders and delights of the nearby spa town, Scarborough, where they'd spent their honeymoon.

"Ooh, but it were wonderful. T'shops an' everythin'," and Polly, all-smiles, sat next to her husband, as full of energy as a wound-up clock-work toy as she giggled and chirped fifty-to-the-dozen. "We went over t'Valley Bridge," she boasted, "and even went into… oh, what's that place called, Adam, where there were all them things for to see?… Ro… Rotunda Museum."

"It sounds… just the spot ter visit," Hannah humoured her.

"An' we went ter t'Spa, ter an orchestral concert… an' every morn-in'—well, almost—we saw a pierrot show on the sands. Oh, it was lovely, Evelyn. You should 'ave bin with us. *Carrick's Original Pierrots*. The men were dressed in white baggy suits wi' red pom-poms an' ruffs round their necks. An' they 'ad a sort o' black scarf on their 'ead under a white point-ed cap, an' they started their show wi' a pierrot comin' on the stage an' sayin'…." she paused for breath before turning to Adam, and in her childish way pleaded, "go on, Adam. You do it, love. You can do it better na' me."

Adam Dacre cleared his throat. "Ladies and gentlemen," he began to imitate the seaside entertainer, "…for your delectation and delight, we proudly present that epitome of seaside spectaculars, the personification of popular pleasure, an extravaganza of effervescent entertainment and elocution, a marriage of music and mime, we give you… the Pierrot Show!"

"An' then," Polly broke in, "Mr Tambo-Man would shake an' rattle 'is tambourine an' the show would start proper. Oh, we 'ad a lovely time, didn't we, Adam?"

"Aye."

"An' we saw the castle—"

"An' the 'arbour."

"An' t'boats an' big ships. Oh, it were wonderful. An' Adam says we may go again some time." and suddenly feeling self-conscious, Polly went quiet.

"Well, that'll be summatt ter look forward to," Hannah tried to rescue her feelings.

"An after all that, will yer be ready fer comin' out wi' me first thing Monday mornin' or dooan't yer want ter be a 'local' fisherman any more?" Adam's father joked.

"I'll be ready, dad."

"Yer will look after him won't yer, Mr Dacre?" Polly asked, suddenly concerned.

"Polly, your man'll be safe, never fear."

"Yer very kind."

"Aye… an' we've all on us bin busy while you two 'ave bin in Scarborough," Jacques Dacre continued, "fer we've taken all your weddin' presents ter Ring o' Bells, an 'Annah's bin all week getting' t'spot ready for yer."

"That's very kind. An' I mun learn to cook now, I suppose."

"Oh aye," Hannah was quick to agree with her. "Adam's a good appetite." She looked at her brother, and seemed to sense that something was amiss.

"I can make sandwiches," Polly boasted.

"Well, doy, yer'll soon learn." But Hannah had her doubts.

Polly chirruped while dishes were washed and put away. Adam had bought her some china dogs to put on the mantle shelf, and a figurine of little Red Riding Hood, and she'd seen, and oh, it were lovely, a tea-cup and saucer that said 'A Present from Scarborough' but when they went back to the shop the following day it had been sold. Father and son went to the Cod & Lobster, and Evelyn and David tactfully disappeared while Hannah tried to have a "motherly" talk with her sister-in-law.

"And… everythin' was all right wi' you an' Adam?"

"Oh yes, 'Annah."

"There were no 'problems' on yer weddin' night?"

"No. Why?"

"Just… Polly, don't be shy. Yer can talk ter me—ask me owt—yer know."

"What about?"

"Well, on what couples get up to when they're wed. Sleepin' together an all that. It's nowt ter be shy about, now yer married."

"No, I know it isn't."

"Well, was everythin'—yer are a 'proper' 'usband an' wife, are yer?"

" 'Course we are," Polly giggled. "Adam loves me."

"Good. An' I'm not goin' ter pry any more. But I'm here if yer need me."

"Right. I mun call at t'privvy, an then… when Adam and Mr Dacre get back… me an' Adam mun get 'ome."

"An' yer double bed's got new sheets on. They wor among yer presents."

"That'll be nice—t'bed all made up, I mean."

All Polly Dacre needed to concern herself with was keeping her new husband at a distance. Their nights in Scarborough had, for her, been embarrassing, to the point of shameful. Never had it occurred to her that they would have to undress in the same room, or lay side by side in a double bed with Adam... well, wanting to "touch" and do things. Kissing was all right, but he wanted them to take all their clothes off, and cuddle up together, and... and she daren't bring herself to even think when he intended them to do after that. She'd wanted to cry. Adam was rubbing against her, stroking her thighs. She'd held herself rigid. Petrified.

"It's all right, doy," he'd kept whispering in her ear, snuggling closer with each kiss.

But it wasn't. She wanted him to be nice, not start trying to "do" things.

"Relax, Poll-doll. You want me to love you, don't you?"

"Mmm."

"Well then..."

"When we're back in Steeas. 'Don't seem right, 'ere."

"Oh, Polly," and Adam had put his arms round her. "What's the matter, doy—you frightened I'll hurt you, or we'll stain the bed-sheets? Polly, I'm no more experienced in these things than you. Let's just... cuddle each other."

"That'd be nice."

"And no... 'you know'.'"

But Adam had seen her without clothes, and she'd cast a sly glance and seen his—and she couldn't even bring herself to think about it. Nor was it small and limp between his legs, but—oh, if it was going to be like that when they went to bed, what was she going to do?

What *was* she going to do?

Thinking about (and secretly envious of his brother) David Dacre stared at a cut-throat moon and a wasp's nest of stars lighting the inky canopy that entrapped Staithes. Despite the season, there was a razor-sharp wind causing the breakers to spit spume, and dredge up shingle and bladder-wrack from the North Sea along with the more recent rubbish the fishermen had thrown overboard. Adam and Polly would be tucked up in bed, and by now Adam would have—the lucky dog!

Still, he consoled himself, his time would come, for he was only sixteen, and everything before him, and when he'd served his time at the blacksmiths and could shoe horses as easily as his employer, and bend curves, and make metal do as he wanted, then he would—oh, but marriage was a long way away, nor, in the meantime had he a sweetheart who would let him do that—what Adam would be doing with Polly. His mates boasted—but he knew it was all talk, just as one of them told tales of what happened to young lads who went to sea and were among men who had no recourse to woman to satisfy their lusts. There was one thing—he'd never so much as go out in a coble.

He'd also heard stories… that when a coble had had a run of bad luck then the wives of the crew would, at midnight, after slaying a pigeon work a magic charm, and conjuring up a witch, entreat her to remove the evil that hovered over the craft. Much more to be feared were the crashing waves rising like monsters from the deep and smashing boats over Pot o' Steel as though they were made of matchwood . Despite his being born in a fishing village, and as a young lad running naked over the flat scaurs of rocks before jumping into the breakers, the sea terrified him. The constant at-best-rocking at worst pounding over the slipway and surging half way up the High Street. Then it would recoil, only to again spring out of its lair. A wild thing! No-one could tame the sea.

Even in his dreams, the monster would insidiously creep, encroach, and gently enfold him as he felt himself being lured, then slowly but forcefully dragged deeper and deeper into its depths. He'd awake with a start, wakening Adam, his bedmate. He'd be shaking, yet could say nothing more than it was a bad dream—"the sea" had a hold over him—could command silence. His big brother would put a protecting arm round him, and David would shiver when he thought of what only seconds before had seemed so real.

He'd have no Adam now to keep the demons at bay, and as he stared toward the barely discernable horizon David Dacre thought—no, he knew—that one day the sea would claim him.

For the not-faint-hearted, it was to be an amorous autumn.

A season of carnal longing, lust and hedonistic fulfilment, when all things ripen, are luscious, and ready for the taking. Even the vibrancy of summer paled when contrasted against the purple spiked buddleia en-crusted with peacock butterflies. The yellow September sunlight was a fitting backdrop for dahlias with their tousled heads and ostrich plumes of asters. Gardens were a riot of colour. Drowsy wasps hovered over bowls of ripe pears in the honey-toned stillness of kitchens smelling like chapel harvest festivals. The seashore glistened, the morning light dancing off the waves as fishermen with salt-bleached hair and salt-bleached eyes went about their business, the backs of their hands and their faces a near copper colour. The gold of autumn!

Hannah's days were long and full, for she was now laying down provisions for winter. There were fruits to preserve, or turn into jams and chutneys, and with every batch she made, she allocated an extra one for Polly and Adam, and also the captain. Then there was his house to keep clean, when she had time for such things, for it seemed that most of her afternoons at Hillcrest were spent in the gentleman's bed.

After their lovemaking they would lie together, their passions temporarily fulfilled, listening to the distant sea quietly booming like a lazy bassoon. Gone was the staccato splash of waves on the rocks, this sound was mature. Sonorous. As resolved as a perfect cadence.

After deep relaxing breaths, Hannah's fingers would lightly trace the contours of her lover's torso. She could feel his body suddenly tense then relax under her explorative touch. She lightly brushed the hair over his abdomen, but modestly went no further.

"Don't stop, Hannah," he'd plead.

"Nay, but I mun be away soon,"

"But not until… just once more."

"Yer'll get me a bad name."

"But don't worry, love. I'll do the right thing. I'll ask you to marry me."

"What? Again?" she joked.

His hand was cupping her breast, the tip of his tongue caressing her nipple. He stopped only to look up at her and whisper, "I love you."

"That's as may be."

"But I do," he insisted. "Let me show you again just how much."

Once more she gave herself to him, her body arching as she felt his flesh deep inside her. Hungry for his kisses, her lips greedily sought his mouth, her nails clawed as she drew him closer. Their bodies rocked in rhythm, her sounds of pleasure grew to screams of ecstasy, their breathing became laboured, then her orgasm seemed to envelop her, to take over her body and soul. Finally, like receding waves on the shore, there was calm.

Now she must just lie in his arms, where she felt safe, and loved.

The sun was casting long shadows when the lovers finally stirred.

"I mun go now," she whispered, "affore tongues start waggin'."

"What the hell. Let them."

Round and pregnant, the harvest moon shamelessly lit up the village, bathing the rough stubble in the fields above Cowbar with a phosphorescent glow. The young lovers embraced then kissed, their bodies, if not their minds, as one. She gave lovelorn sighs, and wished that he'd say the words she was wanting to hear. That he loved her… enough to stand up his dragon of a mother and tell her that she was the girl he wanted to marry, and that they had an "understanding".

He was hoping… that if he were to promise… to "stand by her"… then she might yield to his advances. Feeling bold (and lucky) his hand began to fumble inside her blouse. Instead of shoving him away as she'd done on previous occasions she drew him closer.

"Somebody… might see us," he whispered.

"Not if we go inside the barn," and with the innocence of children their feet crunched over the cornfield, the full mother-moon lighting the way to seduction. She felt… that she would soon have a "power" over him. He would be ensnared by her lovemaking—be her slave. He'd heard the other lads in Staithes boast about their exploits, and from their tales, knew what was expected of him. Inexperience was not to be a barrier to this night of passion.

Within the shelter of the building he threw his jacket over the floor of straw, she her shawl. Evelyn hoped he'd know what to do and get on with it, for if she were late arriving home, then suspicions could be raised, and he'd heard that the first time a woman—and he imagined it would be the first time for her—then they were suddenly undoing each others clothes. Yet try as he might, nothing was happening, he was as limp as piece of wet seaweed But her fingers were massaging, stimulating. Somehow, she was under him, her legs wide apart.

She was coaxing, already taking on the dominant role. "Push" she whispered, as her body became even more accommodating. Then, for Timothy Howarth, things had started to happen. He was… hell, he was going to manage it after all.

When it was over they pulled apart. He felt deeply ashamed, disgusted by the act he'd just performed. Her arms were reaching out. "Don't let's go yet."

"But… we mun get back before me mother—"

"Please, just a few minutes."

"An' when we get ter t'beck, we'd best go our own separate ways, That way nobody'll suspect owt."

"All right, Tim, if that's what you want."

"Aye. It'll be safer, I'm thinkin'."

Evelyn knew better than to argue. Little point when he was now hers.

Christmas—and for Hannah, another feat of cooking and baking. Realising that Polly could scarcely boil a pan of water, then she and Adam must share their Christmas table, and, and hoping such a guest would raise no undue speculation in the village, Owen was also invited to part of the Dacre household for the day.

He arrived, somewhat apprehensive as to his reception, not knowing whether he was to be received as a future in-law or as Hannah's employer.

David opened the door to him. "Coom in, Captain. Merry Christmas ter yer."

"And to all of you." He wore a fancy waistcoat with an Albert-and-chain under a blue checked suit, the beard was neatly trimmed, his cheeks glowed, and Hannah looked on her fine figure of a man and wished she could throw her arms round him, thus ending any doubts the family might have regarding the nature of their friendship.

"Yer'll 'ave a glass o' wine?"

"Yes please, Hannah."

"An' when Polly an' Adam arrive, then we can start, an' I hope yer 'ungry."

" 'Annah 'as been busy," her father complimented her, "I dooan't think t'oven's been empty fer t'last seven days."

"Aye, an' I mun go an' top copper up wi' boilin' water affore it get too low, or else t'puddin'll be spoiled," and she jumped up to see to what she regarded as the best part of the meal. Dark with fruit, mixed with brandy before being wrapped in a floured cloth and now hanging from a cutdown broom handle it was suspended in the boiling water. She hoped Owen liked pudding. She'd saved some brandy so she could set it alight before bringing it to the table, and there'd be some for the sauce—it was beginning to sound like a drunken meal.

When the potatoes were mashed, the greens done, the roast parsnips looking the colour of polished walnut along with glazed carrots, and the turkey, (a change from the usual goose) sat on a huge meat plate, Polly and Adam then made their appearance.

She had changed little since their marriage, was still all giggles and ringlets, and if the family had hoped for a "roundness" in her figure, then they were to be disappointed. Still, Hannah told herself, it was early days. Yet Adam seemed so loving and caring. Soon she'd be able to tell them what they all wanting to hear… but Christmas would be a lovely time for such an announcement. It would also be the ideal opportunity for herself and Owen to—but it wouldn't, because her life still wasn't her own. There was her family to care for.

She'd been hearing rumours about Evelyn, and no use asking her if there were any truth to the gossip until the two of them were on their own, and there was David and his silly talk about going to join some regiment and "see the world" as he called it. His world was here, in Staithes. There was Dad—and Polly need to learn how to cook and bake, so she could feed Adam. No use relying on someone else all the time, for one day… and it was getting nearer, she'd have to say yes or no to the constant proposal of marriage Owen was offering . Polly's first test as a housewife would be Boxing Day when aunt Bridie would be calling at Ring o' Bells for afternoon tea. Under Hannah's supervision Polly had baked aunt Bridie's favourite (and her aunt's test of a housewife's capabilities) seed cake. Hannah hoped the house was tidy and dusted and—and Hannah stopped bothering about other people, and began serving the meal.

He was perched on the edge of his armchair, his mother in an equally uncomfortable position seated opposite. They were in the Holy of Holies, the "parlour" above the shop, a room reserved for Christmas days and funerals.

The high windows were flanked with brocade that was never drawn and heavily draped with cream nets to stop both prying eyes and also the sunlight, which faded carpets and furnishings, highlighted specks of dust on the walnut what-not, and dared to intrude on those other-than-designated days. The chimney had been blazed before lighting the fire, and now in the hearth two tiny flames huddled together for warmth. A pottery plaque with a pink edge warned "Prepare to Meet thy God" while in the other alcove a matching one proclaimed "God is Love". The horsehair sofa, black and shiny and looking almost polished, was to be viewed only—it was certainly not for sitting on.

His starched collar was now beginning to rub. The rough tweed suit, even with long combinations underneath was prickly, his waistcoat was tight, and when he moved his shoes squeaked, which both pleased yet irritated his mother at the same time. (She knew of his every move, but the actual sound annoyed her.)

After a long silence—he'd earlier dared to whistle, till she fixed him with a look—Lizzie Howarth finally managed, "Seventeen year, terday."

He thought he'd escaped the annual reminder, but Lizzie Howarth had not forgotten the great wrong done her, nor was she to let her son forget.

"Spoilin' t''appiest day o' year. Leeavin' me wi' a village shop ter run on mi own, an' a ten-year-owd lad still needin' a good leatherin' every Friday neet ter rid him o' t' week's sins. What did I do ter deserve that?"

"Nowt, Mam."

"No. An' it wor 'ard goin'. They were long days slavin' in that shop keeping' us out o' work'ouse. But one day, it'll all be thine. When owt ails me I'll want thee ter be set up wi' somebody sensible, fer tha not reight bright, even though I shouldn't say such things."

He wanted to suggest—but knew Evelyn Dacre wasn't the girl his mother had in mind. She'd have him destined for somebody plain, from one of the Bible Meetings she attended. Unattractive, God-fearing, wrong side of thirty, and never seen a man without trousers.

It was better to remain silent than to risk incurring her wrath on such an afternoon. Besides, he'd been giving the matter serious thought. Evelyn Dacre was—well, becoming too demanding. What had happened in the barn above Cowbar seemed to be assumed every time they were together. She'd come into the shop for a bar of chocolate (for which Tim refused payment, unless his mother with hovering, for where money was concerned, she had more eyes than a potato) and holding the bar, and his hand, she'd whisper, "See you tonight."

It was easier to agree to her suggested meetings, for at least then she would leave him to get on with his chores, and it would keep the secret from his mother, who would want to know too much, not that he dare tell her—

"Tha can 'ave an apple," and she nodded toward the bowl of fruit, "or an orange, but not both. An' tha mun eat it in t'kitchen, mind."

"I'll 'ave—"

"Not that one, that goin' back in t'winder ter tempt folk," and her hand went out, for fear he should take the shiniest fruit. "Tak' one thro 'bottom, they're all t'same."

"...Aye."

"As tha read thi bible this mornin' Timothy?"

"Yes, mam," he lied.

"What as tha read?" she wanted to know.

"Proverbs," he was quick to reply.

"That's a good lad. We mun not neglect daily tasks."

"No, mam."

"An I might open up in t'mornin' for a couple o' 'ours. Somebody's sure ter want summatt. It's been an expensive day, terday. Yon farmer should be ashamed, chargin' what 'ee as fer an' owd hen. Tha mun enjoy it, there'll nooan be one next year."

She chuntered as she went downstairs, and left alone, Tim moved to the window and peered down the street, imagining the party there was sure to be at the Dacres. Evelyn had asked him to call on her that evening at their house, but he knew better than to accept such an invitation. For it were as good as a "promise", to call on her, an open declaration of his intentions, and he wasn't altogether sure what they were.

Evelyn seemed to be taking over his life. So easy for her to come into the shop in the pretence of buying some small item, only to whisper that they must meet, when he was in no position to refuse, and when they did meet, she was only more demanding, and for ever wanting the two of them to do "somethin' different".

How many "different" ways could she dream up of performing such a basic act?

"Lie on one side, with your weight on one arm, then you got the other free— so you can 'do' things. Touch—stroke. We can stimulate an' play wi' one another, an—" and sometimes she was kissing more than his lips, and wanting him to reply in a similar way. He'd return home feeling deeply ashamed of what had taken place between the two of them, and vow that it would be the last time they would meet. It was secret, and it was wrong.

Not until seeing Evelyn had he even thought about... sex! Not even as a teenager had things stirred, or had he wanted, or even felt the need to satisfy such animal instincts—because they'd not been there. They would have to have words, the two of them. Perhaps it would be best for him if his mother did find him a wife. At least, she'd choose one who was not at all demanding in that department.

At the end of their perfect day, Polly and Adam, arms round each other said "Goodnight" to their family and Capt Danvers-Griffiths, as Polly still called him, and made their way to Ring o' Bells and some unopened presents still to be investigated. "And next year," Adam was saying to her, "we'll invite everyone to Christmas Lunch at our 'ouse, an' you can let 'em see what a good cook you've become."

"But I'm not."

"No love, but by next Christmas, who knows?"

She was silent, and Adam knew deep inside that Polly would never master such things. She made the cottage look pretty, bought flowers and dolls instead of food, was sweet and girlish when he returned from fishing, would even scrub his back when he bathed, but would never… for theirs was an unusual marriage. Unconsummated.

Polly was still a virgin!

Despite Adam's devotion and great patience, Polly was, for some reason she was unable to explain, frightened and repelled by the thought of what other married couples did, and what Adam was expecting from her. They'd never so much as argued about such a thing, for Adam would stop his advances when she froze. He'd say he was sorry, or she'd make some excuse that it 'wasn't the right time' and hope he'd know what she meant. Any excuse, so she didn't have to let him do "that" to her.

"But don't you want babies?" he'd once asked. "I thought we'd agreed—were goin' to—"

"Course I do, silly."

"Well then? Where d'yer think babies come from, Polly?"

"I know all 'bout that. But you've got to patient with me, Adam."

"Polly, love. We're 'usband an' wife . It's what married couples do. It might hurt just a bit the first time, but I'll be so gentle, I do so want to love you."

"You can kiss me. 'Ow's that?"

"An' cuddle, like this?" and his hand went under her nightie and up the inside of her thigh.

"No, Adam—not like that," and she pulled away from him.

Some night's he felt like sleeping on his own, or he'd go to the Cod & Lobster and later, instead of coming straight home, would walk along the High Street and toward the bridge over the beck. He'd see figures come out from the shadows. Love was available, for a very reasonable price. A man from the miners' cottages at Cowbar was selling his fourteen-year-old daughter. Husbands, their wives. Before he'd set sail on his Iceland trip there were girls on the harbourside readily available. His soon-to-be shipmates were anxious to have their last fling, but he'd thought about Polly and was able to resist temptation.

More desirable then ever she now seemed, this first Christmas evening of their being married, and Adam hoped—oh, he so hoped—that tonight Polly would finally yield to his advances.

Chapter 5

Another recently married couple had returned to Staithes, even if only to work.

The Knights' earlier trip to London in the hope that picture dealers might be interested in their work had been fraught with disappointment and frustration, their only encouragement coming from one gallery—yet even they could offer nothing more substantial than simply words.

They faced a cruel winter, their meagre funds now reduced to necessities: painting materials. Their only consolation in returning to Yorkshire being the warmth and hospitality of their landlady, and their ties with the other painters. The "respectability" of married life had now opened certain doors, for they were regularly invited to Sunday afternoon teas with the Jacksons, or the Hopwoods who lived in nearby Hinderwell. They had earlier met up with Silkstone Hopwood whilst visiting an exhibition of Dutch paintings at the Guildhall, when he had invited them to join him on a planned painting holiday in Holland. It had seemed tempting, but unattainable. It was not an easy life, being an artist.

Yet they were painting conscientiously and had rented a derelict property on the harbourside for a studio. Harold was working on a particularly good picture, while Laura faithfully observed, and in sketchbook and in oils recorded, the day-to-day life of the fishing community. A young woman, recently widowed, wearing the traditional mourning bonnet; a Staithes funeral; the pet monkey that escaped from Barber Row and ran among the rocks evading capture; and a particularly striking portrait of Evelyn.

After several weeks of the daily trudge to their studio they took stock of their work. Their best pictures were to be submitted to the Royal Academy and, if accepted and hung, then Laura must somehow conjure up enough money for their train journey to London for the varnishing day.

Weeks passed. Their tickets arrived. Both of them had had their work accepted.

Wearing patched-up Sunday best, and travelling on borrowed money, they boarded the train from Whitby to King's Cross, their clothes soaked from having walked from Roxby to Whitby in a torrential downpour. The ensuing train journey was uncomfortable and unbelievably cold, and still feeling wretched the following day they were greeted on the Academy steps a colleague who informed Harold that his picture had been sold for a hundred pounds. They were overjoyed. They would have the wherewithal to finance the trip to Holland after all.

Good Friday, 1904, saw the demise of Reuben Dacre, who had, according to his widow, "Nooan bin 'issen fer soom time."

" 'Course, doy," she was quick to point out to Hannah, who had called to express her sympathies on behalf of her branch of the Dacre family, "I'm nooan complainin'."

Seeing a somewhat mystified expression on her niece's face, her aunt continued, "It's a shame 'ee's deead, 'cos 'ee wor just startin' ter behave. They do say as dogs an' 'usbands do as they're told, if they live long enough. There wor no longer any unnecessaryness when it wor time for a good night's sleep, if tha gets mi drift. I 'ad years an' years o' puttin' up wi' a man as 'ad nobbut one thing on his brain. If tha gets wed doy, an' thee 'usband does go astray, dooan't thee worry. It means less o'—" and she gave a knowing "cough". "That there."

"I'll… remember that," Hannah finally managed, at the same time recalling something else.

"I noticed…" her aunt confided, "a reight change coom over him… after Adam's weddin'."

"…Really?"

"Aye. 'Didn't seem t'same man. I dooan't think 'ee 'troubled' me ageean. Funny how weddin's affect folk."

"Mmm."

"An' 'ow's your captain gettin' on?" Steeas' most recent widow suddenly brightened up.

"Nay, aunt 'Ephzibah, 'ee's nooan… well, not yet."

"Dooan't wait ter long, if yer've a chance o' 'appiness, 'cos not all men are like Reuben wor. I think yer've backed a winner there. Me mother allus said, 'If yer've a good 'usband, blind him in one eye. If yer've a bad 'un, blind him in both.'"

"That seems good advice. But I really came ter ask about t'arrangements for t'funeral. Fer dad's wonderin'—"

"Thursday if we can manage it, if not Friday. But it'll be affore t'weekend. Jonas is at Loftus wi' t'undertakers as we're sat here talkin'."

"Is it goin' ter be a big do?"

"No. I dooan't know what 'ee's left—but I do know as 'ee allus kept me short. I'm wastin' nowt on fancy flahs an' gurt funeral teas. There'll be no boiled 'am an' trifles. It'll be plain an' simple. Like 'ee wor."

" 'Appen it's as well," Hannah agreed with her choice.

"It is. An' I can't pretend ter be broken-'earted, 'cos I'm not. 'Ee led me a reight dance, allus threatenin' ter leave me fer soom woman at 'Inderwell as 'ee said 'ad ta'en a fancy ter 'im. At 'finish I said 'Bugger off. But tak' thee two lasses wi' thee. Dooan't leeave me saddled wi' 'em. If she wants thee, she mun 'ave all 'trappin's.' "

"That seemed fair."

"But 'ee wouldn't. I'd be a lot better off nah if 'ee 'ad, 'cos she'd be payin' fer t'funeral." She shook her head philosophically. "Nivver 'eed, doy. We'll 'ave a cup o' tea, an' yer can tell me all yer news. Is Polly expectin' yet?"

"No. Leastways, they've said nowt ter me."

"Well, there's time enough. They're nobbut young," but as her aunt began busying herself with tea things, Hannah wondered yet again if things were as they should be between Adam and Polly. That they were still in love was evident, but her sister-in-law seemed so... immature. A baby to her would be as a doll, just a plaything. It was Adam who struggled to keep the cottage in some semblance of order, nor could Polly bait lines, she was physically sick at the thought of gutting fish, and useless when it came to the hard work involved, and expected, of a fisherman's wife. It was herself and Evelyn who carried her, but time would come when her younger sister had her own man to care for. And, Hannah realised, Owen wouldn't wait for ever.

The tea was strong, aunt Hephzibah had made some shortbread fingers. The two of them drank and munched, until, as a sudden afterthought her aunt asked, "do yer want ter look at 'im?"

Hannah thought quickly. "Well, I think... best ter remember 'im as 'ee wor."

"Nay, doy—'ee's a lot better nah. 'Ee's deead."

"...Where is 'ee?"

"Oopstairs, in bed. All laid aht. Looks grand. She's done a reight good job 'as Sair-Anne. Ah know she's a gossip, but she can lay folk aht. 'Ee'd nooan bin deead five minutes affore she wor bangin' on t'door. 'Tha'll want me best quality service,' she says, 'for 'ee wor a good 'usband.' I says, 'I want 'cheapest yer can do. 'Ee wor a sod.' That put 'er straight. Coom on doy, 'ave a look at 'im."

Laid out in a four-poster bed with faded maroon drapes, Hannah beheld her dead uncle. There was an uncomfortable silence as she sought for words of condolence, but found none.

"It's a shame 'ee's deead. Fer t'last few month... well, I dooan't know what changed 'im"—but her aunt's look spoke volumes.

Feeling excited, yet apprehensive when she thought of the possible outcome of her excursion, she looked from the compartment window to see fields, villages, open countryside, and even views of the North Sea move into, and from, her vision.

The speed of the train—the rattle it made—*getmetowhitby, getmetowhitby* it seemed to say as it gobbled up the miles. Now, because no-one was watching, Evelyn took the brass curtain-ring from her purse and slipped it on the third finger of her left hand. Unless given close scrutiny it would serve its purpose. She stared at her reflection in the window and again practised her "look". That of a destitute woman fallen on hard times, with two young children, a husband unable to find honest employment, and a wicked landlord about to evict them. Too many mouths to feed, without another expected in a few months. The sorrowful face stared back. She wanted to laugh, but knew that would spoil the effect.

"Think depressin' thoughts," she told herself, and she tried to imagine death, and terrible pain. Having her arms pulled from her body, burning coals placed on her skin, her tongue being torn out—ooh, it was awful. A fellow traveller, a gentleman in a striped suit, bowler hat on his knees was giving her curious looks. She stared beyond him, and sighed wearily.

Soon, she told herself, the train would pull into the station on the West Cliff, she'd alight, and then, as she meandered into the town itself, her quest could begin. And, she reminded herself, she must buy Polly something for her birthday, as that was the excuse for her coming into Whitby.

They were approaching Sandsend. The gentleman was still staring.

A lace handkerchief? A piece of carved Whitby jet?

Still, the present would depend on how much she had left in her purse, and Evelyn imagined that that which she had come to Whitby to hopefully purchase would cost more than mere coppers. It could even be… two… as much as five pounds, in which case she'd have to return, her mission unaccomplished. If the price were so high, then she'd have to go to Timothy for the money. No use approaching Hannah: she'd ask too many questions.

She fingered the curtain ring, to signify to the striped suited gentleman that she was a respectable married woman and not the sort of person to engage in conversation with strangers, no matter how honourable their intentions might, or might not, be. She drew her shawl round her shoulders, then looked again in her purse. She'd fifteen shillings and some bits of change. She was a woman of means.

Walking from the station, she passed and paused by the West Cliff Saloon, where, it was advertised, a band would perform twice daily, weather permitting, and there was also a theatre visited by "Leading London Dramatic and Concert Parties". Day tickets, sixpence, periodical tickets on moderate terms. On the far headland she could see the church and ruined abbey, to her left, the sea, on her right, an arc of fine residences. She tried to imagine the people who would live in such houses. They'd need an army of servants, the ladies would have maids, and would dress in fine silks. Fifteen shillings and bits of small change would be nothing to the likes of them.

Not sure of her ultimate destination, Evelyn allowed herself to be drawn into and part of the sightseers and sudden bustle of people as she began to move from the outskirts and into the town proper. She passed advertised apartments at Belle Vue Terrace, and the Granby Hotel, with "Breakfast, Luncheons, Dinners and Teas provided at the shortest notice, also spacious rooms, good bathrooms and accommodation for cycles at very moderate tariff"—and almost directly opposite, Botham's Café, where "Visitors may rely on everything being of the very best quality, and the price moderate". She saw Atkinson, Family Grocer, D. Lawson, Saddler and Harness Maker, selling 'Saddles, Bridles, Martingales. Every stable requisite in stock." A.H. Drewett, for "Pianos and Organs by all leading makers. Tuning and repairing a speciality".

There was a branch of the Scarborough and Whitby Breweries, Ralph Lawson, noted for prime Yorkshire hams and bacon, and the West Cliff Fine Art Gallery of E.E. Anderson, Artists' Colourman, Carver and Gilder (he was the recent painter in Staithes)—but none of these were able to supply what Evelyn needed.

At the end of Skinner Street she turned left into Flowergate. On her right was The Angel, "High Class Family and Commercial Hotel, with Electric Lighting throughout, and an Hotel Porter who met all the Whitby trains". She passed Spantons, "Hatter, Hosier and Gentleman's Mercer. Cycling, Golfing Boating and Bathing Requisites in great variety". Mrs Day, Milliner. Furs, lace collars etc.; H.A. Spiegelhalter, Watches, Clocks, Jewellery and Silver Plate. Mrs Thornton, Milliner and Dressmaker. Baby Linen, Corsets—*corsets?* The last thing she wanted. There was R.C. Cook, Boot and Shoe dealer; Agar and Son, Cabinet makers, Upholsterers and Undertakers, House Agents and Appraiser; Arthur Hemmingway, Baker and Confectioner, Excursion and Choir Parties Catered for Special Terms; W.H. Duck, Family Butcher—but still, not the shop for Evelyn.

Flowergate now became Golden Lion Bank, then streets seemed to converge, and she crossed over the swing bridge onto the East Side, for in the old part of the town, tucked away in one of the narrow streets would, she imagined, be the sort of shop she was looking for. On Bridge Street she passed W. Sawdon, Watchmaker, and the St Hilda Serge Emporium, selling a cloth renowned for "Beauty and Appearance, and exceeding Hard Wear, unaffected by Sun, Sea-Air or Salt Water. Ideal for Seaside, Travelling, Yachting, Cycling and Golfing. Absolutely fast in the dye, made in various qualities, and pattern books sent on application. To be had from the Sole Proprietors: Jas. N. Clarkson and Son, Whitby".

She turned into Sandgate, and peered in the jet workers. Their window displayed samples of their craft. Necklaces, brooches, even miniature models of the ruined abbey, while toward the back of the shop she could also see the workers themselves sat at their benches. Across the street was a shop selling sweets. Humbugs, coltsfoot rock, pink and white sugar mice, hundreds-and-thousands, bars of chocolate, crystallised fruits, toffee, clotted-cream fudge. It made her mouth water.

Better than herrings and honey, or sucking on a piece of coal—then she caught an unmistakable smell of southernwood. She twitched her nostrils. And there was a scent of... hops? Or was it just a combination of various odours? It was emanating from the herbalists she was now approaching.

She stood and sniffed: her day was not going to wasted.

For a long time Evelyn inhaled the many fragrances as she stared first in the window, then inside the open door of the shop. She saw bunches of herbs hanging from hooks in the ceiling, and sitting safe and comfortable on mahogany shelves dark blue bottles with gold lettering. Syrup of Squillae, Syrup of Rhoead, Syrup of Tolu. There were fancy-looking Apothecary jars bearing what she took to be Latin inscriptions; pestle and mortar, a set of brass balance scales, marble slabs, specimen jars holding secret potions and (she supposed) possibly love charms. Phials of pills, jars of already made-up preparations, bottles of various mixtures. While below the marble slabs and working area lived drawers of skullcap, devil's claw, flowers of bergamot, wormwood, elderflower and peppermint, malt and hops, and in tall jars twists of barley-sugar looking like walking sticks, and broken bits of Spanish juice resembling coal. There were jars of pomades, blocks of goose-grease and elderflower masquerading as bars of soap, and bottles of glycerine and oppidildock which, the labelling claimed, were a boon for chapped hands, and Evelyn was tempted to get dad—then, her strength suddenly draining from her, she must now tell the woman behind the counter what she was hoping to buy.

She had a kind, motherly face, a halo of silvery hair, and was spreading smiles as think as butter on a cold morning. "Now then, doy, what could we get you?"

Trying hard to remember her earlier rehearsed words but failing
miserably, Evelyn blurted out, "I don't rightly know how ter tell yer,
Missis. But I'm in a bit o' trouble," and she opened her shawl to reveal
exactly the nature of her predicament."

"Eee, but tha'll nooan be t'first young lass in that situation."

"I can't 'ave this bairn," Evelyn blurted out, no longer feeling the
need for any possible pretence, "I'm nooan wed. Can't yer 'elp me?"

"Best ah can do is advise thee ter go ter t'man as got thee into trouble
an'—"

"No, that's no good. Please Missis. Me mother's dead, God rest 'er
soul, but when me dad finds out, then…" and the tears began to well up.
"I've been… so silly. What am I goin' ter do?"

"Come on, calm thissen. Come in t'back o' t'shop an' I'll mak' thee a
cup o' tea."

"But that'll nooan get rid o' mi baby."

"It's ter late fer that, I'm thinking, looking' at thee. 'Ow many
month?"

"Four," she lied.

The woman shook her head. "It'd be dangerous, yer too far gone."

"I'll risk it."

"Nay, but it's bairn we mun think abaht," then the shopkeeper
dropped the latch. "Time ter put us feet up, an' we mun 'ave some
currant pasty… an'… talk abaht what yer mun do next."

Silently, with head downcast, she left the herbalist's and slowly shuffled
along Sandgate till she came to the market place and the old Town Hall,
its body, as round as hers was soon to be, surrounded by arches and
columns. It was market day, the base of the building being used by young
women selling butter and eggs. Someone else had brought baskets of
gooseberries to sell, and a woman had loaves of bread and cakes. There
was a stall selling cheese, and meat pies. Evelyn was suddenly hungry, but
resisted the urge to eat, until she knew how much money she had for
such an extravagance as food.

There must be another herbalist. One who would not ask questions,
but just hand over what she wanted. She looked up at the clock beneath
the domed cupola. The day was still young.

From the market square, alleys and yards seemed to lead off in various
directions and the one she took led her to the pier. The well-worn stone
flags, she fancied, would, if they could only speak, have many tales to tell.
Of press-gangs, and sweethearts waving farewell to their lovers who had

signed-on as members of the crew for some whaling expedition, and as she looked toward the mouth of the harbour, Evelyn could recall the story her mother had told her about "the bells". Following the dissolution of the monasteries, the bells of Whitby were sold and ordered to be conveyed to London, but as she sailed out of the harbour, the ship and her precious cargo sank. The bells had never been recovered and—and she could still hear Mam's voice, legend had it that on quiet nights the sea fairies ring them, and their sound could be clearly heard above the waves.

She stared into the restless water and listened to a thickness of silence, then suddenly started as a voice pleaded, "dooan't jump—tha'll get all thee cloathes weet," and she turned to the motherly figure stood next to her.

"I wasn't goin' to."

"Good. 'Cos there's nowt so bad as can't be put ter reights. When I'm feelin' low, I allus..." and the woman's hand went into her pocket from which she produced a silver box "...'ave a dose o' snuff. Clears me 'ead." The gnarled forefinger and thumb dipped into and pinched a few grains of the brown powder, then with a flourish she brought them to her nostrils and sniffed theatrically. After rubbing the tip of her nose with the back of her hand she pronounced, "that's better. Now I can put t'world ter rights. So what ails thee, pet. A trouble shared is a trouble 'alved."

"Isn't it obvious?"

The woman nodded. "Oh, men 'ave a lot ter answer for. They promise yer t'world till they 'ave their wicked way. Knock yer about an' all, does 'ee?"

"Oh no, Missis. Nowt like that."

"Well, that's summatt ter be thankful for. An' is this man o' thine single—or' as 'ee got a wife an' bairns?"

" 'Ee's nooan married."

"Prospects?"

" 'Im an' 'is mam own t'village shop."

"Well then. Where's thee problem, pet?"

Evelyn, as though admitting to some great sin bit her lip, then murmured, "'ee's grown distant, of late."

"But 'ee wasn't when 'ee filled thee belly."

"No. I thought 'ee loved me then."

"Oh, men," the wise old head shook in sympathy before asking, "an' do yer want this bairn?"

Evelyn stared into the waters, and in a voice alien even to herself confessed, "I called into t' 'erbalist fer summatt... but she'd nooan 'elp me. What am I ter do, Missis?"

"Aye, tha's a problem," the woman agreed. "It'll be difficult fer a young lass ter buy a potion ter bring abaht a miscarriage, even if she knew which 'erbs must be 'married' for 'em ter be effective—fer one 'erb must 'ave another ter work with. Just as it needs two ter mak' a baby, then it needs—"

"Do you know… which 'erbs?"

Her companion looked out to sea. "Oh aye, nivver fear. I can mix thee a powerful draught as'll do the trick. Expensive, mind."

" 'Ow much?"

She considered. " 'Ow much do yer 'ave?"

Evelyn calculated mentally. About twelve shillin' an' sixpence."

"Nay," and the woman gave a derisive laugh and got up to walk away.

"Please, Missis," Evelyn grabbed her arm, "look… I'll even gi'e yer this brooch. It wor me mam's." Her voice faltered. "It's great sentimental value. It's all I 'ave left ter remember 'er by." Removing the piece of jewellery Evelyn added, "an' it's real gold."

"No. It's pinchbeck."

"Well, it looks like gold," Evelyn argued.

The gnarled fingers traced the outline of the carved head on the cameo as the woman began thinking aloud. "Nah there's an Apothecary on Church Street, not far from t'Abbey steps. T'gentleman who owns it is a friend o' mine, an' will do me a favour. If I were to… gi'e me thee money, doy."

"Ah can't 'and twelve an' sixpence over just like that. Yer might run off an 'me never see yer again."

The woman was hesitant, the brooch still in her hand. "No, I can understand thee bein' cautious. Come wi' me ter t'shop, but wait outside wi' thee money ready… an' I'll go in for thee. 'Ow's that?"

"Aye. That sounds better."

The old woman was suddenly all smiles. "Come on then, let's get thee what tha needs. An' tha mun scald 'em in boilin' watter, an' drink it while it's still 'ot."

"And then?"

"Tha'll get… a sort o' stomach pain. Nowt ter worry over, for tha'll know then things are startin' ter 'appen. Tha'll bleed, but dooan't panic, 'cos tha'll be all reight."

But she was already beginning to have doubts.

"Timothy 'Owarth?" the stentorian tones rang out.

"…Yes, Mam?"

64

"Coom dahn 'ere."

She stood at the bottom of the stairs, a domineering figure dressed in black. It seemed odd that a body seeming so frail could produce such a sound, as harsh and resonant as the top notes of a violin, and Hannah thought, just as grating.

Wearing her "Sunday piety" face, she turned toward the two sisters, and in a scathing tone warned, "when we get ter t'bottom o' this I'll mak' yer look smart. I'll show t'pair o' yer up fer what yer are."

"An' what's that?"

"I've nobbut one thing ter say ter thee. Deuteronomy 6, verse 16."

"An' I mun reply wi' Mathew 10, verse 21."

"Dooan't thee quote t'bible ter me. Ah read chapter an' verse every day o' mi life. Ah go ter t'chapel every Sunday. There'll be celebrations in 'eaven fer me when ah get oop there—pearly gates'll be open wide. There's soom in Steeas'll not even get through t'back door."

"Yer sanctimonious owd bat. Yer no better na' onybody else."

Lizzie Howarth took deep breaths to calm herself after the onslaught against her person. Finally regaining her voice, she continued, "when my lad cooms dahnstairs an' we get this business settled, then that'll be t'last time yer darken me door—an' that goes fer t'pair o' yer. Dooan't so much as coom into t'shop—not even if yer've t'brass ter pay for every-thin' on shelves. We want nowt ter do wi' yer. Is that clear?"

"Let's go home," and suddenly afraid of what the old woman might say or do, Evelyn pulled on her sister's arm.

"Oh no, doy. We've coom ter see—" and at that instant, Tim Howarth came into view. He stood on the top step, looking down on the three women waiting for him and, suddenly feeling like Solomon about to deliver judgement, he swallowed then asked, "Aye? An' what's to do?"

"There's a young woman 'ere," and his mother gave Evelyn her most scathing look, "an' she says yer know 'er."

"I know 'em both." He nodded to Hannah, then managed, " 'allo, Evelyn."

"But she claims... yer know one another intimately. Timothy, this lass is all big wi' a bairn, an' she reckons it's thine."

"I'm sorry, Tim," and Evelyn put her hand round her middle. "I tried... but... it didn't work. It just made me violently sick. Tim, we're 'avin' a baby. What are we goin' ter do?"

"Yer trollop, yer nowt else."

"It takes two ter mak' a bairn."

"Yer slut," Lizzie ignored Hannah's remark, then turning to her son, promised, "But tha's nowt ter worry over, lad. She'll 'ave been dahn bi' t'beck. T'father could be anybody—an' then she's t'brass faced cheek ter say as it's thee. She's lookin' fer a feller as is daft enough ter wed 'er. Ter tak' on 'er an' 'er bastard."

"Shut up, mother… fer me an' Evelyn—"

"Timothy," the old woman tried to silence him, "tha'd better not coom aht wi' what I'm afeared tha goin' ter say, or else—"

"That I'm t'father ter Evelyn's bairn? Well, it's more na' likely—"

"But yer know it's yours," Evelyn reasoned, "for I've nooan been wi' any other man. Yer wor t'first, an' t'only one."

"Then it must be mine."

"Nay lad, dooan't thee be so daft as ter—"

"Mother," his voice suddenly rose, "will yer shut up? Nah… I'm prepared ter do t'reight thing. If yer 'avin' my child, then we mun be wed… that's if yer'll 'ave me."

"Huh, if she'll 'ave thee."

"I'll nooan tell yer ageean. Just shut up affore yer say summatt as yer might later regret."

"It'll be thee as does that."

"Nah then, Evelyn," and seeming very serious, he asked, "when's it ter be?"

"As soon as things can be arranged," Hannah answered for her. "I know it's not an ideal situation, Tim, but at least yer man enough ter face up ter yer responsibilities. An' yer mun pull together when yer wed. Evelyn here's a good little worker, an' she'll nooan fritter away yer brass, nor will she—"

"An' where are they goin' ter live?"

"Well… we mun discuss it."

"Yer 'aven't arranged that along wi' everythin' else? Yer slippin'."

"Well," Hannah reasoned, "yer'll need Tim ter 'elp in 'shop?"

"Oh aye?"

"Then surely… another pair o' 'ands 'ud nooan coom amiss?"

"An a bairn skrikin' thro mornin' till neet? If 'ee's daft enough ter wed 'er, that's 'is funeral—but 'ee's nooan bringin' 'er under my roof."

"Then yer mun get yersen another slave. For if Evelyn's nooan goin' ter be made part o' t'family, then I'll nooan work for yer."

"In that case…" and Lizzie considered her options, "I'll sell up, an' go an' live in Scarborough. I'll spend all me brass, then yer'll get nowt when owt ails me."

"Suit yersen, mother," and he defiantly put his arms round the soon mother-to-be, "But me an' Evelyn are to be wed, so you'd best get used ter it."

"I'll go ter Scarborough," she threatened.

"Dooan't talk daft," he cut her down, "they'd nooan 'ave thee."

He stood on the bridge staring into the sinuous water, which like an idle temptress shamelessly solicited and beckoned.

The breeze tantalisingly lifting the edge of her skirt, she spread and exhibited her sensuous body bathed in wedding-ring sunlight, arched her rippling skin, then curved and cavorted. There was a flash of white petticoat, followed by a heaving and swelling, then an orgasm of foam being drawn toward the open sea, and like a spurned lover Adam wished, oh, how he wished that this expanse of water were Polly, lovesick for his advances.

That she were naked and laid on their bed, and as he joined her, then her hands would begin to excite and explore his torso. Shoulders, chest, her finger tips would trace his muscles, linger and tease his nipples, his smooth belly. Her kisses would moisten his thighs, her tongue tickle and tease the most sensuous parts of his anatomy. She would draw him toward her, and moan with ecstasy as he began to stimulate her then her soft sighs would become screams of pleasure as he took her. And their loving would be long and ardent, and his reaching a climax be far away, for Polly must be the one who's needs were to be satisfied.

Sometimes he wondered if it would ever happen between him and Polly, for recently he'd taken to sleeping downstairs in the armchair. No sense in them sharing the same bed, the same room even, if she were so… totally "unresponsive" to his attempts at lovemaking. She always seemed to have some excuse. She wasn't feeling well, it was "that" time of the month, or she'd suddenly remembered something she must go downstairs to attend to.

Then afterwards, she'd be especially nice to him, and he'd feel very ashamed of himself when he thought of what he'd tried to do to her. To force her to—that wasn't the way. Polly had to want him, the feeling had to be shared.

He supposed no other husband would have been anything near so considerate. On their wedding night any other man would have been as rough as he liked. A husband had rights, and if his new bride had, only hours previously, promised to obey him, then she should do just that, and that meant being agreeable in bed. He remembered how, before leaving for their honeymoon, his friends had nudged him and said something with a slightly naughty double-meaning. They all had wives who— well, he knew, they must do it, or else how could they talk about it?

And how could he admit… to anybody—anybody at all that he was a complete and utter failure when it came to being a "proper" man? Talk like that between a son and his father didn't seem right, nor could he discuss such a thing with David, who was himself little more then a lad. The captain would probably tell Hannah, who in turn would say something to Polly, and then Adam would feel wretched at having broken such a confidence. Whichever way he turned—but there was no way.

He would see the other men with their unattractive wives, and would find himself envying them. He remembered a shipmate boasting, "an ugly wife is more na' willin between t'sheets, she's grateful fer owt," and he thought of the girls on the harbourside at Whitby—but he wanted to lose his virginity to Polly. She was so pretty, just as the day he'd wed her.

That was the trouble.

And now, come the weekend, his younger sister was to become Mrs Evelyn Howarth, and looking at the state of her, would be a mother before the year was out. At least, one of the family was going to have a "normal" married life—as normal as one could living under the same roof as Lizzie Howarth. But Adam, despite what Tim and Evelyn must have enjoyed, still preferred his state of celibacy than having to live as part of the Howarth household. After she were married, Evelyn would need her family more than ever.

And, as Adam turned into the High Street and toward High Barrass he felt that after he had told Polly his latest news, then she would need his own shoulder to lean on. He'd spent an afternoon in Whitby, where he'd been drawn to the ships in the harbour, some unloading their cargos, others signing on crew members. He'd been tempted (at least there'd be no frustration and disappointments when it came to bed time) and then he heard the name Nathaniel Dacre. He'd edged closer, as the man related the dramatic events.

A fight, and all over nothing, but suddenly things had turned ugly and the man lunged at his attacker with a knife. There'd been blood seeping through his clothes, spilling out of his mouth. The man had jumped into the water to evade capture, but had drowned, while Nathaniel Dacre, stabbed through the heart, was dead. "It were a cursed ship," the man was saying, "they changed her name. No good can come o' that." Adam could recall earlier rumours that Nathaniel had joined a ship—nor could there be two men of the same name. He could well imagine the scene the man had described, for Nathaniel Dacre was a troublemaker, but now he must break the news to Polly and the rest of her family.

She was all smiles as her entered the door. "We've been tryin' dresses on, an' Hannah says Evelyn's can't be let out any more, but there's only another week, and when… .why Adam," and she read the look on his face, "what's wrong?"

She was quite silent as he told his tale. Silent and motionless. Not asking for explanations, nor interrupting—and no tears. The words washed over her. They were calming, healing words. For to her, they somehow righted the wrong that he had earlier done.

"So… it must be Nathaniel, wouldn't you say?"

"Oh yes."

"Polly, while I go an' tell your mam an' dad, d'you want to call on 'Annah an' Evelyn?"

"No. I'm goin' to get into the bath, then leave the water in so's you can get a good wash affore you come up to bed."

He stared.

"Somethin' wrong?" she asked, looking all dewy eyed.

"…No. Leastways, not if you mean… what I think you mean."

"…An' you don't need a clean nightshirt… in fact… you don't need to wear nothin' at all, 'cos I won't be."

"Polly… what's brought all this on?—Not that I'm complainin'."

"…P'raps it's Evelyn 'avin' a baby," she lied. "I imagined at first as we could adopt it, till I knew she was gettin' married. Then I thought… as you'd rather we made our own."

"Mmm. I say, Polly, you do know—?"

" 'Course I do, silly. Now, on your way to mam an' dad, an' don't be long as you're back… D'you want somethin' to eat?" she asked as an afterthought.

"Oh no, Polly love. An' I'm goin' to run all the way there an' back."

The summer of 1904 was fruitful for more than Evelyn Dacre, for the group of artists that were now so much part of the lives of the fishing community had attracted others to join their ranks.

From the West Riding of Yorkshire came Owen Bowen. Originally of Welsh descent, the grandson of a congregational minister and a great grandfather who had opened the first Sunday School in Wales. His other claim to fame was that at the tender age of seventeen he was expelled from the Yorkshire Union of Artists. Now in his early thirties, with his established and successful Leeds School of painting, he brought his paints, brushes, easels, canvases and his genius to the Yorkshire coast, and for the summer months became part of the painting scene.

Landscape painter Lionel Crawshaw was another newcomer. He had studied in Paris at the *Academie Colorosso* and now had a studio in nearby

Whitby, as did the third new member, Edward Anderson, a Whitby man, whose father was a fine art dealer and owned both the Rembrandt and West Cliff galleries. After studying at the Royal College of Art he had only recently returned to the area, having been elected as a member of The Royal Society of British Artists. A seascape and landscape painter who preferred to work in watercolours as opposed to oils, he had a studio in Whitby's Well Close Square, which was to be the venue of their summer exhibition

Evelyn Dacre took deep breaths as she struggled into her dress. She stared into her mirror, a heavily pregnant woman glared back. She would be the "Staithes Exhibition" this year, for in a few hours she would be married, and in as many weeks, a mother. She spread her hands over her belly and wished—oh, but it was all too late, now.

At nineteen years old, she was trapped, for (and she'd realised this since knowing that she was carrying his child) she had no love for Timothy Howarth neither had he any for her. The prospect of forty... fifty years without love was something that she would not wish on her worst enemy, and it was about to be her fate. The day itself had dawned anything but bright. There were squally showers interrupted by weak shafts of sunlight, then yet more rain. There was no cheerful trumpeting and drumming, just a bleak outlook.

An omen.

She ate a scant breakfast, and wished dad could take her in his arms and make everything better. But it was too late for that now. At three o' clock that afternoon—

"An' who knows? Soon, well I might look like you."

Her tinkling bridesmaid's voice stopped her thoughts. "You mean... you an' Adam... ?"

"Well, not... you know... but we do that."

"Why, Polly," and Evelyn suddenly flushed, "we're sharing sisterly secrets this morning."

"An' Adam's very... thoughtful, very gentle you know."

"Good, I'm pleased," and the bride-to-be put her arms round her childlike sister-in-law, then, her mind on other things blurted out, "I 'ope as that bloody woman doesn't cause any trouble this afternoon. Lizzie 'Owarth's nooan too pleased I've 'ensnared' her son—she's even called me a 'arlot."

"Tim's the lucky one to get a girl like you."

"Leastways, he'll no longer be ruled by his mother."

She stared out of her bedroom window into the far horizon, where sea and sky merged and Evelyn somehow likened it unto their forthcoming ceremony.

"Happy the bride the sun shines on"—it was a murky depressing morning.

In a dress of dark blue, one hand held her prayer book, the other adjusted a hat that had given many years of service as Lizzie Howarth "imagined" her appearance (for mirrors in one's house smacked of vanity)— and she was having none of that!

"Timothy," she called in her strident tone, "We mun 'ave words."

"It's ter late nah, mother. There's nowt ter be said."

"Go through wi' this weddin' an' tha'll regret it."

"I'm 'avin' no threats today."

"Well—tha mun think on mi words in time ter coom."

He shoved her aside. "It's ter late nah. It's all arranged."

"This'll go dahn as t' silliest thing tha's ivver done," and her scrawny fingers grabbed his arm. " 'Ave a bit o' sense, lad," she pleaded, "fer she'd nooan look side o' beck tha wor on if shoo wasn't in t' predicament shoo is."

"It's goin' ter 'appen, this weddin'—so accept it. In two 'ours time me and Evelyn Dacre will be 'usband an' wife," and he rushed down the stairs and strode out into the street, and the sea fret that was rapidly enveloping the village.

With Adam as best man and Polly the one and only bridesmaid, the wedding was a subdued, clandestine affair. Hannah had baked from morn till night during the week leading up to the event, and although the Dacre family were well represented, there were very few of the Howarths present. After the ceremony there were the usual speeches at the end of the wedding feast, then later that afternoon the couple caught the train to Whitby, for four days honeymoon. Throughout the entire proceedings, Lizzie Howarth had not raised so much as a smile. Her displeasure at such a union was made painfully clear.

Timothy Howarth might be her son—but she would never look upon Evelyn Dacre as a daughter!

Chapter 6

On the second Monday in October Evelyn Howarth gave birth—to twin boys!

The Dacre family were overjoyed: Lizzie Howarth was furious. There would not only be one child screaming from morn till night, but two. God was certainly punishing her!

Following the cutting of the umbilical cord, each child was taken immediately to the attic and held aloft, ensuring that it would "rise up in the world" and given a token-present of both salt and silver before being returned to its mother. While Lizzie Howarth, anxious that her daughter-in-law could be "churched" and get back behind the counter and start earning her food and board, was more fractious than usual. Nor would the locals have an un-churched mother enter their home, for it was asking for bad luck, as was taking an unbaptised child into one's house. Lizzie felt she was to have a terrible time ahead of her. She was no longer responsible for the goings-on in her own home, being now saddled with the fruits of her son's misdemeanours.

And the Dacres were going to wear her stair-carpet out, traipsing in and out of the house—oh, it was a bad day she'd let those two Dacre women step over her threshold, the only saving grace had been Hannah Dacre's seemingly "sensible" talk about christenings.

"We mun get 'em done sooin as we can—shall I 'ave words wi' minister for yer?"

"Aye—an' they've decided on names. James an' Simon," and Evelyn thought of the two bundles, one in each of her sister's arms, then shook her head and added, " 'trouble is, I can't tell which is which. They're booath bonny bairns."

The following month on her first chapel attendance, the minister offered prayers of thanks for the successful outcome of her confinement and, thus "churched", Evelyn could now resume her normal life. The following Sunday the boys were christened, in no time it was Christmas, then there was "first-footing"—and a new year was about to begin.

Life was hard for Evelyn Howarth.

Seasons came and went, but feeling like some animal trapped in a cage, she saw little of life outside Lizzie Howarth's shop. The boys had reached the stage where they were crawling about on all fours and into everything, Tim seemed subdued, his mother more and more domineering. It was after one of her increasingly violent shouting sessions that her whole body suddenly stiffened as she went a deathly pale, then slumped at their feet.

Evelyn rushed toward her. "Go an' fetch 'doctor.'"

Timothy Howarth held his mother's wrist, searching for a pulse. "Ter late fer a doctor. Tha needs ter get Sair-Anne. She's deead!"

Sair-Anne, the "layer-out" woman, seemed unmoved by Evelyn's sense of urgency. "Nay, doy," she reasoned, "if shu's as deead as tha reckons, shu'll nooan be goin' onywheere," and she took a generous pinch of snuff then wiped her nostrils with the back of her hand. "Nah then, lets 'ave a see, what do we need? 'As Tim gooan fer t'board?"

"Thro 'joiners? Yes."

"Then we'd best be on us way. Eee, Lizzie 'Owarth. Allus thought she'd be ter meean ter die. Ah'll bet shu 'ated partin' wi 'er last breath. Shu would gi'e nowt away."

Tim was pacing about in the parlour. "I've shut 'shop. 'Ave I done reight."

Evelyn nodded, as Sair-Anne, enjoying her moment of glory boldly assumed, "Tha'll want me best layin' out service ah s'pose—wi' thee mother not bein' short o' brass? Ah do a cheap job fer them as 'as nowt put away... but Lizzie 'Owarth—well?"

"Aye... best yer can, Sair-Anne. An' she's 'ad all 'er layin 'aht stuff in 'bottom drawer fer more years na' I care ter remember. But if there's owt yer want—?"

"Summatt ter drink 'ud nooan coom amiss. Brandy."

She slowly sniffed the amber liquid before tasting, then when the glass was drained Sair-Anne announced, "well then... there's a job ter be done," and she began the ritual she'd over the years performed many, many times. The body was washed and the jaw tied up, before the deceased was wrapped in a white sheet and laid on the board down the centre of her marriage bed. White woollen stockings covered her feet, the hair was combed and tidied, then a pillow was placed at either side of the head while another sheet was meticulously folded in patterns of horizontal pleats which ran down the entire length. Then finally a large white handkerchief covered the face. When all was done she called for those who had entrusted her with such a ritual to come and inspect her handiwork, and after receiving payment added, "tha might want ter gi'e me a keepsake in memory o' dear saintly departed," and her eyes rested on the large cameo brooch Lizzie Howarth had worn.

"Oh, aye."

Her scrawny fingers grasped that which she'd envied for more years than she cared to remember, as she recited her usual phrase under such circumstances, "thank yer very much, an' I'll allus think on 'er when I wear it."

The doctor arrived and, as a formality, signed the death certificate. Neighbours—who saw the funeral as the highlight in a person's life—came to gawp, and went away to speculate on how much money Lizzie Howarth would leave.

The following two days were hectic for the Dacre womenfolk, for besides the usual household chores there was the baking of the funerary foods to attend to. The joiner busied himself with the coffin, while the "bidder" went to every house and street corner to announce the day and time of the funeral and invite the entire village to attend, and nigh on hoarse would be heard calling, "will yer coom ter Lizzie Owarth's funeral, fer shu's deead an' laid aht. Friday mornin' at eleven o' clock, fer liftin' an' 'yms, affore shu sets off ter 'Inderwell churchyard. Will yer coom ter Lizzie 'Owarth's funeral?"

Coffin bearers had still to be recruited, and to be kept "as close to the family as possible", and there were the "servers" to arrange, yet throughout all of this, not one tear did her daughter-in-law shed. Evelyn Howarth felt that her life was about to begin.

The morning of the funeral was one of mist: wet and clinging. No wind from the sea, none from the land—just a shroud of impenetrable grey cloud.

Thick smoke lethargically oozing from soot-blackened cracked chimney pots sullied the air. The acrid sulphur permeated the woollen-blanket skies, tainted lips, assailed nostrils and irritated throats and lungs, as Hannah Dacre, head bowed respectfully, shawl drawn close to her body, hurried along the High Street to her sisters. She stared at the shop window draped in black, then was momentarily startled as a figure came out of the mist and toward her. A rubicund face that bore the unmistakable Howarth features. The family were beginning to assemble.

"Now, then"—but he ignored her.

"Yer'll be a relative o' deceased," Hannah tried again. "I'm Tim's sister-in-law. These are very sad times—please accept mi condolences."

"Thank yer very much," he croaked, "but ah reckon as mi sister Lizzie'll be wi' 'er Maker nah. Eee, shu wor a good sort. She'll 'ave a front seat oop in 'Eaven, nivver fear," and Hannah was temporarily lost for words.

The man had obviously inherited the Howarth trait of frugality. His now-shiny suit had seen many years of service, the shirt collar starched and so-soon-in-the-day cutting into his neck, the mourning tie was taut and the overcoat so large, it was probably borrowed for the occasion.

" 'Appen as we'd best get inside," and Hannah made a positive effort to stop herself scrutinising the stranger, "for I've called ter take 'bairns off Evelyn's 'ands. She'll be busy enough today without two little lads ter look after." He followed her through the side door leading to the Howarth's living quarters, pausing at the top of the stairs for the chief mourner to make his appearance. Tim Howarth emerged from the parlour.

"Uncle Amos!"

"Tim, lad."

"D'yer want ter take a look at mi mam?"

"Oh, aye."

"Coom on then, she's in 'ere."

"I'll just 'ave a word wi' Evelyn," Hannah greeted him, "then we mun be away. We'll see yer later." There were others arriving as Hannah and her two charges left. Some more of the Howarth family—and the locals were also gathering—it was going to be a "proper" Staithes funeral, despite Lizzie being such an unfriendly, unloved individual.

When the immediate members of the Howarth family had arrived and were gather round the open coffin, the minister laid his hand upon it as he delivered a short prayer of thanks for the life of Lizzie Howarth. The coffin lid was then placed in position, and the specially baked funeral biscuits, along with glasses of port were taken outside and distributed among the mourners, clay pipes and tobacco for the menfolk, and food for the bearers. The coffin was then carried downstairs and placed in front of the shop on two chairs, and the hymn *Guide Me, Oh Thou Great Jehovah* sung. Suddenly there was a streak of mustard sunlight turning to ochre breaking through the cloud. No angels with long trumpets to announce Lizzie's imminent arrival at the pearly gates (for she was not one for extravagance—that was a cardinal sin!). The coffin was lifted, and behind the bearers walked the eight servers, wearing black hats, white crocheted shawls and black silk sashes. They walked in twos, the shawl across the outside shoulder of each pair. Heading the macabre procession was Tim Howarth, a lonely figure, his wife trailing behind. The procession to Hinderwell cemetery was laborious—and long!

It was several weeks after Lizzie Howarth's demise that the middle-aged junior partner of the firm of Whitby solicitors called on Tim and Evelyn Howarth.

"Yer'll 'ave a cup o' tea an' a slice o' cake?" Evelyn offered as a welcome gesture.

"Er… tea would be very nice, thank you."

"An' I'll tell Tim ter put a sign on' door 'Closed till after lunch.'"

"And if I could just… er… put all the papers out for Mr Howarth's inspection?"

"Aye, on 'table. I'll just shift these bits of things. Wi' twins, their clothes gets all over."

"Oh, quite."

As the stranger busied himself, Evelyn glanced over his shoulder, but everything looked official and "wordy"—best for herself and Tim to peruse at their leisure, and there would be plenty of time for that. Minutes later, while Evelyn, through the now uncurtained window (for she was beginning to make changes) glanced on the happenings in the High Street, the junior partner delivered the crushing news.

She suddenly turned to Tim, unable to believe what she was hearing.

"But there must be some mistake," her husband finally came to life, "mi mother couldn't—wouldn't 'ave done this to us."

"I'm sorry to be the bearer of such… a 'disappointment' to your expectations, but the new will she instructed us to draw up is quite legal. It was made on the"—and he paused to look at the date—"twenty-third of August, 1904."

"Two days after we were wed. An' she's left everythin' ter 'chapel?"

He nodded. "In conclusion to this morning's meeting, I must also serve upon you a notice to vacate these premises within twenty-eight days or the bailiffs will be called in to forcibly evict you."

"Eh?"

"The property is to be sold by auction at some future date," he ignored his remark, "along with the goodwill, stock and fixtures and fittings, the money raised to—"

"…Go ter 'chapel?" Evelyn completed his sentence.

"So… she'd left us wi' nowt?"—and Tim Howarth seemed unable to understand what was happening.

The bearer of bad tidings shook his head in agreement, then delivered his last crushing blow. "There is also, according to the deceased, a strong box containing an undisclosed amount of money, which I must remove for safekeeping."

"That's reight. Well, there's a box, anyroad," Evelyn seemed to take control. "It's in 'er wardrobe. I'll go and fetch it."

She looked at Tim, adding, "she allus kept it locked—I don't even know where 'key is."

"Then you've not—?"

"Good 'Eavens, no!"

Tim seemed a broken man watching the Howarth fortune being stolen from under his very nose, as the box containing the wherewithal to buy their dreams was so casually handed to the solicitor. Their home, their livelihood—everything was to be lost.

She'd been an evil woman to the very last!

They stood in the doorway, arms round one another, then Evelyn, hearing one of the children went to investigate. Her husband, still dazed, muttering, "I'm sorry, doy—I'm truly, truly sorry."

She began preparing their mid-day meal while Tim (for it came to him as natural as breathing) busied himself attending to the sudden influx of morning customers, as news of their earlier visitor had quickly spread round the village.

"It seems daft," he managed to say to her later that day when there was a sudden lull. "What are we doing, keepin' open when it's ter be sold. It's not ours any more. What's the point in keeping it afloat for some-body to buy it when it's auctioned off?"

"Unless… you buy it?"

"What—wi' the few coppers we 'ave?"

She drew a deep breath. "I 'anded over the box this mornin' –but not this" and from her apron pocket she took out the envelope. "Call me a dishonest woman if you want, but I'll nooan see everythin' ta'en away thro us. You've worked and slaved for years, and if we 'ave ter vacate the premises in four weeks time, well, we'll move in wi' mi dad, then when it's up for sale, we'll buy it an' move back in."

He stared, hypnotised by the brown envelope, then finally managed, " 'ow much is there?"

"Enough."

" 'Expectin' 'world an' 'wife ter turn up?" Tim Howarth cast a withering glance at the man nailing the "Sale by Public Auction" notice above the premises.

"There could be a lot of interest. It will be advertised in the Whitby Gazette, and other newspapers as seen fit."

"Yer'll nooan get outsiders coomin' ter Steeas."

"That remains to be seen." The man seemed nervous, as Tim moved closer, adding "besides, there's talk abaht a new "Co-operative Society" thro East Cleveland openin' a grocery an' drapery department in Steeas. That'll knock a shop like this sideways."

The man seemed troubled at such news. He wished the interfering local would go away.

"An' Steeas folk dooan't tak' ter newcomers. It'll be a brave man as dare open this shop... O' course, I could allus make an offer, before it came to auction."

"Such things are out of my hands. You'd need to make an appointment with the senior partner... and if you were to make a formal proposal, well—it would be considered."

When Tim told this conversation to Evelyn she began to have reservations.

"But what's up, doy?"

"Well, if what you say is right, and a worker's co-operative is to open in the village, then they'll take all the trade. They can sell much cheaper than we could. We'd have invested all our money and be left with a shop full of goods that nobody would buy."

"Then," and he fought for words, reluctant to let the chance of being his own master slip away, "what are we going to do?" Once it's sold we'll have nowhere to live, I'll be without job—no money coming in, and the nest-egg won't last for ever."

"Unless..."

"Mmm."

"We stay wi' me dad, till we find somewhere ter rent'—an' save the money for James an' Simon's futures?"

"Well—what would ah do for a livin'?"

"P'raps this Co-operative... would want a helper? Somebody who knows the villagers could be an asset to em'—it's all ter try for, Tim. Besides, we might not 'ave enough money ter buy 'spot, anyway."

"There's a lot in that envelope. We could buy 'alf o' Steeas wi' that—an' 'ave change."

"All the better to hang on to it then. Who knows when we might need it?"

She had, since it had been in her hands, looked on the money as a possible escape—from marriage—and no sense in tying it up in bricks and mortar, for that would certainly make her a prisoner.

The auction sale was held two days after they vacated the property. Timothy said little, but Evelyn had no regrets. She was finally free of Lizzie Howarth—and she now had the wherewithal to make life suddenly much more desirable.

Chapter 7

The Dacre family home seemed uncomfortably overcrowded. Evelyn, her husband and children (made more than welcome by the head of the household) were allocated the main bedroom, forcing Hannah to move into the attic room, and David and his father to sleep in the small bedroom that looked onto the bank and was dark on even the sunniest of days. David resented having to share a room with a parent who snored, and again envied his brother. Adam had Polly to snuggle up to, and David would lie awake at nights… and imagine… himself and Polly. He didn't see her in a nightie, nor himself in a nightshirt, for they'd be naked, the two of them, and would retire to the bedroom and the comfort of the four-poster after he'd coaxed her legs apart and had his wicked way with her downstairs in front of the hearth.

In the bedroom he'd kiss and nibble her breasts. His hands would explore, she would return his fondlings, his member would be hard, as it was every time he thought about her. His hand would go to his groin to help him seek relief, yet even after reaching a climax the longing was still burning. Nothing could quench that fire.

He should find himself a girl—no, a woman!

Not an arrangement made by in-laws where marriage was expected be the outcome, but something that would satisfy this "need"—this "thing" he wanted to do with Polly. He'd heard tales… of the streets of Middlesbrough, where women were to be had, or much nearer to home, down by the bridge Friday nights. He was a desperate young man—but he was not fool enough to dirty his own doorstep, for any misdemeanours in Staithes would quickly come to the ears of his family. He must seek relief in self-abuse—and learn to live weighed down with feelings of guilt, the price such an act demanded.

Two women in one kitchen was one too many. Hannah, who had kept house since her mother died had developed a routine that did not include a sister, brother-in-law and two nephews, while Evelyn, after being dictated to by Lizzie Howarth was not prepared to accept yet another mistress. Being a married woman and mother of two she saw as a mark of seniority over her fast-approaching-becoming-a-spinster sister, and felt a need to assert this authority.

Tim Howarth left the house early in the morning and caught the train to Whitby to the menial job in a chandlers, returned home late at night, ate his supper and went to bed. David was forever moaning, the head of the house was spending more time than was good for him at the Cod & Lobster, the two little lads were into everything (nor was Evelyn as attentive as she should be)—and a "certain gentleman" was proposing marriage almost every day.

Finally Hannah relented.

A date was fixed, the first day of spring. The minister was approached, the banns were read and Hannah made several visits to Whitby to complete her trousseau. "I look well," she joked to her husband-to-be, "A spring wedding. At my age it should be an autumn job."

"In my eyes, you'll always be young and beautiful."

"It's me ling pie—that's what you're after."

"Hannah, when we walk down the aisle you'll make me the happiest man in the world," and he wiped a tear from his eye. "I do love you, you know."

"Aye. I really believe you do."

The bankside and across the beck was painted sunshine yellow, as clumps of daffodils trumpeted the news that all Staithes had speculated on, but not expected to happen. Her affair with the captain was old gossip, marriage was news. Polly Dacre also had "news"—she was to be a mother before the year was out. Adam wept for joy, and resolved to take even greater care of his child bride. Romance was also in the air for the group of Staithes artists, for one of their members Frederic William Jackson married a local farmer's daughter, the pair settled in nearby Hinderwell and he began building himself a wooden studio behind his new home.

As Hannah and Owen left for their honeymoon, changes were again made in the Dacre family home. David looked forward to the privacy of having his own room. His sister, however, had other plans. "They're no longer babies," she argued her case for moving her offspring into the now-spare bedroom "and besides… we're still, well, we've not been married all that long. We need… you know—"

"No, I dooan't. But I can see as you an' Tim are goin' ter take over, if nobody stops you."

"If you resent us bein' 'ere, then we mun find some place else. But who'd look after dad then? Who's goin' ter cook an' clean for yer both now 'Annah's left? She'll nooan want ter leave Owen an' be down 'ere all the time."

"Yer 'ere for good then?" He sulked, and stormed out. It was always the same, he came last. Adam was lucky—oh, he was more than lucky, having Polly. The birds round Jackdaw Well strutted in front of him. Secure—this was their place—even the bloody birds were better off than he was. He climbed steep path up the cliff, turned round to look over Staithes, then headed toward Port Mulgrave and Hinderwell.

What would happen when he found a girl and wanted to settle down? Would they have to begin married life in the attic bedroom with his father?

Why couldn't his brother-in-law get off his backside and find a home for his family? He'd not wasted any time getting her pregnant. If he'd had his fun, he should be man enough to take care her, and not have them under somebody else's roof. Tim Howarth was no more of a man now than when his mother was alive, for his wife was becoming just as bossy as Lizzie Howarth had been. As Hinderwell Station came in sight, David counted the money in his wallet. He had enough, and his mind was made up.

An hour later, from the carriage window, he saw Staithes for the last time. The train went over the viaduct that spanned the beck, and David Dacre looked down onto the patched-up roofs, smoky chimneys, the fish drying fields above Cowbar, and the far horizon where the sea and sky became one.

Life, for him, was about to begin.

The late summer saw Polly big and round like an overgrown fruit. She had a longing throughout the day for raspberries and parsley and at night suffered with backache from the strain of carrying Benjamin, for she was sure it was a boy child she had inside her. She would pause in the afternoon sun to watch the young children playing near the Cod & Lobster, or beyond the scaurs of rock she would see the young boys naked and splashing among the breakers. Then, as though it were a punishment, she must look at that great expanse of rolling water. Somewhere out there in a tiny craft was Adam and his father. Supposing—but she was always supposing. And it wasn't just because she was having a child, for she'd been fearful for Adam's safety ever since they'd been promised. If anything was to happen to him, what would she do?

But she'd other things to worry over: for there were tales she'd heard... about a baby born with two heads. Then there was the story of the child born with a pair of wings. The poor mite had fluttered round the bedroom then, exhausted, had fallen dead at the midwife's feet, its body suddenly limp and lifeless. If she was to give birth to such a child... well, she'd wrap it in a shawl and hope no-one would notice.

She stood watching a cormorant dive, and seconds later re-appear quite some distance away. Then, kneeling beside a rock pool and turning over a stone, Polly stared at the now-disturbed green crabs scuttling to find another hiding place, the waving tendrils of seaweed covering their tracks. Sometimes in the pools there were fish trapped till the next in-coming tide, or gaping mussels. Occasionally there would be a seal washed ashore—and the locals would club and stone it, for they believed such creatures to be at best predators, at worst witches in disguise and about their mischief.

At the water's edge as though on stilts, oyster-catchers paraded and inspected the contents of each wave as it was flung over the rocks, and the cormorant silhouetted against the white spume gave a sharp twist to its long neck, stretched and shook its black body. There was something in its pensive loneliness that aroused her compassion, and she stood watching as the tide, like a sheeted ghost, crept insidiously over the sea-weed covered rocks.

Carried along the wind was the rattle of the slow wagons from the ironstone mine further along the cliffs, where she could see yellow foam spilling onto the scaurs. Not even an inland occupation such as mining was without the fear of accidents, for there had been fatalities at the mine, or tales of men trapped, having to have limbs amputated due to rock falls—and she thought yet again about Adam. What if he were to lose an arm or a leg? Supposing he were underground and there'd been an explosion and...?

But he was out there with his father. She hugged her tummy and headed for home.

Oh, her head was full of silly thoughts.

There was news going round the village that the Knights had returned. They had their old studio, a converted stable and loft on the edge of the sea wall by the beck mouth, and, when the weather would allow were seen with their easels set up on the quayside, or they would be trudging to Hinderwell to capture some scene. Laura felt that time was of the essence. Her work took on a new urgency, for since their painting trip abroad the North Yorkshire coast had somehow lost its earlier magic. And like some seer, she felt that this would be a summer of sadness, followed by a season of sorrow.

Evelyn would hover when in their vicinity, hoping Laura would ask her to pose. The extra money would come in handy and provide an innocent diversion to what was becoming a mundane existence. Timothy Howarth was not the most intelligent man in the world, or (as she'd resigned herself into accepting) the most ardent lover. He seemed these days to go to bed only to sleep—and then he snored!

She needed to be loved!

And words themselves were not enough, he had to show it, but he was forever making excuses when she—well, he said he didn't want to father any more children.

"But… that doesn't mean we don't have to—I mean, we can be careful," and she would touch him, but he was cold to her advances.

"No, doy, I'm tired. Been a long day."

He didn't seem to realise… that she had needs—it wasn't just the man who enjoyed "that".

She wanted to feel him inside her, and for him to make her—but it was useless. He knew nothing about the thrill one was supposed to experience when they were making love—she'd have to get Adam to have a man-to-man talk with him. Polly was loved. Even though she was pregnant they'd not stopped doing that for when the two women were talking about babies and things, she'd admitted that she and Adam—she'd even described the actual position they'd adopted so as not to harm the baby. Oh, her sister-in-law was lucky, for not only was she pretty, but she'd a man who knew how a wife needed to feel, and was able to satisfy her. Polly Dacre, in Evelyn's eyes, had everything.

It was nearing the end of the herring season, and Polly hoped there'd never be another. The smell hung over the entire village, on Adam's clothes, about his person—he was even sweating herring. She would see them drying in the fish fields above Cowbar, in alleyways and back gardens—herrings were everywhere!

They would be on spits in front of the kitchen range, grilling in front of the fire for evening meal, again for supper, then rolled in oatmeal and fried for breakfast. The pan, the plates, the washing-up water—everything would smell of herring. To escape she would walk up the bank and head toward Dalehouse, a tiny hamlet some ten minutes walk from the village where she'd pick blackberries, or, when she could reach up for them, clusters of rowans for Hannah to turn into jelly. Such cooking was unknown to Polly, the best she could manage was stewed fruit, but with cream from the farm?—well, Adam was more than pleased with her efforts. He was looking forward to the baby arriving, but that was weeks away, yet aunt Bridie was already talking about "leavin' 'im a nest egg". Polly peered among the brambles, some strewn with gossamer-like cobwebs as she carefully leaned to pick the ripest of the autumn fruits. Late summer wasps, drowsy and lethargic, hovered. In the fields she saw pheasants, and among the hedgerows the last of the foxgloves and bright yellow clumps of ragwort. The earlier green bracken had turned brown, as had the carpet of leaves that crunched beneath her feet. It was a dying season, and Polly looked at her purple stained fingers and nearly full basket. She'd had a good morning, she'd call at Hannah's and then—and she suddenly felt Benjamin. It was time to return to Staithes!

Hannah was out, she left the rowans on the front step, took the short cut along the top of the bank, then down the stone steps that led to Ring o' Bells. She'd be glad when the house came in sight, what she wanted now more than anything was to put her feet up, for it had been a long walk, and she'd been—and then she felt… not so much a "pain"—more a sort of warning—that Adam Dacre was very soon to become a father. But Benjamin wasn't due for weeks, Adam was out in the boat. Hannah—well, she could be anywhere. Led the life of a lady these days. Evelyn would be at home. She'd know what to do.

"Coom on, Sair-Anne, Polly needs thee. 'Bairn's coomin' early."

"I'll be wi' thee in a minute, doy," the voice came from upstairs, "ah'm crouched on mi pittle-pot."

Adjusting her clothes, the village layer-out and midwife appeared calm as Evelyn constantly stressed the urgency of her being needed at Ring o' Bells.

"An' 'er waters 'as broken, tha says? Well, we'd better get a move on an' not stand 'ere talkin' all 'day."

"D'yer need owt?"

"Just ter button me booits oop."

"Coom on, Sair-Anne, dooan't thee dawdle."

"Ah've delivered more bairns in this village than tha's 'ad 'ot dinners," the old woman reminded her. "Ah delivered thee, dooan't forget."

Minutes later Sair-Anne, after her "examination", authoritatively announced, "shu'll be soom time yet. 'Be a false alarm."

Polly felt another sharp pain, and drew a deep breath. "I wish Adam was 'ere."

"It's 'is fault tha in 'predicament tha are now—but this is women's work, we dooan't want any men around. Nah then, doy, ah'll tie this sheet 'ere 'top o' 'bed. Tha can pull on it when 'baby starts ter coom."

Polly's forehead and hair were wet with perspiration, her whole body was racked with this all-consuming pain, the likes of which she'd never before known. After what seemed to her a lifetime Sair-Anne announced that they should send for the doctor. Having delivered babies for the best part of her life, she had a "sixth sense" and knew better than to place herself in position that might reflect bad upon her "calling" if the birth should not go as expected.

The doctor arrived. The child, several weeks premature, was turned, then delivered by forceps. Polly was haemorrhaging, but managed to hold the little girl in her arms. It was a night of waiting for Adam (who was being comforted by his sisters) as Polly breathed her last.

He was now a father—and a widower.

The funeral was, as near as Staithes would allow, a private affair. Polly's father and two of her brothers were sat at the back of the chapel. Aunt Hephzibah, wearing full funeral black, looked much older. Aunt Bridie sat beside her favourite nephew, who appeared to have distanced himself from what was about to happen. He seemed to be in the world but not part of it. Hannah and Owen were also sat in the front pew, with the head of the family and his son-in-law. Evelyn was at home caring for the infant and her own two lads, and having no clue as to his whereabouts, they were unable to contact David.

When the service ended, with head downcast Adam bravely followed the coffin to Hinderwell cemetery. Aunt Bridie later confided that she'd poured the best part of a bottle of brandy down him to numb the pain. He was not weeping: just dazed, as if in a trance.

Not wishing to in any way cause him further distress, Hannah had nevertheless had thoughts (and come to a definite decision) regarding the baby girl. She must wait for the right moment—making sure it was before her sister could voice such a suggestion.

It was several days later when Hannah called on an unwashed, unshaven brother. "I've brought a few things, a casserole an' the like."

"Thanks, Hannah," and he seemed truly grateful.

"It's an awful thing that's 'appened ter thee Adam, an' I'm truly sorry. Sayin' 'pain'll go away doesn't bring thee relief, but both me an' Owen feel for yer. They do say as 'time brings sweetest mem'ries' "

"She's still... all over the 'ouse yer know—wherever I look I can see 'er."

"Aye, I can believe that. It wor 'same when me mam died. Dad went through it an'—"

"But they'd had a life together, an' he'd got us."

"An' you've got a little girl, an' we need ter think about 'er. 'Ave yer decided on a name yet?"

He shook his head. "We thought it'd be a boy—we never considered girls' names. What about... Ruth, d'yer think?"

Hannah considered. "Aye, if that what yer want."

"Mmm."

"An'… well lad, I don't want ter push yer, but… she needs someone ter care for 'er. Yer goin' ter be out wi' me dad—yer can't take 'er wi' yer. Me an' Owen 'ave been talkin' –an' 'ee suggests," and she took a deep breath, "that yer let us care for 'er. Yer'll allus be 'er father an' 'ave first claim on 'er, we're nooan tryin' ter take 'er away from yer—we just want ter elp'. I might as well tell yer, me an Owen can't 'ave a family. It's my fault, not 'is—but be that as it may, we want yer ter think abaht what we're offerin'.

"Thanks, Evelyn. An' there's summatt else. I can't live in this 'ouse. Polly… she's—oh, it's too much. I wor thinkin'… would Evelyn an' family move in 'ere, an' me move in wi' mi dad? Does that sound sensible?"

"It's a good idea, lad," and Hannah put her hand on his shoulder. "Tha goin' ter pull through, never fear."

There was yet another fishing tragedy in the village, and because they had taken these people so close to their hearts, and were sharing their grief (yet not prepared to completely throw in their lot with Staithes) the Knights decided to move. To Newlyn, Cornwall.

They were seduced by a more gentle climate, the light and warmth, and the not insignificant fact that there was already an established colony of artists in the area. Painters such as Stanhope and Elizabeth Forbes and others whom they knew.

It was the end of one season, the beginning of another.

Chapter 8

The winter was long and cruel, with boats tied up on the beck, their skippers in the bar of the Cod & Lobster. The north wind screamed up the High Street rattling roof tiles and chimney-pots while waves with a head on them like fresh yeast raced over the slipway and like bad-mannered in-laws one was at loggerheads with, rushed into houses in Church Street without having first been invited. Hannah stared over the rolling world of white water to the horizon where sea and sky merged, and her thoughts went to her father and Adam, one now old with arthritic hands curled like crab claws, and permanent "sea-boils" round his wrists from where his guernsey chaffed, the other—?

Adam Dacre was a very unhappy young man.

She'd bring baby Ruth to see him hoping it would lift his spirits, but when she realised this was having the opposite effect, then—yet the little mite was his daughter, part of Polly was still with them. Then there was David, but where, exactly? Nothing had been heard of him since—well, Evelyn had said it was a silly misunderstanding over "summatt an' nowt" but wouldn't be drawn further. Still, Hannah told herself, chickens do come home to roost, eventually, and it was only a matter of time before he came running down the bank and everything in that department would be back to normal.

Although now a married woman and "mother", she still felt a loyalty to her family and their troubles. It was better that Evelyn and Tim should be in a home of their own than with parents. Perhaps everyone living on top of one another had been the reason for David's disappearance.

Perhaps.

Then there was auntie Bridie, suddenly becoming very argumentative with everyone. And aunt Hephzibah, who was doing strange things, and wandering. When the locals found her miles from home they'd try to persuade her to return, only sometimes she'd start being awkward and stubborn, hit out at those trying to help, and shout and scream. Or she'd cry like a baby and say she was a confused old soul who couldn't find her way home, and she'd no coal for the fire. Hannah sighed, as she held Ruth closer. It was time to return to Owen and the comfort of her own home. She had a man who loved her. She was lucky.

The yellows of spring were meticulously captured on canvases as the now-familiar artists recorded clumps of daffodils, spikes of forsythia, and creamy banks of primroses. Artist Owen Bowen built a caravan on wheels, and using a pair of shafts from an old hearse had a "mobile studio". Henry Silkstone Hopwood, after wintering in North Africa with fellow artists William Mayor and Spence Ingall was again seen in the village capturing a coastline cursed by storms and lashed by cruel seas. The gulls forsook their homes on the cliffs and defiantly nested on roof-tops between chimney-pots, the high spring tides flung giant jellyfish onto the beach, which were left on the sand to be inspected by dogs and cats, and rejected by both. Weak shafts of morning sunrise would quickly die leaving an anaemic sky and a brooding, foreboding expanse of water and, as Evelyn Howarth surveyed the scene, she likened the state of the elements to her own position.

She felt trapped in a marriage that had no "high spots", just a dreary day-to-day monotony of caring for the twins between baiting lines for dad and Adam and making sure they had something to eat at the end of the day, keeping Ring o' Bells spick and span, and "bein' there" for a husband she no longer loved, but merely "cared for" as one would look after a stray dog.

Oh, how she envied Hannah!

In her posh villa at the top of the bank, with a man who treasured her, not merely expected her to do his washing and slave and clean for him without giving anything in return. She supposed—imagined... they would make love, and without the complication of Owen feeling he had to father children in order for Hannah to be fulfilled. They already had their family, for although they claimed that "she was still Adam's child" Evelyn knew different. Money could buy anything, if there was enough—and that was something else that had been causing friction between herself and Tim.

His mother's old shop!

The present owners, probably regretting their move to Staithes (and also because of competition from the Co-operative store near the beckside) had decided to move on, the property was once more for sale, and Timothy was again anxious to know just how much money Evelyn had "tucked away".

"Not so much as yer might think," came her tart reply when he'd dared to enquire. "Besides," she'd reasoned, "we're 'appy 'ere."

"But—"

"No, Tim. I mun look after dad an' Adam, they're only a few doors away—an' you're all reight where yer are."

"Ah dooan't like goin' ter Whitby every day."

"Well... there's nowt near enough ter buy yer mother's owd spot. Besides, I wor glad ter get away, if 'truth be known. It doesn't 'old any 'appy mem'ries for either on us. I shouldn't speak ill o' those departed, but yer mother wor an evil owd cat. She made my life 'ell—an' a lot more went on na' you ever saw—'cos besides bein' evil, she wor crafty."

"Well, I know yer didn't allus get on, but—"

"Nobody 'got on' wi' Lizzie 'Owarth!"

"But... even if we was to somehow—?"

"Not if we were ter 'ave it given" she ended the discussion. "Besides," she was quick to add, "we need summatt fer a rainy day. An' who knows, when 'lads get older? We might need it fer their education—after all, their cousin'll more na' likely end up at some posh school. Oh, little Ruth'll want fer nowt."

"No, ah dooan't suppose she will."

"No 'supposin' about it."

Feeling she'd won the argument, Evelyn, later that evening was again tempted to take the envelope from its hiding place and count the contents. Not that the amount would have increased, as it would had she deposited it in a bank, yet hidden away in Ring o' Bells in a place that only she knew, it gave the money (and herself) security. To deposit such a large sum with a bank could give rise to speculation and awkward questions. Better to leave things as they were.

Evelyn pulled her shawl closer to her body and stopped her daydreaming.

Money? It did buy happiness, if there was enough. It could buy an escape from the life she now led. Not that she wanted fine houses and silk dresses—just to be free!

Free from the smell of fish, the mewling of gulls, being trapped in a cage with the cliffs behind, the sea in front. But most of all she wanted to be free of Timothy Howarth.

Her sister also wanted things. Like any other proud mother Hannah, on every conceivable occasion, wanted her baby to be seen and admired. And must now make almost weekly train journeys to Whitby to buy new clothes, toys—anything she thought the child might possibly need. Shawls, sun-bonnets, tiny pink bootees, dresses with pink frills and bows, a baby's bath and (ordered from a store in York) a perambulator. Owen also doted on the little one and would be totally absorbed simply watching her asleep, sucking her tiny thumb. Or the two of them would make silly noises to one another, and he would claim she was understanding everything he was saying to her, and insist that she was not only the most loved baby in all the world, but also the most beautiful.

She had Polly's looks, and this seemed to torture Adam whenever he called to see her.

"She's just wakened up. I'm goin' ter change 'er, an' then yer can 'old 'er for five minutes," and Adam would stand feeling awkward in such fine surroundings. Hannah had done well for herself: her home was a palace compared to High Barrass.

"Ah just—is she all reight?"

"Mmm, she's doin' reight well. Sit in this chair, see, an'—" and she turned to her charge, "we'll nooan be a minute—'cos we want yer smellin' all sweet fer yer daddy," and as she fussed of the child, her father would already be thinking of an excuse to leave.

"I've brought you some money."

"Adam, yer dooan't need ter—"

"Oh, but ah do," he insisted.

"Well, just this time, then."

He placed the few shillings on the table. "It'll buy 'er... well, summ-att."

"Aye." And Hannah busied herself as she enquired, "an' 'ow's things? Are you an' dad managin' between yer?"

"Aye, things are as well as can be expected."

" 'Ee's nooan spendin' too much time in 'Cod, is 'ee?—An' you're not drinkin' na' more na's good for yer?"

"No. I'm... you know."

"Aye, I know, lad."

His arms reached out for little Ruth, and Hannah wished he'd had a bath before he'd called, but knew she must bite her tongue. The baby gurgled, Adam had a mental image of her mother and felt great tender-ness—and hatred. If Polly had never given birth to the bundle now in his arms then she'd still be alive—they'd be living and loving at Ring o' Bells and everything would be wonderful. Death was cruel: living was a thousand times worse. But life had to go on.

There was the usual round of chapel anniversaries, then in no time at all, it was June, and the Fair Week. Evelyn and Tim, with two boys who, despite being twins, bore little resemblance to one another (for the family likeness had vanished a few weeks after their birth) and dad and Adam were to enjoy the hospitality of Hannah and Owen. Hannah (who now had a dressmaker in Whitby) wore pale blue silk especially for the occasion and a hat trimmed with lilac ribbon and ostrich plumes. Her younger sister felt more than a twinge of jealousy. Owen was wise enough to know to take second-place and allow Adam to fuss over his child.

Jacques Dacre looked on, thought much, but said little.

"Come on dad, tuck in," Hannah sensed that all was not well with the head of the family. "This pork's coomed thro a farm at Roxby—can't get more local na' that."

"Yer've put a rare spread on," he complimented her, "enough 'ere fer a weddin'."

"That's as maybe—but there'll nooan be another—weddin', that is, for some time I'm thinkin', unless David—" and she stopped, and there was a long silence. "Anyroad," she tried to make amends for her careless tongue, "we might 'ere from 'im any day."

" 'Could be... making his way in... whatever—and come back a rich man," Owen tactfully suggested.

"Aye." But Jacques Dacre had his doubts.

Wedding plans were, however, afoot for one of the group of the painters, for Rowland Henry Hill, who hailed from Halifax and lodged in Runswick Bay during the summer months had, whilst in Runswick, met his future wife. She came from a prosperous Sheffield family, and they were to marry in the September and set up home near Hinderwell.

Another member of the group, Ernest Rigg, moved to Sussex. Whilst Russian Arthur Friedenson, regarded as almost "a local" for so long he seemed to have been part of village life, was also growing restless. Like Rowland Henry Hill, he had also met his wife in Runswick, and the two of them were "making plans".

Marriage, however was the last thing—the very last thing—on Adam Dacre's mind, as through the monocle of time he stared into swirling mists rising like spires of grey lace. Alone in his boat, he listened to the sea murmuring a slumber song as he was gently rocked and lulled.

The whispering waves calmed, soothed, washed away the hurt as he thought about Polly, and—because his thoughts must follow that pattern—Ruth. It was their loving that had created her: something beautiful—and yet the sweetest flower must wither and die.

He had read somewhere that swans mate for life—and so it would be with himself and Polly!

There'd never be another woman in his life, or his bed even. And he knew... that one day Ruth would distance herself from him, for Hannah and Owen could offer her so much. Hannah was going to make a loving mother, and Owen an indulgent father. She'd want for nothing.

There was a stirring... the wind was getting up. The thick grey vapours, like something steaming from the head of a giant chalice, were beginning to clear. He could not only hear, but also see, the waters: a sort of oily blackness all around him. He remembered his several-years-ago Greenland expedition, when he'd been saving up so that he and Polly… and he suddenly realised memories could be sweet!

And, as he told himself yet again, love would never die.

Chapter 9

Days became weeks, then months. Time was marked only by the changing of the seasons. Spring tides again raced up the slipway and hurled long trails of seaweed on the staithe, the cliffs took on a springlike appearance as though painted yellow. Gulls screamed; jackdaws paraded; the yearly Fair came to the village; Jonas Dacre wed some pasty-looking thing as skinny as he was fat; and Jacques Dacre, after a bout of summer pneumonia, took to his bed and died.

Adam, now seeing himself as head of the family, must man the fishing boat single-handed, the funeral bringing back painful memories of his late child-wife. And the pattern of life in Staithes and its inhabitants took on yet another change. Toward the end of the year, news reached them that Richard Bagshawe, a familiar figure among the group of artists who had taken the village to their hearts, had died in Whitby. And earlier that year Arthur Friedenson had moved south.

Evelyn Howarth drew her shawl closer and realised she must also be on the move, for Hinderwell churchyard was no place to loiter. Every week (but sometimes she must miss, for some reason or other) she would come to lay flowers and tend her parents' grave. It had become *her* job because Hannah seemed far above such things. And anything to do with the dead, or graves, would cause Adam great anguish, for he was still so very much in love with someone who was no longer of this world.

For such pure, bonding love Evelyn was not so much sympathetic as envious, for any fleeting feelings she had once had for Tim had long since gone—having been replaced by the harsh reality of day-to-day living. Sometimes she felt cheated, for married life had killed her dreams. She looked around her, at the fallen and now rotting sycamore leaves at her feet, the rime-covered tufts of grass, the holly tree without berries and the yew trees near the lych-gate, where she could again see her father's cortège. Then she made a sudden effort to control her thoughts, and concentrate on what has to be, rather than what had been.

" 'Bye dad," she murmured, then gave a sudden shudder—it was as though someone were walking over her own grave. She hurried to the road, for there were no such things as "omens"—besides, she must need to keep fit and well to care for the twins.

There was a cruel, unforgiving wind as she approached the station, for her day wasn't over yet, it hadn't even begun.

The train rattled into the station, she being the only passenger to board, and as she settled herself in a seat near the window Evelyn speculated on how best to spend the money in her purse. She must resist things like chocolates and perfume: winter clothes for James and Simon came first. It was hard. Life was a constant struggle. The austerity and harshness of living. A life—no, "existence"—with no dreams, no hopes, and no escape.

Der-der-der-der, der-der-der-der the train rattled in sympathy—and agreement—as she settled herself in the corner by the window watching the world go by.

At Whitby's West Cliff Station Evelyn alighted and looked around her. The sea was just as pewter as the one from her upstairs window, the horizon blurred and indistinct. Nearer to her, figures moved. The town was going about its business—and so must she. And some minutes later she was looking in shop windows in the town's Flowergate. There was a feeling of Christmas in the air, somewhat early, but nevertheless present, and she stared at the two elegantly dressed women coming toward her, and felt decidedly "country-ified". There was a rustle of silk from the swish of a dress, and she caught a scent of poppies. One of the women wore a fur over her shoulders, and Evelyn marvelled at the tight-corseted waist. " 'Never haul a boat up the slipway in that," she thought to herself, "Nor those shoes," and she suddenly felt ashamed at her own clumsy footwear. But these fine ladies of Whitby wouldn't have to gut fish or bait lines—nor be lumbered with a husband the likes of Tim Howarth.

She approached the quay, if she were to do her shopping across the bridge then she would be more likely to find a bargain and perhaps even have some money left—and then she saw him!

He had just turned into Grape Lane. She took deep breaths—it wasn't possible that he could be here, under their very noses, yet none of the family were aware. She rushed forward. Two sailors were obscuring her view—she had momentarily lost sight of him.

But he was here. She'd seen him. And now she must rush, her walk became a run as she frantically looked this way and that. That head of hair, it was unmistakable. David. It was David, her baby brother. Well, no longer a baby from what she'd seen, but he'd always been tall for his age, and now must be—and suddenly, he was there again, she saw him disappear into a jet-workers.

This was a surprise—and would be for him when he emerged and she threw her arms round him. But to be in Whitby, only a few miles further down the coast from his family, and to have not even—wait till she got hold of him, the young man would have some explaining to do. When she thought of the trouble and anguish he'd put his family through, all because of some… well, only he could explain what had gone wrong, and as soon as he—and the door-bell clanged and a head of auburn hair emerged as Evelyn pounced.

Too late she realised her mistake, for the man was totally unprepared for such action as he was being subjected to. For, after grabbing him, she suddenly recoiled: it wasn't her young brother David, but a complete stranger.

Oh, what had she been thinking of?

As though she'd mistakenly plunged her hands into a copper of boiling water, Evelyn automatically drew back—but felt it was too late, for the damage had already been done.

"I'm so sorry, so very, very sorry... I thought you were—but you're not."

"Not what?" the young man asked, when he had recovered from the initial shock.

"My brother. You're not my brother, are you?"

He blinked, and looked again into the searching eyes scrutinising him. "No," he managed, "I've never seen you before."

She turned away, and said sadly, "No, I realise now—I've made a most awful mistake... and I am so very, very—"

"Yes, I think we both know that. I say, are you all right? You seem to be... somewhat 'agitated'."

She drew a deep breath. "You must forgive me. My brother just... disappeared some years ago. The likeness between the two of you is unbelievable."

"Well," and the young man tried to make light of the situation, "if I'd a sister like you, I certainly wouldn't disappear."

"But he has. I keep thinking every Christmas, or his birthday that we'll see him."

The young man held out a thread of hope. "Perhaps this Christmas?"

She nodded, still staring, trying desperately to hang on to something that wasn't there.

"His name's David," and it sounded like a plea. "David Dacre."

"Well, mine's Jacob. Jacob Steinhauer."

"And I don't know how he's managing to earn a living... or if he's alive, even," and her lower lip started to tremble. "If he'd just let the family know he's all right—he doesn't have to come home if he doesn't want to, but so long as we know..." and she felt a pair of strong arms round her, as the stranger offered, "I was going for my lunch when we sort of "met." Nothing much, just a mug of tea really. Would you like to join me," and minutes later Evelyn found herself pouring her heart out to this comparative stranger, while he, in return must tell her his life story from his earliest memories to the present time and his working in Whitby as a jet carver.

Unable to take her eyes off him, she clung on to his every word—for this was the nearest she had been to her young brother since that morning he'd stormed out of the house never to return. The physical similarities between the two men, it was uncanny. Eyes, the Dacre nose—it was all to much to take in at once—but if she saw him again?... and she found herself asking, did he live in Whitby? Were his parents alive? Had he any brothers or sisters? Was he... married?—and there the likeness between her brother and this Jacob character ended. He and his younger brother been brought to this country by their father who worked with fur, and could never understand why his new customers must have their garments with the fur on the outside for show, instead of inside for warmth.

"No. Are you?"

His question brought her back to reality. She stared, then struggling to pick up the thread of the conversation without confirming or denying her marital state, she went on, "I live just a few miles further along the coast". She fancied he must have noticed her ring—yet among a fishing community when the sea claimed so many lives, a wearing band of gold signified nothing. She now considered herself "married in law only"—for most nights she couldn't bear Tim Howarth anywhere near her. She had married in haste and would, no doubt, have many years to repent.

Chapter 10

Having now completed what seemed to have become her daily ritual of calling at Ring o' Bells to see her sister, then calling at Adam's to spend some time tidying his house and making sure he had enough to eat, Hannah would then, as though drawn by some unforeseen force, walk down to the beach to stare at the expanse of water.

At times angry and dashing against the cliffs, but today the sea was calm, reflecting the hard blue of the December sky and lulling the onlooker with a false sense of security. The shy breakers teased the rippled sand as cormorants displayed and dived, and there was a stillness in the air, making her remember a poem she'd learned at school: *No stir in the air, no stir in the sea*. But Hannah wasn't to be fooled as she thought of Adam somewhere out there, wrestling against the elements, trying to make a living.

It was a hard life, and in Staithes more than anywhere else. If men were not risking their lives at sea, then (and from the tales she'd heard) the local ironstone mining was also fraught with danger. There had been casualties, fatalities among the workmen just as happened within the fishing community. But the area offered little else by way of employment. There were the shopkeepers and publicans, and farmers, who also had to work hard to survive. But at least, with fields of turnips and potatoes, hens for their eggs and a cow for milk, they could eat—and thinking of farmers and the like, she must call on one to order the Christmas goose.

The family would this year be dining at her table, for Hannah felt it would be a difficult time for them all, and being the eldest, she must try to hold them together.

And now there would be even fewer mouths to enjoy the meal she would prepare. No mam, dad, no Polly, and, she supposed there'd be no David either. To expect him to suddenly appear was too much to hope for. The silly lad, to have up-sticks the way he had, and to let no-one know where he was or anything. Perhaps she'd lay an extra place at the table, though that could imply that it were for dad, and make everybody weepy.

Yet (and she'd noticed it a couple of times) one member of the Dacre family was particularly cheerful. Evelyn was positively blooming. Like a young girl in love, and Hannah wondered… would she be sharing a "secret" with the rest of her family when they were all sat down to lunch? Was there to be another brother or sister for the twins? Hannah hoped the baby would be a girl, a playmate for her Ruth who was the absolute image of her mother at that age. Blonde hair, turn-up nose and a rosebud mouth, when Hannah looked at her she could again see Polly.

Out of tragedy had come, for her and Owen, something wonderful, and Ruth should want for nothing. Though Hannah had a nagging fear, an absolute dread, of how she herself would cope when the day came that Ruth must, for several hours most days of the week, be parted from her to attend the village school. And with that in mind, and so as not to waste a precious mother-and daughter minute, she stopped her day-dreaming. Time to get back to Ruth and Owen—she'd been away from them for the best part of the morning.

Jacob Steinhauer had also had a busy morning, trying to bring some semblance of order to the hovel he shared with his younger brother.

At least, he'd changed the sheets, and their bed (by jet-worker standards) was clean—but it was a job where the worker was always in the black, powdery dust. It embedded itself into one's skin, under nails, in eyelashes and round nostrils—and he'd long since stopped thinking what it did to the lungs. But he was able to earn a living and care for Mathew as best he could, and anything was better than the lad being in the poorhouse. They'd been orphaned at an early age, and had clung together like intertwined saplings, and he even felt guilty sending the lad out for the day and telling him not to return till late afternoon. But Mathew couldn't be with him and Evelyn when "that" might happen.

Not that he'd—well, if the day did go as he'd planned, he hoped she'd be more experienced than he was, for he'd never… didn't even know what women looked like. He'd heard his work colleagues talk, even boast about their conquests, and since meeting Evelyn and realising how he felt toward her, he wondered, should he some night stroll down to the harbourside where he'd be certain to find some woman more than willing, at a price, to complete his education? His workmates told tales of the quayside doxys, as they called them. Painted pretty as figureheads and rotten as rust, their kisses laden with pox, the mark of their sinful profession. He thought of Mathew, alone in the world should anything happen to him. He was his protector, he had to keep healthy.

He must empty the tin bath still in front of the hearth—and perhaps Evelyn would like some tea. He looked in the canister, there was just enough—and he ought to dust the pot dogs and—the bedroom!

He must look again, and make sure there were none of Mathew's dirty clothes hanging about, and that the pillows were arranged and tidy. Evelyn wouldn't want to do "that" in a pig-sty, and his hand went to his groin as something started stirring. Men sometimes—but he didn't want to start that today, besides, it was said to drive them insane. Better to remain celibate than become an idiot. He again smoothed down the sheets, and had a sudden mental picture of them lying naked locked in each others arms, and her fingers reached down to his pubic hair. He wondered… would Evelyn…? But no, that was surely a man's thing. Girls would be all smooth, and… beautiful… and lovely.

Scarcely had he completed the last of the many chores he'd set himself when there was a knock on the door. He rushed to open it, then stood back and said shyly, "Hallo Evelyn, come on in."

She was all-smiles, carrying a shopping basket that seemed to be laden with her purchases. She placed it on the table then removed her shawl as though making herself at home.

This could be his lucky day.

When it was over he wanted to straightaway withdraw, but she was still pressing against him.

"Not yet," she whispered. "Don't you want to do it again?"

"But it's gone all—" and further protestations or excuses were superfluous as his tutor, so skilled in the art of lovemaking (and her talents wasted on a husband who slept and snored every night) was anxious to more than complete her protégé's initiation. She drew him even closer, "push," she whispered, then began animal-like moans as their copulation resumed, till she suddenly gave a cry and pulled his hand over her pulsating abdomen as she achieved an orgasm. Her back arched, her body writhed, she could feel him deep inside her, he was thrusting, her nails tore into his back, she wanted to scream—and then there was calm!

When it was over he hurriedly dressed, feeling acutely embarrassed as she started to examine his now flaccid member. "You're very well endowed," she complimented him.

"You should see Mathew—and he's years younger than me."

"And has he also been—?" and her fingers touched the tip of what had earlier given her such pleasure .

"Well… it's part of our religion."

She seemed puzzled. He thought it best not to enlighten her.

Minutes later, like some married couple they sat drinking tea as she rummaged through the contents of her basket, then taking the parcel from the bottom shoved it into his hand. "And I've bought you something for Christmas. I knitted it myself."

"…Thank you."

"It's… just…"

"I won't open it now, I'll save it till Christmas morning," and here's…" and he fished in a drawer, took something out and placed it in her hand. "I haven't had time to wrap it, I only finished it yesterday"— and in her palm, Evelyn looked at, and admired the carving. "You need… a gold chain? Or even a black ribbon to wear it on, but I couldn't afford—"

"Oh Jacob, it's beautiful. And I'll always think of you when I wear it," but she was already beginning to wonder how she could claim to have come by it. Still, Tim Howarth was too stupid to even realise that it was an obviously expensive item of jewellery, even if he were to notice it.

Jacob glanced at the mantle clock. Evelyn, sensing that she might be outstaying her welcome said suddenly, "well, I must be away. I've still some shopping to do." She pulled her shawl round her shoulders, and basket over her arm gave him a kiss as he was about to open the door.

"Evelyn—it was all right, wasn't it? I mean, I've not—"

"Jacob, everything was fine—and we shall—"

"Do that again?" he finished her sentence. "I hope so."

She hurried through the narrow streets then over the swing bridge, and as the employees were leaving the store where Tim now worked she stepped out of the shadows. He seemed surprised to see her.

" 'Bin buying this an' that for Christmas, was how she explained her reason for being in the town. "Hannah's looking after the lads. She's making them their tea, and we're to collect them on our way home." She was more-than-usually talkative as the two of them headed toward the West Cliff and the train as she sympathised with Tim having such a journey every evening. " 'Better if you could get a job in Steeas. Easier."

…And easier for herself, for that way she would lessen the risk of her meetings with her new lover being discovered. For she knew her affair with him would not be short-lived, and only time would tell what the outcome might be.

Time does not stand still, not even for lovers.

Cruel Staithes winters make way for spring, and that budding season must in turn step aside for high summer, then the gold of autumn for the yearly cycle to begin again. The fair week came and went, and like stragglers after a party the few remaining members of that group of artists who had earlier settled in the village were still to be seen occasionally. One of them had married a local farmer's daughter from nearby Hinderwell, Frank Henry Mason, although he was based in nearby Scarborough still made regular visits to the area, but Laura Johnson and her husband Harold Knight had forsaken Staithes for Newlyn. Evelyn would contemplate... on what might have been, if she had set her sights higher than a shopkeeper—who was not even that these days, but merely a grocer's assistant, along with several others.

Each time she met Jacob she feared discovery. Some innocent harmless remark, or the two of them being seen together, then word getting back to her husband, or even Hannah prying—and finding out more than was good for her. Still, she supposed, if—when—news reached Hannah, then there would be a sisterly lecture before confronting Tim with such a revelation. And if it were known, then what could she do?

To just leave everything and live with Jacob was unthinkable—as was life without him.

She wanted the best of both worlds—but realised that, playing such a dangerous game as she had embarked upon, she could end up losing both.

The arthritis that plagued Owen "according to the weather" seemed worse and more persistent, forcing him to hobble about the house (and down into the village proper) on a couple of walking sticks.

As she saw him struggle, Hannah realised he was now an old man, and she would walk with him along the cliff path leading to High Barrass where he'd make his way to the staithe proper to join the company of the other old men of the village, who like babies in prams, were put out into the summer sunshine. They'd pull on pipes or take a pinch of snuff, and through rheumy old eyes would see... a world that used to be.

Fishermen had tales to tell, and he'd reminisce and relate his yarns of sailing the China seas, then some old Staithes local would "remember" the two fishermen who caught a mermaid, and were reluctant to release her. But on finally being persuaded to do so, on reaching the open sea she prophesied "the sea shall flow to Jackdaw Well." He'd pause for effect before ending his tale with, "an' watter rushed o'er staithe an' demolished thirteen 'ouses affore reachin' 'well—but it gat there."

His listeners would shake their heads in wonder. That was indeed a tale to tell their grandchildren.

Whilst in such amicable company Hannah could call on her sister to get the latest (if any) family gossip and also keep an eye on Adam's housekeeping—or lack of it. Still, her brother must labour more than most, having no wife to aid with the fishing chores, and although his sisters helped as and when they could, such assistance was sporadic, and not to be wholly depended upon. For Evelyn, it seemed, had become a law unto herself, with her jaunts into Whitby. No reason—she just "fancied it", expecting Hannah to have the lads after school.

She must go into Whitby herself, one of these days, and find out what she was getting up to.

She just stood and stared at him, unable to believe what she was hearing.

All week she'd been planning, searching for some seemingly innocent reason to jump on the train to see him. New clothes for the twins? But they'd more than enough. Knitting wool, so's she could make them matching jerseys?

A visit to the herbalist on Church Street? That seemed the most feasible, for she could tell Tim she was having "women's problems" and he'd just take that as something he should know nothing about, so would not in any way argue. Besides, she told herself, it *was* a "woman's problem"— the problem being... satisfying this desire. Craving for (and dare she say the word, even to herself?) *sex!* It was something only men were allowed to find pleasurable, a woman just being a means they would use and abuse to this end.

No good looking to Tim: he didn't know the first think about—but Jacob, after his earlier over-eagerness was now becoming receptive to her needs, realising that such closeness was not to be rushed and was infinitely more pleasurable when the climax was delayed. He was even now prepared to explore new... then his voice brought her back to reality.

"Well—say something," and he gave a nervous smile.

"I... can't think. But why, Jacob? Don't you love me?"

"It's not that, it's... look, Evelyn, if we continue this relationship, how can it end?"

She considered—and was silent.

"It's only a matter of time before your husband finds out. And then... and he is your husband, the man you meet when you leave here, isn't he?"

"You mean, you've been spying on me?" And, from deep within her, the Dacre spirit was rising, about to come into its own. "Of all the deceitful—"

"It wasn't like that. One afternoon after you'd left I'd to get some things in for Mathew's tea, and I saw you come out of the shadows to meet him, and then you put your arm in his. And I realised I was just... something for your amusement."

"No, Jacob, it isn't like that."

"It isn't any more. Besides I've started seeing someone."

"And you think you can just cast me on one side?" The voice was angry, the words threatening.

"I think we've said all we have to say to one another. Look, I don't want to hurt you. Let's part as friends."

She paused, mouthed the words: "You used me!"

"No, you used me—to satisfy your own needs. What's wrong with your husband, anyway? Isn't he man enough to—?" and he suddenly recoiled as her fingernails tore across his cheek. There was a spurt of blood, then for her final parting shot she spat in his face.

Just as she had been a gad-about, Evelyn Howarth suddenly became a stay-at-home wife who, having drunk from the cup of happiness, was now left with the dregs of sorrow.

Staithes was the punishment for her daring to try to rise above it. She was reduced to living with a husband she no longer cared for, while knowing that the man she loved would be happy with someone else. It was a bitter cup, and she longed—oh how she longed—for an end to it all. For life had killed her dream. There could be no life with Jacob, for he was to be married at the end of the month. What was she to do?

She still had the nest-egg, and she thought... about catching the train to Middlesbrough. And from there, well, the world could be hers. London, perhaps—or even abroad. America!

Anywhere but the confines of this fishing village, which was to her now little better than a prison. Her brother was only a few doors away, Hannah called every day, Tim was under her feet every night—she had no time to herself.

Yet even if she did manage to escape and walk along the cliffs, she just thought about *him*.

To jump, and end it all. That would seem the best solution.

Chapter 11

It had nothing to do with the folks in Staithes, none of their doing, so why should they be involved? They didn't start wars, they just wanted to be left alone to get on with their lives. If there was any friction or trouble in or between families, well, Hannah told herself, they sorted it out between themselves as she had done when she needed to have words with Evelyn. It had been a misunderstanding, and it was all put to rights with no harm done.

The unsavoury business with Polly's brothers when they'd tried to rape her knowing Adam was at sea and unable to protect her? Well, that was something altogether different, but she'd dealt with it, as she'd done with most things, being the eldest and having had to hold the family together after mam died.

Yet this talk… about war (and Owen seemed more informed than those running the country) and as he read and digested the events in the daily newspapers he painted a bleak forecast. But so long as it didn't reach Staithes, or Owen and the other men in the village didn't have to go and put things right—because, well, Tim Howarth couldn't sort out his left foot from his right. Didn't know hay from straw.

And as for the rest of the men in Staithes?—For the most part they were either fishermen, or worked at the local ironstone mine, something that had been part of the village for a long time employing many locals and even outsiders (for over twenty cottages had been built at the top of Cowbar to accommodate them, together with those at Lane End approaching the village). And there were handsome wages to be had, so she'd been led to believe. A good miner could win fifteen tons in one day, and at fourpence a ton and working five days a week—well, he was not readily going to give that up to enlist for some silly war game. And it was regular work, not dependent on the weather, and the tides, as fishing was. Staithes was best keeping well out of things—and as for this Arch-duke Ferdinand or whoever he was?—well, the aristocracy were a law of their own making and far removed from the likes of ordinary folks.

They needed to do as she did—sort things out between themselves before it got too late.

Owen Danvers-Griffiths was also trying to "sort things out" and make, if not sense, then at least a realisation of what was happening, and the dining room table became a clutter of maps, newspaper-cuttings and anything else that was in any way relevant and could help shed possible light or reason on the position the country was getting itself into.

Lord Kitchener's appeal was for one hundred thousand men for the war. No men between the ages of nineteen to thirty to be refused, providing they were physically fit: old soldiers up to the age of forty-eight, and late NCOs of regulars and ex-soldiers were also urgently needed. There were also among his papers (not that they were any real use to him) the Terms of Enlistment for this present War, assuring any new recruits that they would be discharged with all speed the minute the war was over.

Fine words—but the captain had his doubts. Nor could he visualise an end to hostilities by Christmas. But everyone had doubts and worries, even the fishermen is Staithes, who were worried they might be suddenly hauling an unexploded mine in their nets!

The end of October was marked with the tragedy of the wreck of the *Rohilla*, a passenger ship, prior to being fitted out as a hospital ship, and on her maiden trip under the Red Cross Flag. There was a terrific storm at midnight as she approached Whitby, placing her in a perilous position, and because of this war no lights on the headlands or warning signals from the shore. It was also rumoured that she'd struck a mine, and the ship, then heading for the shore, grounded. Her signal gun boomed across the sea, to be answered by rockets from the Coastguard War Station, awakening the residents of Whitby and the lifeboat crews and the like who were soon at their posts as hurried consultations took place. Nothing, it was decided, could be done till first light, when a rescue attempt could be made. Then, on reaching the stranded vessel the four nurses and the stewardess were safely lowered into the lifeboat, followed by the surgeons. With those rescued safely ashore, another attempt was made before conditions worsened, and then, the rising tide on Friday noon saw the saddest part of the drama, as the populace of Whitby lined the tops of the steep cliffs in a state of utter hopelessness as they saw giant waves tear the ship apart, and men, some lashed to bulwarks, none of whom possessed lifebelts, tossed into the angry waters and drowned.

The tragic day passed wearily, the cliff-top watchers helpless as the dreadful scenario further unfolded. Although efforts were still being made to reach the doomed vessel, terrific seas were still bursting on the wreck. Saturday 31st broke with the same appalling weather conditions, rescue attempts also being made by the Hartlepool steam trawler *Mayfly*. That evening, appeals were made for helpers with lamps to patrol the beach for any survivors that may have jumped overboard on the fall of the tide in the hope of reaching the shore.

Four men were taken from the water, then another two, and as a powerful motor car lamp cut through the dense darkness a man was seen knee-deep in the water. The colour-sergeant of the Devons, along with a private of the same regiment, and one or two others.

There were yet more survivors Many of the locals who had been waiting with lights on the slippery scaur now rendered assistance.

Later that night came news that the North Shields motor-lifeboat, the *Henry Vernon,* had left, reaching Whitby at one o' clock on the Sunday morning. When daylight came (and with the second coxswain of the Whitby boat being familiar with the rocks, shallows and currents of the region) the *Henry Vernon* approached the wreck and, carrying a supply of oil, poured this onto the sea to still the waves while the final rescue attempt was made, and with the remaining crew on board, made for open sea and safety. On reaching the shore many survivors needed hospital treatment, the ship's mascot, a black cat being brought ashore by one of the sailors.

Fifty had been rescued, fifty-one, including the mascot, the events being faithfully recorded in the dining-room at Bank Top.

And now, among the euphoria surrounding any Christmas festivities were the newspaper cuttings and stories of the latest German atrocity, for on the morning of Wednesday, December 16th the look-out man in Whitby's East Cliff saw two large men o' war some three miles from shore coming up the coast from Scarborough. Their flags were small, the sea fret making him unable to decipher their nationality. Suddenly, they changed direction, bringing their stern guns to bear on the cliff as the leading ship opened fire, the second one following, the shots directed at the Signal Station. Hitting the cliff directly there arose a cloud of dust and debris, then there were more shots which took the top off the Station, practically demolishing it, the occupants having already vacated the building and lying flat on the ground as a safety precaution. One man, however, received injuries from a fragmented shell, and died on his way to hospital. Some children were also injured, one needing his leg to be amputated the following morning.

Everything in the enemy's line of fire was targeted, as close-on two hundred shells were discharged, and although the attack lasted only minutes, its effect was far-reaching. Shells fell into the harbour, and some that flew high even reached villages on the edge of the town. Residential properties beyond the railway station were hit, some complete terraces demolished. The Parish Church miraculously escaped, but the ruins of the West window in the abbey were damaged, and a corner of the Gatehouse blown out. Many shells flew over the railway lines, and one exploded in the cattle dock. Telegraph wires were brought down, some sheep were killed in a field near the abbey, and a pig that had half its back sliced off by a shell fragment had to be slaughtered.

At the County School, shells fell in the playing fields. Fortunately the children were inside the assembly hall for morning prayers and the building was untouched. Fortunately also the gasworks, although in the line of fire, were undamaged, as was the electric light station. Whitby was quickly becoming a seaport town of bombed streets with houses reduced to rubble, the inevitable fires and smoke, dust and carnage, injuries, the air torn by the cries of innocent people suddenly made homeless by German ships who, having previously caused similar destruction further down the coast in Scarborough, were anxious to return to their base without fear of possible interception or molestation, necessitating their destroying the Signal Station, thus rendering it incapable of raising any alarm.

On a brighter note, Capt Danvers-Griffiths was also to record that Frank Mason, who had actively been painting in Staithes a decade earlier, was now an official War Artist, and that Rowland Henry Hill who, with his father, had watched the desperate efforts to rescue patients and nurses from the stricken *Rohilla*, had felt so moved that he must paint the scene.

Great men, great artists!

Chapter 12

Being a coastal road, the salt air usually kept it free of black treacherous ice, fortunately for passenger and driver, as Owen and Hannah braved the wintry weather and embarked upon their Saturday evening's entertainment at the Whitby Music Hall.

The occasion: Owen's birthday treat.

In the theatre bar gas lights hissed and gave out their white light, satins and watered silks rustled, necklaces sparkled, hair immaculately coiffured sported the occasional plumes of osprey or some diamante comb. Owen look particularly smart in his evening attire, while Hannah felt confident in her pale blue brocade while she carried a wrap of sable. Suddenly Owen finished his cognac in one gulp, and murmuring, "I think we should be—" began escorting her to their seats in the front stalls.

Hannah looked round, half expecting to see some familiar face, but in that was disappointed. Then minutes later, gavel in his hand and giving a warm welcome to all the "ladies and gentleman of the audience", the compère introduced the first of the evening's entertainers. A juggling act, there was the Amazing Alphonse followed by a young woman who, even to Hannah's musically untrained ear was definitely off-key. She glanced at Owen, who smiled in agreement. When the interval arrived they again repaired to the bar, and the second half of the evenings entertainment was "patriotic"—and even more so, the highlight of the evening being the recruiting song *I'll Make a Man of You*. The singer, Miss Florence Somebody-or-other, was corseted and in blue-striped taffeta. Trying to look attractive even though no longer young, she had a good pair of lungs as she belted out the words, "But on Saturday I'm willing, if you'll only take the shilling, To make a man of any one of you." Then, with a chorus of similar woman with heaving, half-covered bosoms they went into their much-rehearsed routine. "Are there any able-bodied men in the audience?" "Do you have a man digging the garden when he should be digging trenches?" another one asked, then onto the stage marched a very smart-looking soldier followed by a recruiting sergeant.

The young soldier stood to attention, and Hannah drew a deep breath.

"Name and number," the sergeant bellowed.

"Lance Corporal David Dacre, number—" and Hannah suddenly felt faint.

"I'm doing my bit Sir, to serve my King and country," Lance Corporal Dacre shouted the words out for all to hear. "working alongside a grand bunch of fellows. My mother and my sisters will be proud of me when the war's over," and in reply to the sergeant's next question he replied, for the entire theatre to hear, "my advice? Be a man, enlist today!"

Then there was a salute as he crossed to the side of the stage, while the singers again came to the fore "Are there any able-bodied men in the house?" the singer repeated her earlier question, and the first of the new recruits rose from their seats, glanced round self-consciously then took their first faltering shuffle toward the steps leading onto the stage.

The theatre orchestra played patriotic music, recruiting officers magically appeared, the men were greeted by the women before, like lambs to the slaughter, they took the King's Shilling.

Hannah seemed unable to believe what was happening. Her breathing became difficult, the dress was suddenly too tight, the air stifling. That she should see him, after all these years, and—a soldier?

But men in Staithes were fishermen. They knew nothing about fighting and going to wars and the like. In desperation, she turned to Owen. "What are we going to do?"

"Ask him what he's playing at."

"Do you think he really is a soldier, or is it just part of the evening's entertainment? Perhaps he's just joined them... like one of the singers, and he's acting the part of—"

"We'll find out—come on," and, through the ranks of young men, the two of them purposefully strode toward the sergeant-major and his dummy.

Things had to be explained, and Capt Owen Danvers-Griffiths was not a man to be fobbed off.

Though he'd managed to escape his family, David Dacre was no longer leading the charmed life he had become accustomed to, for in the early hours of the morning the sergeant and two of his henchmen burst into his room, causing his bedmate to drag the bed covers closer to her, as he himself received the beating of his life.

"I'll teach you to mess around with what isn't yours," and a fist smashed into his face, "and as for you, you little whore, I'll—"

"Leave him be," Miss Florence screeched, no longer ladylike. "Call yourself a man?—can't do a bleedin' thing in the bedroom these days. Can't even get 'ard."

"Bloody trollop!"

His nose, now spurting blood was no longer numb, but he reeled as his assailant's knee smashed into a delicate part of his anatomy. "When I've finished with you, young 'un, you'll only be fit for work in a harem!"

And the two men held him, as their sergeant did his worst. Finally he nodded to them. "He's had enough… for now. Let him go," and he slumped into a pool of his own blood.

Several days later he was released from hospital, but Lance Corporal Dacre's punishment for sleeping with his sergeant's woman was far from being over—it had not yet begun!

Scarcely had the bruising subsided than he was to be "transferred", given a different uniform and a rifle with a newly sharpened bayonet, then, with others destined for the battle-front, the following afternoon marched to the railway station, and late that evening arrived in Hull. A change from a twice nightly show and an easy life, but, he told himself, all things must come to an end, as would this latest predicament he managed to get himself into.

With the others, he lined up on the platform and marched toward the docks, expecting to board some troop ship, but instead he and the rest of the men were packed like sardines into wharfs and sheds, with neither bedding nor blankets, just their greatcoats to keep out the night air, and the following morning were transferred to various billets around the town. Training began, drilling and parades long and arduous, and after several weeks the platoon moved to a position at the mouth of the Humber, where they were kept busy digging trenches and putting up barbed wire to safeguard their position, and at night manned searchlights across the river, thus when any ship came into view it could seen as plainly as in daylight.

The boredom being relieved by a shell throwing up water in front of a ship coming up-river and not showing the proper flag signal, or watching to rats darting and foraging among the riverbank. Then there would be rumours that "a spy" had been caught snooping, but nothing further or more definite, speculation seeming more interesting than the real thing.

Eventually came the order to move out. A new billet, a new parade, and every Friday evening every man in the billet had to dress in full fighting kit and fall in ready to march off to the station. This was a practice alarm. Again, the platoon was moved, for batches of men were being sent off to France almost weekly, and at the end of the month Lance Corporal Dacre was among them.

They travelled to Southampton, and on arriving, went straight to the "ship"—a cattle-boat that had been given an extra whitewash. The men were issued with lifebelts, and ordered to wear them until told to remove them. The journey to Le Havre was about six hours, two destroyers escorting them every nautical mile, and the men disembarked to French cheering before arriving at their base camp, a distance of several miles.

Situated on a high point, equipment weighing the men down, they arrived exhausted to a camp under canvas and inches deep in mud. Food was rotten and sparse (fortunately) and Woodbines were sixpence a packet, as and when they were available. There was one army blanket per man, and friends huddled together for warmth—yet the worst was to come.

Route marches were almost killing, so much so that one eagerly looked forward to being drafted for the front line, and Lance Corporal Dacre was one of the first. Given twenty-four hours rations, bully-beef, biscuits, tea and sugar and extra ammunition, with his comrades he marched to the station, to be packed into cattle trucks for a sixteen hour journey, after which the stiffness turned to a numb sensation before the train reached its destination when the men (literally) "fell out". Guides were waiting to escort them to the battalion, and the Lance Corporal plodded on, following the shadows of the men in front of him, oblivious to the occasional flashes in the sky or the distant rumble of guns.

He suddenly pictured Staithes, and Old Rall stood at her door exchanging village gossip—but that was a life far removed from the hell he was now living.

He came back to reality. They were approaching a village in which the regiment was resting, some of the men already there had even come to meet them, and suddenly he recognised one of his earlier friends, and by the end of the night, they two men were putting the world to rights before yet another sleepless fitful night.

News reached them that Fritz would shell the village the following day, which he did.

This became a regular occurrence, as in the early afternoon there was a bang in the distance and the whistle of a shell in the air travelling toward them. More were to follow, sending bricks and glass in all directions. When it subsided and they were able to assess the damage they saw a wrecked house where a shell had gone straight through, killing the occupants. Broken furniture, broken crockery, broken lives!

Then one night they were to move into the trenches. The platoon formed in the village street, and after the roll call, began their march, singing songs to try to keep their spirits up, but there was a sense of unease. Not actual fear, but something very close. Then came an order to halt, and as they fell out they drew on their last cigarettes before going into the trenches proper, slithering and sliding in the mud at the same time balancing the pack on their back and helping struggling comrades. The night sky was suddenly lit with enemy flares as they dropped on their knees, rifles and machine guns spitting staccato death bullets. The noise came nearer as they jumped into the trench.

It was muddy. It was under several inches of water—and it was about to rain.

The following morning taught the Lance Corporal a sharp lesson in military warfare, as one of the men out of curiosity popped his head over the parapet… and held it there just a second too long, for a German sniper pulled his trigger and his comrade was no more. He was buried behind the line.

Of her two cousins, Ruth preferred Simon. He was her playmate and companion, and although there were occasions when James was with them, it was Simon whose company she sought. James was "bossy". Simon would play games.

She stood, giggling at her favourite cousin's attempts to build a counter for their café. It would need to be higher, with stools in front, and shelves behind, for they'd need lots of things to sell. And there would have to be a pan on a stove for poison soup, and they'd sell poison sandwiches. They were going to poison everybody. Every German who came up the slipway would be in need of some sort of refreshment, and here was an ideal place to run a café and stop them in their tracks before they reached the village proper.

Germans!

She didn't know what they looked like, but uncle Owen had a table top full of things about them, so there must be pictures. They ate children, she knew that, and she also knew that she and Simon must be extra careful when they were playing on the beach—yet aunt Hannah need have no fears, for Simon would protect her. She loved her cousin Simon lots and lots and lots.

There were four days in the trenches, and the same number of rest days, with not many casualties, as, at that point, no out-and-out combat, nights being cold in no-man's-land as one listened for the slightest sound, strained ones eyes as the night sky was suddenly pierced with a beam of light from the enemy lines. Lance Corporal Dacre was an early war "casualty" with terribly swollen feet, needing to have his boots cut off by his comrades before being bundled into a motor ambulance and taken to a military hospital, his two dead feet seeming as nothing compared to the other men's injuries. Men had lost limbs, their sight—one poor sod had lost his mind.

His "treatment" seemed to consist of his feet being bathed and powdered, then he lay on his bed with his feet propped up and outside the bedclothes. The doctor, who came round daily would, as part of his visit push a needle gently into them to assess their response, if any—but when he'd been told of the lad who was recovering after having to have his feet amputated because of this condition, this patient's feet took a turn for the better, and he was eventually declared fit and well and able to rejoin his companions.

Life, and war, was to go on as before.

Chapter 13

David's letter was brief, and after being handed round and read by the members of the Dacre family was duly filed away in the "war-room" as the captain's dining-room was becoming known.

So much stuff had Owen collected, and he seemed more knowledge-able on world events than did politicians or newspapers, and even "local" news like the miner's hospital seemed to take second place. This had been built near the road leading into the village, a much needed thing, for accidents, even fatalities at the local ironstone mine at nearby Grinkle were not uncommon. The building, surmounted by a glass dome and cruciform in shape was built of red brick, and although intended primarily for miners, other patients could be admitted, and it was to be supposed, even Staithes fishermen who could have been involved in an accident.

And the sea (always a cruel master) was now fraught with new danger, from enemy ships and unexploded mines being caught in the nets and hauled in.

The coastline was now a tangle of barbed wire and other barricades, and as Evelyn surveyed the boats moored in the mouth of the beck she wished that Staithes could get back to what it had been before all this war business. Besides, the Germans would never invade Staithes, if they were to land on this coast it would be Scarborough, or even Whitby—but never Staithes.

There was nothing here for 'em.

There was even less for her now, for hadn't Tim gone and done the daftest thing—he'd enlisted. She had to admit, she felt "cool" toward him, even before her brief but pleasurable indiscretion in Whitby, but some women—men as well, needed "something" to bring excitement into their lives. Everybody needed to be loved, and if one's husband was no longer responsive, nor understood or could satisfy his wife's needs, then little wonder she had to go elsewhere. But for him to go off to war?—well, that was a different thing entirely.

And there were the two lads to consider, not that he had—not at all. Supposing anything happened to him, how would they manage? For he may not be the world's greatest lover, but he was prepared to work and put bread on the table, and he didn't beat hell out of her every Friday night after being in the pub. She was suddenly beginning to realised when she'd been well-off.

But when the war was over and he was back with her (and he wouldn't fall in love with any French girl and abandon her and the twins)—besides, who but her would have him?

Evelyn again prided herself on her frugality, and the nest-egg she'd taken from Lizzie Howarth's bedroom that had remained untouched, except for the odd occasions when she'd counted it. The amount was always the same, and that pleased her. Not a pound, not even a penny had she touched. It was for the lads, when they came of age.

Hannah and Owen may well provide for Ruth: Lizzie Howarth would do the same for her James and Simon.

It was spring, 1916, and the Lance Corporal was again on the move. He had sailed into Marseilles and with a couple of his comrades immediately went to find some girls to satisfy their needs before the battle in front of them. Later that day they were again packed into cattle-trucks for the long ride that lay ahead of them through the heart of France, and after three nights and two days, their journey finally came to a halt.

After a long march they rested the night in some barns, then the following day moved on to another village, then—and the mood of the men changed, then were getting closer to the Somme front. Tents and wooden huts were to be their new homes, more intense training began, and he and the rest of his men were, for the first time, issued with steel helmets. Then, several days later each company was provided with new maps, kit was inspected, new field bandages were issued, rifles cleaned and oiled before, as evening came, they moved off up the line, the arrival announced by shells overhead as they crossed open fields before reaching the front lines, with evidence of the dreaded *Minenwerfer*, the huge trench mortars that fell out of the sky like great chunks of death. Here they were on-duty ten days at a stretch, and so began another pattern in the Lance Corporal's life, and it became a hell which he miraculously survived.

There were rumours of a "great advance" that, it was said, could mean an end to the war, and as the day of the "great advance" came nearer, on the day before the thing was to kick off, loaded down like pack mules they reached the wood at Auchonvillers and dropped into the long communications trench leading to the front line. Suddenly out of nowhere a shell came screaming at them, a high explosive shrapnel shell. The nose cap hummed and thudded to the floor, and the iron balls the shell was loaded with sprayed all around them. There were cries of pain as some of the men were hit, then wounds were temporarily dressed before the casualties were sent to the nearest dressing station, and for a second, Lance Corporal Dacre envied them.

The following day the fun began. Guns of all kinds were being fired indiscriminately, the was the din of several hundreds of shells whizzing overhead were like express trains hurtling through the sky, the ground moving from the thud of the shells hitting the earth, the enemy trenches being churned up in a cloud of flames and smoke. The German trenches could plainly be seen in the light of the burning shells, the barbed wire entanglements blown into a knotted, twisted mass. Great howitzers dug deep into his lines before exploding, spraying tons of stones and soil into the sullied air, and tearing a hole in the earth the size of a house.

Then suddenly, there was a new noise. The roar of an aeroplane, as from a great height and like an angel of death the illuminated craft came into view, the usual red, white and blue rings lit up, the first one the Lance Corporal had seen. Another diversion to lighten the monotony was the day was when the men were requested to move out of the trench… to be photographed! The war correspondent making this request having promised them a measure of rum, and cigarettes, they were happy to oblige. Then came the news that a huge mine that had been prepared over many weeks would be blown the following morning, the signal to go over the top.

The enemy guns were coming to life. Machine gun bullets whistling overhead, then suddenly, at the appointed time the earth shook as a great blue flame shot into the sky, carrying with it great chunks of earth and tons of brick and concrete mingled with wood, metal wire and fragments of sandbags. And as the shout of their comrades in the front line reaching over the top soared over the noise of the battle, the Lance Corporal and his men moved forward. Oblivious to the bodies strewn in their path, the cries of their wounded comrades, for the war had taken on a new scenario, the whole atmosphere had suddenly changed. There was no stopping to help one's comrades, but an uncontrollable push to get to the front and into the battle.

On reaching the front line trench, there was no need to climb out on top, for the trench was battered flat, the wire entanglements in fragments, as Lance Corporal Dacre led his men into no-man's land bullets made horrible hissing noises, shrapnel tore at the sky, shaking the ground, throwing up pieces of dead, and soon-to-be dead men. The wounded screamed, longing for their end. Then there was a call for the fit men to line the bank of the road, the officer issuing the orders menacingly waving his revolver. Some volunteer must signal for reinforcements, while the rest of the men were again ordered to go over the front line.

There was a calm after the storm as the men munched bully beef and hard biscuits and shared each other's water. Then they collected their dead, removed their identity discs, and placed their bodies together—comrades in life, undivided in death.

The following dawn the battlefield was strangely quiet, friend and foe as though "resting" after the carnage of the previous day, then suddenly the Lance Corporal heard voices the other side of the barricade, and cautiously peering over, saw three Germans. He called to them and sighted his rifle, the Germans jumping toward the ditch through which they had crawled, but only two of them made it. That afternoon, they retaliated with a "coal box" coming through the sky like an express train hitting the ground only a few yards from the barricade. Then the air was sprayed with all manner of things, and in the background, the distant drone of yet another weapon of destruction on its way. Others followed, then a shell dropped in the middle of the road, followed by another, and yet even more. Some of the men were killed outright, others horribly mutilated, and another shell hurled three dead bodies across the road.

As dusk fell and the bombing ceased they tried once again to move the still alive but wounded men, though it was a further twenty four hours before the men were relieved, walking out of the trenches a sad, tired and almost officerless platoon.

And now she must wear a mourning bonnet and dress in black—for that was "the way" to do things. There could be no big Staithes funeral as there had been for her aunt Bridie, nor even the more modest affair when her father had died, because... there was no corpse, no husband to weep over as a widow was expected to do.

His "body" was somewhere on the battlefield of a foreign land—and such a cruel twist of fate, for he'd only left England the month before he'd been blown to pieces. But now, there were the two lads to care for single-handed, and Evelyn again prided herself on the box full of Lizzie Howarth's "legacy", feeling it would be needed more than ever over the coming years to help secure the twin's futures. Yet, and this gave her a certain consolation, her late husband had been so stupid he probably wouldn't have felt a thing as the bomb hit him, wouldn't have noticed it at all.

It was becoming part of a now familiar scenario, the train journey, trip in a cattle boat then a long march to wherever he was needed, with little between by way of enjoyment. Sometimes they could steal a few hours in some brothel and there be pampered before behaving like men were supposed to act in such places. The girls were, on the whole, more than agreeable to his requests, for he found the act just between two people slightly boring. Much more enjoyable if the girl at the same time also "entertained" a couple of his comrades. And the men could not only indulge in the act of copulation, but also look on and admire the prowess of their mates. Their naked bodies—the girl being subjected to such acts as they performed, each trying to outdo the others, the ornate gilt mirrors, the "wickedness" of such places—but a soldier had to have some enjoyment, for the next sniper's bullet could be for him.

New men were now joining the battalion, to jolt along in cattle trucks, then marching, marching and more marching to that bloody awful front. A bloody awful abattoir—a bloody graveyard!

Slippery duck-boards zigzagging around muddy craters and wrecked gun carriages, burned out aeroplanes shot down in flames by the enemy, bits of equipment, broken rifles, rusty bayonets, barbed wire, discarded clothing, even rotting limbs, reminders of tin-hatted grimy men pulling on fag ends, unconcernedly urinating in front of their comrades or defecating like cattle, while in the distance one long, desolate waste. Fires still burned, the stench would last for ever. Hell was far preferable to such battle-grounds—and one battle-ground the same as any other he thought to himself, as he surveyed the now familiar scene.

Great shells were humming overhead, whiz-bangs seemed to be coming straight at them, matched by the battery of their own guns coming from behind. Then out of the sky came a great shell straight toward them. The earth was torn from beneath their feet as the fireball exploded toward them, the corporal felt his breath to be on fire before a blackness mercifully enveloped him.

Part II   1918

To everything there is a season, and a time to every purpose under the heaven...
a time to love, and a time to hate; a time of war, and a time of peace.

Ecclesiastes 3:1,8.

Chapter 14

She was now forty years old, with a face and figure to match.

With a near-invalid husband to care for, a twelve-year-old niece who was more like a daughter, a widowed sister, a brother who simply lived from day to day, the magic having left his life on the death of his wife, and soon (and she knew it would fall on her to care for him) a brother who had been maimed in the war.

And what was he going to do with his life, should he return to Staithes?

What could he do?

He certainly wouldn't be able to earn a living, not in his condition, and she supposed… if he were to get a pension, at least he'd have some sort of independence… pride?—Oh, it was all too much for her at times. The war had taken many young lives, and reduced lots of strong young men to near helpless things, her brother was certainly not the only casualty of the battles. Other local lads had enlisted, many seeing it as an escape from the drudgery of the appalling conditions of the ironstone mine, or the precarious and fluctuating conditions of earning a living from the sea. Then there had been Tim, who's army career had indeed been short lived, and now Evelyn had the twins to bring up on her own. Life could be cruel.

But at least the lads were working, and bringing home some sort of wage. James seemed to be the stronger, more protective of the two, already the man of the house, while Simon was still a schoolboy who loved to be with his younger cousin. He would share his sweets with her, play games, let her do silly things, and would always readily take the blame if they annoyed Owen by being particularly noisy, or if the two of the had wandered off and caused concern by their absence. And thinking of Owen—well, what would he do to fill his days now he had no more war bulletins to cut out of the paper? The "war-room" could revert to its original purpose, and again be their dining room, the mahogany table laid out with Irish linen and silver candelabra. She could even display the cranberry epergne centrepiece, begin to live again—the austerity of the war would, she hoped, soon be over.

But some foods were still on ration. Sugar had been for the past twelve months—and Owen had such a sweet tooth—and the beginning of the year had seen tea, butter, margarine, lard and bacon, then jam and syrup suffer the same fate, though the butter and margarine allowance had recently been increased from five to six ounces per person per week. But it was now coal that was in short supply, and suddenly scarce. Further along the coast, at Skinningrove, "sea-coal" was often washed ashore, and though little more than dust, when packed into paper cones and arranged over already bright embers then left to burn (without poking with fire irons), it was a manageable substitute.

So much make-do-and-mend. Old scarves and jumpers were pulled apart and the wool re-used and knitted up again. Clothes were altered— but she'd managed to buy blue and white gingham to make Ruth a dress, for Owen had the wherewithal to buy, even when things were in short supply.

And this morning? Well, he'd given her what most fisherfolk would call a year's wages, so that she could "go out and buy something for Christmas."

She caught the early morning train to Middlesbrough, much easier and more sensible, she reasoned, than being behind the wheel of their automobile (in which she drove no further than Whitby, or if Owen fancied a trip further up the coast, then to nearby Saltburn.) Throughout the journey she was again deep in thought.

About David.

All very well, his deciding he wanted to come back home—but where was that, exactly? Adam was now living in what had been the "family home", Evelyn and the twins in Ring o' Bells, (which by rights belonged to Adam) and she was in a villa at the top of the bank—then where was David going to fit into all this? And if his injuries were half as bad as she was being led to believe, then he'd need looking after like a baby. Of course the army didn't want him any more, he was no use to them. This "cost" of the war could have those picking up the bill paying for a long time.

Eventually the train pulled into the station at Middlesbrough. Hannah stirred herself. No time for wool gathering and supposing this then supposing that, she'd a busy day ahead of her... and she tried to recall... there was a shop that sold little almond biscuits and the like, she'd get Owen some to nibble with his morning sherry, and she suddenly imagined the taste of sugared almonds, she could visualise the pale pinks and mauves—and if she could get some Sage Derby—or any sort of cheese, and some cream crackers?

And marzipan to cover the top of the fruit cake she'd made months ago and put in an airtight tin, and some—well, if she managed to get even half of those things, then the morning would have been successful.

They were glad it was all over—and they'd never started it in the first place!

It upset the fishing—"they'd" never thought about that, had they? What with "gurt" unexploded mines floating about and even getting tangled in the nets, the salmon season over, for they were floating up the beck, dying after spawning, their skin horrible marked, the flesh not even fit for fish-cakes, and as this run of bad luck that seemed it was never going to end—one Staithes family took the only course of action left to them.

Assisted by Old Rall and her crony Sair-Anne, the wives of the crew and owners of the coble assembled at midnight, and in deep silence handed the pigeon to Old Rall. Her scrawny fingers felt the bird's neck, then, with the feathered body in one hand, the talons of the other holding the head, she gave a decisive, deathly pull and twist, and the bird was no more. Then someone came forward, and whilst the bird was still twitching, tore away a handful of feathers before making the cut. There was further probing before the heart was located and removed then stuck with pins and placed on the charcoal fire. Suddenly, and to heighten the sense of macabre, Old Rall held up her hand prophetically and pointed to the door, to signal that the evil spirit, unable to resist the powerful potency of this charm was present—and prepared, for some gift from those who had summoned her, to take away the evil she had plagued the family with.

The following morning the coble was launched, Rall again being present and muttering something incoherent, and the first fish caught that day was kept separate from the rest of the catch, and when the men returned, it was placed on the fire and burned as a sacrificial offering. The incident, and the family having to resort to such measures, was not spoken of. The only suggestion that such a thing could have taken place was the sudden increase in the catches.

But Adam Dacre was above such superstition. So many tales he'd grown up with and he now disregarded them all. The two mermaids caught and brought ashore, the baby that was born with a pair of wings and flew round the room, the Hob-man a few miles further along the coast who lived in one of the caves and cured whooping cough, and the fairies at Beck Meetings. They were tales, nothing more.

Like the tales he was hearing about his brother—apparently!

Christmas came and went, nor was there any sight of David Dacre.

Chapter 15

Lights glowed from the narrow alleyways as guernseyed figures with skeps of baited lines moved toward the staithe ready to cast off. Men and engines coughed, and a dog pranced about as the fleet of cobles took to the open water, Adam Dacre looking back just the once, onto white Boulby cliffs, and only minutes later the snow blizzard obliterated the land. The sea was lipping and choughing, and he was again thankful that he was now an "in-shore" fisherman. Above the heavy swell, the clouds hung like woollen blankets—but January could be a cruel month. He, along with several others, had stopped long-lining and had starting lobstering, albeit earlier than usual. The wind was blowing and a strong tide carrying the pots fast astern, and it was not easy to get them overboard, but when at last it was done and the marker flags set on a bundle of corks, he was able to turn his thoughts to the earlier conversation he'd had with his sister. Not that he'd had much chance to voice an opinion, for Hannah seemed to have already decided. When David arrived in Staithes (for she now had a day, the time of the train from Middlesbrough even) she'd be the one to meet him, and his home would be with her and Owen until they were all of them able to decide "what 'ud be fer 'best."

Well, being under his sister's feet day after day wouldn't last long, and he supposed that Evelyn, now the two lads were working would not want to relinquish the "freedom" widowhood was giving her. For although Adam said little, he missed nothing.

Yet if he himself were out at sea (for he had a living to earn) then what would David do during such times?

One would grow tired of sitting on the staithe, eventually become bored by the sound of the sea and the company of the old men of the village, for a soldier's life was supposed to be full of excitement and action, and there would be neither of those for the poor lad. Nor did Adam, not for one moment imagine David would be happy or comfortable in the company of Hannah and her captain husband (for at times, he even felt that Ruth was in their way) while Evelyn?—Well, from the remarks she'd made when she'd been doing what she considered her "daily duty" by cooking him a meal and tidying his house was not at all happy at the prospect of having her prodigal brother under her roof. Which brought the problem round to him, and as he stared at the flags on the bobbing corks he contemplated.

Besides, if David should need help with things like… getting in and out of the bath, then he didn't imagine he'd want his sisters to possibly see him with no clothes on, for, he imagined, he would still have his dignity, even if he were not able to—and he was not able to even think the end of his sentence, so terrible did it seem.

He suddenly remembered his own days of "freedom"—the fishing expedition to Greenland which now seemed a lifetime away. To return to Staithes was magic—like his earliest fishing recollections, when he'd seen his net like a diamond shroud in the water as it enveloped a silver salmon, and from a rocking boat he stared landward toward Penny Nab, impenetrably black till a great golden glow rose over its edge, illuminating everything. A wasp's nest of stars, purple black lobsters—and in Greenland, the Northern Lights.

And he could now "see" something else. That his brother, on his arrival in Staithes would move in with him. The bedroom he'd always thought might be for Ruth never had been, for though she called him dad, her "parents" were Hannah and Owen. Having made such a momentous decision, he took a backward glance at where he'd sunk his lobster pots, he had others to haul up from the previous day's catch, then he would head for the shore. He could now see the floating buoys and he rowed toward them.

Hannah needed to have words with her brother on another matter, as she felt he should have some (if not the final) words regarding his daughter's education, and if he were to agree to her suggestion, then she would have more time to devote to her now invalid husband.

He seemed dumbstruck at her suggestion. "Schooilin' in York?—But… what'll it cost, for I'm nooan—?"

"Owen an' me, we'll tak' care o' that. All you need ter do is—"

"But what does Ruth say? She's never bin away thro Steeas, an' ter dump 'er in some posh schooil fer weeks on end—"

"But it'll nooan be that way, she'll be 'ome weekends. We'll arrange all that."

"Well…"and he was not convinced, then finally asked, yet again, "an' what does Ruth say?"

"I've not mentioned owt yet."

"…'Appen as yer should!"

"And if she's in agreement?—" and Hannah was not one to let go when her mind was made up.

"Then… we mun talk further. But I've nooan promised owt, think on."

"Then that's what we'll do, Adam," and feeling she was ending the discussion on a winning note, she suddenly changed the subject by asking casually, "is everythin' ready fer David, then?"

"Well, as near as it can be, 'till 'ee arrives next week."

"If yer want me ter lend a 'and."

"No, there's nowt we can do till 'ee turns up," and he seemed adamant that her help would not be required in making his brother comfortable. "Besides," and her read the look of disappointment on her face, "we dooan't know exactly 'ow David'll manage, do we? Comin' back ter Steeas might be all ter much fer 'im."

"Aye," she finally had to relent, "yer could be reight Adam, we mun see 'ow things work out."

She would gain nothing from arguing or antagonising him, but she could now confidently start writing letters to the school in York that Owen had mentioned earlier. There would be an entrance examination… and if things went well fancy uniforms to buy… and her little girl would have playmates who came from well-to-do families a world away from fisherfolk.

She deserved something better than Staithes, did Ruth.

He was helped off the train by the ticket collector, and feet firmly on the platform, stood stock still. Then he turned his head in the direction of the voice, calling out, "over 'ere, lad", and the Dacre family rushed forward, then momentarily drew back as they saw the horribly disfigured face shiny from the burns. There was also the scarred hand holding the stick. But as he moved toward them, these marks appeared as nothing… when they realised the greatest affliction of all.

Their brother was now blind!

Adam was the first to break the deafening silence, as he called out above the hiss and hoot of the train as it slowly began to move, " 'ang on ter me, tha'll be all reight. Let's tak' thee bags," then arms reached out as his two sisters hugged and kissed him.

"It's good ter 'ave yer back wi' us," and Hannah blinked away the tears while Evelyn, still stunned, just held his hand. She couldn't believe it—but Hannah and Adam must have known—they should have told her what to expect.

"Well, and how is everybody?" and his speech was clipped, the Staithes accent was gone, his years of self-imposed exile from the village had made their mark. He was not the young lad who had, all those years ago run away.

"Oh, we're all reight lad," and Hannah, taking control and making light of the situation said simply, "Nah, lets get thee dahn 'ome, an' then we can catch up on all that's been 'appenin'. An' thee two nephews an' niece'll be callin' on thee affore 'day's aht."

Evelyn looked at her sister, then questioningly pointed to her own eyes, and Hannah nodded.

"Now then, tak' thee time, 'cos it's rough underfoot, an' we dooan't want thee fallin'," and with Adam leading the way the family procession took the cliff path that led to the alleyway above High Barrass. Net curtains twitched, someone rushed to tell Old Rall the news. She stared in near disbelief, and managed an incredulous, "Nea!" which in Old Rall's vocabulary could mean absolutely anything. She shook her head, her three chins wobbled. At least, it would give her something to speculate over with Sair-Anne.

Within the week his re-appearance became history, as a far more important event occurred, and again the Bidder went round the village, this time calling, "Will yer coom? Will yer coom to Bridie Dacre's funeral—fer shu's deead! Thu'sday mornin' eleven o' clock. 'Bearers as bin picked, an' 'ymns yar's ter sing. Yar's ter gather ootside 'ouse fer funeral biscuits an' port, an' clay pipes o' baccy afoore 'liftin'." Then, to add weight to her invitation, she added again, "will yar coom? Will yar coom ter Bridie Dacre's funeral—'cos shu's gooan an' dropped dahn deead."

The matriarch of the Dacre family must now be put to rest according to Staithes rituals, and the entire village would turn out to see (and be part of) this macabre circus.

Hannah had once again to organise things, though much of her duties were seeing that her aunt's wishes were carried out to the letter. In the mahogany chest-on-chest was the laying out linen, the shroud and white stockings, the white porcelain rose to be held in the clasped hands, and a luxurious and unbelievably extravagant (even by Staithes standards) flowing golden wig the corpse was to wear.

Aunt Bridie would look better in death than in life!

Also, in her aunt's neat handwriting was a list of names requested as servers, the order of the service itself, and the name of the stonemason who had already made (and had received payment) for the rough marble headstone. In the last paragraph was the name of her solicitors and her bank, where copies of her will had been deposited, and this was to be read out after her funeral had taken place.

The Thursday morning saw thin rays of anaemic sunshine as the village took on its cloak of mourning for what was about to take place. A woman, old again as time, appeared in black astrakhan, with jet round her throat, some distant in-law by marriage. Then, in their moth-balled finery, the two cronies Old Rall and Sair-Anne, followed by an old man in a pilot-cloth coat over a guernsey and polished boots that squeaked. The coffin was laid outside the house, and the whole population of Staithes, so it seemed arrived in time to see the huge bunch of lilies arrive, and then the members of the Dacre family began to appear. David in one of Adam's suits that didn't fit, Evelyn (still in mourning bonnet), while Hannah, in black silk with beadwork, took her place next to the open coffin so that people could look at the corpse then express to her their sympathies.

Hovering in the background like ghouls were the eight servers, dressed in black with a white shawl draped over their shoulder. When the time for "lifting" came, they would in twos precede the cortège, shawls draped over the right or left shoulder forming a chevron, as they headed the procession through the village.

In one of the yards were hanging salted rows of black-jacks. Grey kites, flags flying at half mast and silhouetted against a now sympathetic grey sky. The undertaker was hovering, glasses of port or brandy were being consumed, food in the way of thin funeral biscuits was being offered, then someone hummed several notes before finally arriving on "t'pitch" and the assembled mourners sang *Guide Me, Oh Thou Great Jehovah*. There was an impromptu fanfare of gulls then the coffin was lifted, the servers took up their positions and the cortege made its way to the churchyard in the nearby village.

Later that day the family met at the solicitor's office for the reading of aunt Bridie's last will and testament. There were no surprises, except perhaps the enormity of their aunt's fortune, which, in its entirety had been left to her nephew Adam.

No longer would his sister be able to play Lady Bountiful—he'd now probably more money than she had.

Chapter 16

The spring tides raced up the slipway and into the bar of the Cod & Lobster. For days there was white water, and the boats unable to cast off, and David Dacre was certainly not short of company, and because of tales of sudden wealth, neither was his brother.

But Adam Dacre was shrewd enough to realise (and accept) that a suddenly inherited fortune would not be enhanced, or accumulate, by indiscriminate spending. Besides, he reasoned, he had managed before his inheritance, and he viewed it as something to safeguard then one day hand on to his daughter, and it went untouched apart from the occasional evening he would have in the pub with David. Nor was his brother the "burden" he had first imagined he would be, for Adam was soon to discover that his brother's blind eyes could see more than most sighted people when it came to baiting nets, and occasionally he would accompany him to the lobster pots and help him haul in the catches.

Spring turned to summer, and earlier speculation regarding the estate of Bridie Dacre was something that was now rarely discussed, for life had not stood still. There had been chapel anniversaries, the Fair Week with roundabouts and swings, and the brass band from the local ironstone mine, and Hannah, true to her word had made enquiries regarding Ruth's further education, and she would be attending a school in York as a "weekly boarder" and come home Friday evenings. To make this arrangement possible, Owen and Hannah bought a new motor car, the one that had served them for the past number of years being now unreliable, for the world was moving at a faster pace. So a new vehicle was needed.

On learning that Ruth would be away during the week, Simon moaned like a lovesick boy, for he and his cousin were special to one another, and the two of them seemed to spend every second together of the precious time that was left. Summer evenings would see them standing on the bridge holding hands and watching the moored boats bob up and down on their moorings, and in the new moon, like young lovers they walked toward Cowbar. They said little, their silence spoke volumes. Then, at the end of the evening, Simon would walk with her to the top of the bank to take her home, and Hannah would be waiting with some supper for them both.

A grand lad was Simon, more thoughtful than the other half of the pair—nor were they as close as one might imagine. For there was "something" about James that disturbed her, and she often worried that this premonition might, when least expected show itself—with consequences that could be fatal!

Adam drained his glass, and probably because he'd drunk enough to loosen his tongue asked, "Is there owt yer miss, David—apart from not bein' able ter see? Yer know, owt yer'd like ter do, anywhere yer'd like ter go?"

His brother thought, gave a discreet cough then, as a smile come over his face he replied, "Well, now you ask, there is one thing."

"Anything I can—?"

David mumbled something, and Adam sat bolt upright. "Eh? Come again—but don't use 'that' word."

"All right, let's be very polite then. I miss… going with a woman. You know, having a good—"

"Bloody 'ell!"

"Well, don't sound so shocked, it's a perfectly natural function. Men and women do it all the time."

" 'Appen—but they're wed first."

"And it's my sight that's gone—but 'down there' I'm just like any other feller. I've never had a wife but I've performed with lots of women. Look, stop sounding so bloody prim and proper. I want a woman! I know men… 'abuse' themselves when they—but it's not the same. Is there nobody in the village? Men used to sell their wives by the bridge Friday nights to get some weekend ale money. Does that still happen?"

" 'Ow the bloody 'ell should I know?"

Temporarily defeated, David asked lamely, "What about you? Have you never—?"

"God no! Not since Polly died," and not wishing to sully her memory, Adam decided, "we'd best get 'ome, an' forget this conversation. Come on, yer leet gi'en tupp. Tha needs shovin' in t'beck ter cooil thee dahn—"

"I could do it with my eyes shut! Besides," he suddenly joked, "there's been more than one occasion when I've done just that, and told myself I was deflowering some dewy-eyed virgin instead of an old whore who'd pleasured several men that evening before me."

"David, keep thi voice dahn, somebody might 'ere thee."

"They'd only be jealous. And sometimes with the lads from the platoon, three or four of us might even service the same girl. Do it while the others looked on. Next weekend, what say we go into Whitby and—"

"No, David—definitely no."

"How do I look?"

"This is madness."

"It could be a good night," David Dacre was having nothing spoil his evening of (hopefully) debauchery and pent-up lust, as he stroked the shape of his beard after his brother had trimmed it. "Is it… all right?"

"Oh, aye."

"And this shirt? It's not too—"

"She'll be more bothered abaht what's in the breeches," and, this being the nearest thing to a joke Adam had made that day, David grabbed him by the shoulders and said simply, "Thanks, Adam."

"An' tha says nowt ter Hannah, not even Owen."

" Our secret's safe, don't worry."

"An' if tha gets a dooase o' clap? Well, it'll be thi own fault. If tha starts pissin' puss tha mun tell me."

"How shall I know, if I can't see?"

"Yer meean, I mun watch yer—like when tha wor a little lad aimin' fer 'pittle-pot an' missin'?"

"Well, that's what big brothers are for, isn't it?"

Adam looked at the money in his wallet, and thrust some of it into his brother's hand. "Fer 'pleasures of the flesh.' "

"No, really. I've—"

"Go on, tak' it. What's it cost, gettin' thee leg over?"

"Oh, depends. An all night job? Well… ?"

"But it's nobbut a quickie terneet?"

A smile crossed the younger brother's face. "Don't worry, Adam—and by the way, I shall manage without any assistance. You won't have to watch."

"Thank God fer that. Coom on, let's get thee ter Whitby."

It seemed very much a situation of "the blind leading the blind" as the two men, after walking from the West Cliff station and making their way to the harbourside suddenly stopped as Adam looked around him, then in a defeated way asked, "Nah, what's next?"

"Well, can you see any girls doing business?"

"Eh?"

"You know!—Stranding around waiting for clients."

"David, this is Whitby. It's respectable! There's nooa knockin' shops."

"You know what they call them, then," his brother teased.

"Look, shall we go into a pub? An' there might be some lasses 'avin' a drink that's on t'game."

"Why not? Lead the way. And don't pick the good-looking one for yourself and leave me with the spotty-faced one."

"Dooan't thee include me in this."

"After all"—and David ignored his remark—"we can't be the only two fellers wanting some woman for a quick fumble. If this pub doesn't seem the place, then we could try somewhere on Church Street—or even ask someone."

"Not bloody likely."

And so began a trudge of public houses in the vicinity of the harbour, with Adam feeling suddenly bold as he blatantly stared at various women trying to decide if they were, as David had earlier politely described them "hoping to do business". Finally, in the bar of a pub near the town's swing bridge David Dacre's quest came to an end.

"There's a woman standin' next ter 'bar. Shu's on 'er own."

"What does she look like?"

"Shu's wearin' a red frock—sort of… silk. An shu's… starin' rahnd, as though shu's lookin' fer somebody."

"This sounds promising. We could be in the right place."

"Well, what do we do, then?"

"Just …" and David's memories of earlier whoring came flooding back to him. The chase could be as exciting as the kill. "Just… er… is she attracting any interest? Any fellers approaching her, or is she—?"

"There's a feller talkin' to 'er nah—oh, owd on—'ee's goin'."

"Then… go and get us a couple of drinks, and stand next to her and… make some casual remark about—oh, bloody hell, you'll know in an instant if she's available."

"An' if she is?"

"Then invite her to join us."

David brought his glass to his lips to drain the last drops of Whitby ale, which seemed warm and tasted of hops. But, he consoled himself, it wasn't the beer he was here for.

His nostrils picked up the cheap perfume—this was another good sign, then he heard, "an' this is me young brother, David—did 'is bit fer King an' Country, an' lost 'is sight, poor lad."

He felt a soft hand thrust into his, and a woman's voice commiserating, " 'War took some lovely young men. My name's Mavis. I don't live far from here."

"That'll be 'andy for yer, then."

"Has my brother bought you a drink?" David tried his best to cover for his brother's tactless remark, "if you'd care to join us, that is."

"I don't mind if I do—port and lemon, please," and David felt the chair next to him move closer. "And which was your regiment? And I can't imagine you as a private—a young man like you would be sure to get promotion. See lots of action."

"Especially in Paris," and he thought of the brothels he'd frequented. "Yes," he agreed, "Lots of action."

"Life has its 'ups and downs' wouldn't you say?"

"I certainly would, Mavis. I think we understand one another. And after Adam comes back with your drink, we could take our time, and then... you could let me escort you home. After all, young women in bars can easily get a bad reputation these days."

"Oh yes, there are some very narrow-minded people."

"And I'm sure you wouldn't want to 'compromise' your reputation by being seen in the company of two men."

"Ooohhh, nothing like that."

"And... I'd show my appreciation in a most sensible and generous way."

"Really?"

"After all, as the evening wears on and men become the worse for drink they don't always treat young ladies such as yourself with the respect they deserve."

"Oh, they don't."

"Dooan't what?" and Adam's voice cut the conversation as he re-joined them.

"Know how to treat young ladies such as Mavis. But in a few minutes... we're going back to where she lives. Well, I am. I just need to," and he turned to Adam, "make a call—and as I'm not able to fight my way through the bar, you'd better come with me. We won't be a minute, Mavis. And when we get to where you live, I'm sure you'll... be able to look after a blind feller. Show him where everything is?"

"Ooohhh," she giggled, "I don't mind if I do."

The height of summer had become the glory of autumn, and men would take to their boats as the morning sun like something from a refiner's crucible poured over the horizon to become a gilded net before spread-ing itself over the sea. There were herring catches as never before, plenti-ful in every household for breakfast, mid-day and evening meal. Fried, grilled, rolled in oatmeal, eaten with spoonfuls of black treacle by a soon-

to-be mum and accompanied with boiled onions and stout by retired
Capt Owen Danvers-Griffiths. He would spit out the bones, and dribble
over his food as would a baby, and Hannah felt so helpless as she looked
on.

She was now needing Adam to help to get him in and out of the bath
for his weight was more than she could manage, and on such occasions
thought it a very sensible move, their sending Ruth away to school.
Adam had not raised any objections to his daughter completing her education away from the village, for the child was bright, and Hannah had
great plans for her, when the time came. She missed not having her at
home, but—well, time would tell.

Her absence was felt much more by her cousin Simon, who moped
round the village till Friday evenings when he would call and see her, and
they'd tell each other their news. She was learning to speak French, he
was saving up for a Christmas present for her, and they would be insep-
arable until the Sunday afternoon, when she Hannah must take her back
to York, and Simon was alone again, and quite inconsolable until the
following weekend.

Then, after a fall, Owen took a turn for the worse, and Hannah
braced herself for what was to come. His end was swift—and she was a
rich widow!

Owen's death had been imminent—totally unexpected was David's announcement the following winter that he was planning to get married.

Adam suddenly choked on his tea, as his brother took him into his
confidence.

"Eh? But who to?"

"Well, Mavis. Who else?"

"But she's… er… on t'game. Tha can't marry a woman o' that sort,"

"Why not?"

"Well," and no longer choosing his words, Adam lunged, " 'Cos shu's
bin wi' that many bloody men. Shu's nowt but a common whore—an'
probably riddled wi' syph'—it's a wonder tha's nooan caught owt."

"Well, I'm not perfect, you know. And she's wasn't the first—I have
been around."

"Aye, but tha's nooan done it fer money, though."

"How do you know?"

"David," and his elder brother tried to talk in a reasonable manner,
"women like Mavis… they don't get 'married'. Besides, what'd yer do fer
a livin', t'pair o' yer? Are yer goin' ter keep aht o' way while she entertains

all t'fellers shu picks up? You live in t'kitchen while she's laid on 'er back earnin' a living for t'two o' yer. There's a name fer men as do that, yer know."

"Shut up!"

"An shu's nooan comin' 'ere, I'll tell yer that fer nowt."

"I wouldn't dream of bringing her here."

"Good. That's settled then."

"And when next we meet, I am going to ask her to marry me."

"Yer mad!"

"Look on it… as a good thing, from your point of view. You don't really want a blind man under your feet, do you?"

"David, I've nivver at any time—"

"No, I know you haven't, but… just think about it. I'm blind, who's going to want to marry me?—who's going to want to marry Mavis when they know the life she leads? We get on well, make each other happy—so where's the problem in our getting wed?"

"I just can't…" and his brother was, for once, lost for words.

The bar in Whitby was becoming rowdy, for cruel winters with boats laid up always made men fractious, and Adam finished his drink then left. He heard a smack of fists, and turning, saw the fight breaking out in Church Street. The scuffle was already attracting a crowd of onlookers, but these days anxious to steer clear of trouble, Adam hurried about his business. He was certain it would be another hour before David appeared, and he hoped the lad had not done anything daft—or suggested anything that could in any way be construed as a proposal of marriage. The trouble with David was, he was headstrong, and when he said he wanted any-thing—well, nothing could dissuade him. Years ago because he wanted a bedroom of his own he'd run away from home, and now, well this crack-pot idea of marrying some common whore? Absolute madness!

Adam felt conspicuous and cold as he stood on the street corner, perhaps he should walk toward the park or go down to the quayside—but that could be equally dangerous as the pub he'd just left. The rain was turning to icy sleet, he wished his brother could get his "love-making" (as he now politely referred to it) over and done with. He and this Mavis were as bad as newly weds. The ground was wet and slushy beneath his feet, there was a biting wind coming of the sea. He again he looked at his pocket watch. Time was either going very slowly, or standing still.

"Bloody 'ell, David," he found himself muttering, " 'ow long does it tak' thee ter get thee leg over?"

The following morning, on entering his brother's room, Adam saw the bed had not been slept in, nor did David make an appearance as the day wore on, and it was late afternoon when the two policemen appeared.

A body had been dragged from the harbour in Whitby, and from the personal items in the man's pockets, was believed to be one David Dacre, of Staithes. The rest of their words were wasted on Adam, as he must accompany the policemen to the town's mortuary to identify the corpse. Adam took only one look, then nodded. Yes, this was his brother. This was David Dacre.

The police needed to make further investigations before the body could be released for burial, but could they take this opportunity to express their sympathy at the family's sad loss. Adam felt decidedly sick, and said as little as possible, for he must call and see this Mavis, in the hope that she could shed some light on the events leading up to this accident. And what of the rest of the family? What could he say to them—or did they already know?

Then, two days later there were further and, he hoped (he *so* hoped) unconnected and sordid revelations on the front page of the local paper. One Mavis Pickersgill, a common prostitute well known to the Whitby police, had been brutally murdered. Her neighbours could confirm that she had been entertaining men on the Friday evening, and the police were now anxious to interview her clients, in order to eliminate them from their enquiries

There was one they couldn't interview, and only Adam Dacre was able to put the pieces of the jigsaw together. Another Dacre secret that must be taken to the grave!

For fear of antagonising her brother, and such a thing compromising the relationship she had with his daughter, Hannah Danvers-Griffiths said little, but thought long and hard.

That Adam could have been so stupid as to have let a blind man roam around the harbour late at night? It was asking for trouble, and although he could not in any way be directly blamed for David's drowning accident, she felt he was, nevertheless, partly responsible.

But these feelings she must keep to herself, for the family was already torn apart. They needed something to unite them. Her accusations and recriminations would serve no purpose, for when she looked at Adam it was obvious that all was not well with him.

His days were arduous, and, she reasoned, one in his position (for aunt Bridie had left him "very comfortable") should be able to take life easy.

But not so Adam Dacre!

For he was a troubled man. He was weighed down by guilt and remorse, and after months of carrying his shameful burden, finally he must explain to his elder sister the undisclosed events surrounding their late brother, and the reason for the more-than-occasional trips into Whitby, and like a humble penitent in the confessional (and hoping for absolution) he told his tale.

"But… this can't be reight, Adam—tha's got 'old on wrong end o' stick."

"I'm tellin' thee—"

"But what wor 'ee doin' mixin' wi' that sort o' woman?"

"Dooan't act so bloody straight-laced. Does tha think shu wor knittin' 'im a guernsey. Tha knows damned well what they wor up to."

His sister was having "palpitations" (as the doctor called these things she was now suffering), and she took deep breaths, then staring straight at him, she asked, "An'… tha wor a party ter all this?—tha took 'im whoorin'?"

"Damn thee… it wor a man thing—summatt tha knows nowt abaht."

"An' ah dooan't want ter know."

"Be that as it may, 'Annah—but that doesn't alter me tale. David wor goin' ter ask this Mavis ter marry 'im—'ee wor goin' ter propose that very neet. Nah, put two an' two together. They must 'ave… 'ad words? Started arguing? Shu might 'ave laughed at 'im an' 'ee put 'is 'and rahnd 'er throit ter shut 'er up—then when it wor ter late, realised what 'ee'd done, an' jumped in 'arbour ter drown 'imself."

She was silent for a long time, then asked, "Did 'police know… 'ee wor—'ad been seein' this Mavis Whatever-they-called-'er?"

He shook his head "No. I said nowt. There wor nowt as could connect 'em—an' dead man can't tell tales. There's nobbut thee an' me know—an' we can only guess what really 'appened that neet."

"But… ah think tha's 'it 'nail on t'eead."

He stirred the embers, then put kettle over them. "It's an awful weight I've bin carryin' all these months," and he made a helpless gesture with his hands, then asked, "what are we goin' ter do, 'Annah?"

Her answer was immediate. "Nowt! Tha did reight gettin' it off thee chest, fer a problem shared is a problem 'alved, but what's passed between thee an' me goes no further. Not even Evelyn mun know."

"…An' we say nowt ter 'police?"

"Cert'nly not. An' if it's weighin' on thee mind tha mun talk ter me—but say nowt ter nobody. It's our secret."

"There's a couple o' crabs, if yer want 'em," he changed the subject, "well… tak' all tha needs. I'd a good day terday."

"Aye, that'll be grand. An' Adam," and she took his hands, "tha gettin' sea boils on the wrists. Tha needs ter tak' good care o' thissen. Tha very special, tha knows."

Chapter 17

Weeks turned to months, then became years, and the seasons brought sorrows (and highlights) to the fishing community. Old men and women died, babies were born, but the North Sea ruled: a cruel master and the mainstay of village life.

Old Rall had now been called to her Maker—and would no doubt be stood by the pearly gates exchanging gossip and pulling the angel Gabriel to pieces behind his back. Occasionally one of the group, who some twenty years previously had tried to capture the village on canvas, would be seen in the vicinity. And Rowland Henry Hill, who lived in nearby Ellerby, had by now become part of village life and caused no surprise as he carted his canvases to wherever he was working. Adam Dacre was looking decidedly older. His elder sister carried herself well, despite her now matronly figure and halo of silvery hair. Whilst Evelyn who, it seemed, never had so much as a minute to herself, had survived one war but was now in the midst of another.

A war that constantly raged between the two young men living under her roof.

Big strong lads that any mother would be proud of. And, being twins, very similar in appearance, but totally opposite in personality. James, who loved the sea, had embraced the life of a fisherman, while Simon, the more gentle of the two, worked in the local ironstone mine, and they would spend hours extolling the virtues of their particular calling and belittling any other.

"Fishin'?" Simon would query, "well James, there's nowt left, is there? Thro what I 'ear, 'errin' shoals as bin driven away bi' naval vessels durin' war."

"Tha's bin stuck dahn a mine ter long," his brother would retort, "it's affected thee brain—made thee soft in t'eead. An' if tha wants ter see what fishin's abaht, then coom dahn ter 'staithe soom dark, slipp'ry mornin'. 'Neet mist still shroudin' 'watterside, an cobles loomin' oop like monsters thro 'deep, piled 'igh wi' crab-puts like gurt rat-cages."

"Why, that's nowt," Simon would tease him, "Nah, if want to see real men, then yer need to go dahn 'mine. Sometimes it's so 'ot an' so deep, they're workin' wi' nowt on. Bollock naked—or it could be just opposite, an' yer could be as cold as a frog."

His twin would make a derisive gesture as Simon would continue, but no longer joking, "there's a sort o' 'darkness', James, that yer cannot describe, fer it's different thro owt yer can imagine. Yer touch yer nooase, yet ter can't see yer 'and—an' yer've a ball o' clay stuck ter yer side wi' a can'le in."

"Ah, but, brother… just imagine, if tha can… bobbin' up an' dahn in a coble on a raw winter's day. Eyes filled wi' salt an' they're ter sore ter rub 'em. Waves lippin' an choughin' as yer drop yer ender set on a bundle o' corks. Yer look rahnd fer a marker, but 'land's all gooan—fer 'bloody blizzard's blocked aht all o' Steeas."

"But that's on a bad day," Simon would scoff, "why, in t'mine? Well yer in constant danger o' 'roof collapsin'. A lad 'ad 'is arm sliced off when a rock crashed dahn—an' another 'ad 'is legs smashed ter pulp. They shovelled 'em up ter stop 'rats eatin' 'em."

"Oh, but that nowt," James refused to be outdone, "what abaht when 'arbour's all white watter, an 'fires lit on 'staithe ter burn us off? Wi' an angry sea spewin' and spoutin' like a blowin' whale. Yer need yer initials in every bit o' clothin'—fer when 'sea washes yer oop… in bits."

"Will yer stop it, 'pair o' yer? Ah've 'ad enough."

"Oh, tha's got it easy, Simon," his twin carried on, unheeding the warning, "nowt ter do these days 'cept leead bloody great 'osses oop an' dahn 'pit."

"Oh aye—coomes wi' me promotion. Ah tak' Flossie a pocketful o' grass every mornin' an' at end o' me gi'e 'er 'ard corn an' linseed in 'er food. 'Er cooit's beautiful. But," and he added a downside to his job, "it's parky walkin' ter Grinkle on a winter's mornin'—but coom summer, an' all t' birds singin'? Well, that's a diff'rent kettle o' fish."

"Huh, tha'd nooan 'ere birds singin' if tha wor goin' same spot as me. Just bloody gulls screamin' an' squawkin'."

"Well, then."

"But—" and not to be outdone the firstborn continued, "when yer pull in yer first 'aul, an' net a shroud o' watter an' a gurt 'alibut—well, that's summatt."

"Aye, till yer get back ter find there no buyers that day, an' fish is rags!"

"Will yer stop nah—'pair o' yer," their mother would again call for order, saying one was no better than his uncle Adam, the other just a tease, and they would suddenly feel ashamed of themselves, and usually repair to the Cod & Lobster to cement their wonderful relationship. Brothers were special to one another, twins even more so.

It was a spring of high tides, when waves raced up the slipway only to be dragged back by the weight of the surf, when they would crash and thunder, leaving the beach trembling, the cliffs echoing and bruised. The scaurs would be stripped clean of seaweed, the beach littered with the occasional dead seal, and driftwood to be collected for fires.

This was the time Staithes fishermen concentrated on long-lining for cod, haddock and turbot, and the lines, all five hundred fathoms of them, would have been weighted at either end then left on the sea bed for several hours before lifting; each craft, depending on its size, working three to six lines. And James Howarth would haul them in and wish… that he could be his own master, or at least, be "the other half" of a boat.

But that would need money, and the family—well, his part of the Dacre family—didn't have any. He supposed his mother "managed" from week to week. There was always enough food in the house, but no luxuries. Luxuries belonged to his aunt Hannah, with her fancy villa and motor car, and her packing his cousin off to some posh school. Yet when she'd finished her fancy education she'd still be a Dacre, and no different from the rest of them.

He could remember tales… of how his uncle Adam had joined a fishing fleet and gone to Greenland, and thinking about it suddenly decided him.

He would need, perhaps, to go to Whitby to find one of the bigger boats that would be sailing north to Aberdeen in June before sailing south following the shoals of herring, ending up in Lowestoft during the autumn. If he were away several months, with nothing to spend any money on, then he could return a rich man. He must tell no-one of his plans, until they were finalised

Hannah Danvers-Griffiths was also making plans. Being a woman who had the wherewithal to spend as she felt fit, and as a drowning man would clutch at straws so she must now seek a second (and hopefully more learned) opinion, and so as not to raise any fears or speculations, it seemed to her better to suggest the trip to London was nothing more than "a 'oliday".

Evelyn started in surprise at her sister's invitation to accompany her, for she could not remember any previous sisterly concern. "Tha wants me ter coom wi' thee ter… London for a 'oliday?—An' tha'll pay? Train fare, 'otel bill—the lot?"

"That's what I said, an' that's what ah meant."

Evelyn, at a loss for words managed finally, "tha's gotten ter a funny age, 'appen as tha should see a doctor."

"Ah'd sooiner see 'Houses o' Parliament, or Bucking'am Palace."

"Well, ah mun find summatt ter wear. Ah dooan't want ter show thee up."

"We could go ter Middlesbrough, or... York even, an' get some new outfits. I'll get some new stays, an'—"

Evelyn shook her head. "Tha'll need more na' stays ter get thee figure back. Oh, what time's done ter us. It's wicked."

"Ah'm thinkin'... next month?"

"Well... go on, then. But dooan't thee go booking rooms at some posh 'otel, 'cos I'll be certain ter show thee up, wi' usin' wrong knife an' fork."

"An' ah thought we could go ter t'theatre—or see a musical or summatt."

"Eee, an' why ever not? We're nobbut 'ere once—let's live!"

Evelyn Howarth spent the rest of the day in a state of turmoil. Had she done the right thing? Would Simon be able to manage without her having his evening meal on the table when he came home from the mine? What if James were to suddenly arrive several weeks prematurely, for he was a hothead, and if life among the herring fleet was not to his liking, then he would have made his voice heard. Perhaps—but there were so many things to think of, hundreds of excuses she could find for needing to change her mind and stay at Ring o' Bells just in case—and then she stopped her fanciful thoughts.

She was going to go on holiday—and she was going to enjoy herself.

Chapter 18

The long train journey to London was not without its lighter moments, as the younger of the two sisters, feeling deliciously wicked being suddenly freed from the confines of Staithes and "widowhood" and all that it entailed, flirted shamelessly with the younger man sat in the compartment opposite them.

The checked suit and bowler hat reminded Evelyn that there was more to life than mourning bonnets and ling pie. There was a world outside Staithes, but out of her grasp. He was smiling at her, and brazenly, she smiled back. His shoes shone, he'd a naughty grin—and Evelyn Howarth wished her sister would suddenly disappear, and this young man could then come and sit next to her, and her hand could casually brush against his thigh. Nor would he instinctively pull back, but would welcome her suggestive advances—and so as not to ruffle the knife edge creases in his trousers he'd—

"Nooan be long, nah," and her sister's voice came like a slap across her face, bringing her to reality.

"Sorry?"

"Sooin be there. We sud be in King's Cross Station in t' next ten minutes."

"I nivver—not in me wildest dreams thought I'd ever set foot in London," then in near panic Evelyn asked, " 'Annah, what are we doin' dahn 'ere, reight fair?"

"Well… we're on 'oliday," her sister lied, "we've coom sight seein'. 'Ouses o' Parliament, Westminster Abbey, art galleries, owt tha wants—we might even… go ter see what they call a West End musical."

"Eee, 'Annah."

The train slowed down, then minutes later pulled into the station, and rather them struggle with their luggage Hannah hailed a porter and stood back as he piled their cases onto his cart. He looked at her questioningly. "We need transport, young man, ter tak us ter our 'otel. We're stoppin' in t'Imperial.—Nah, it says it's within walkin' distance o' King's Cross Station, but not wi' all this trammil we 'ave with us."

The engine suddenly screamed, making them jump. Evelyn looked around her—at the ornate metal pillars supporting the high vaulted roof and the pigeons that seemed to have taken up residence, the posters adverting various things, the people to-ing and fro-ing, the smell of London, the dialect of the obvious locals, the parcels being unloaded by uniformed porters, and man walking past was smoking a cigar—and as she inhaled she suddenly thought of Owen puffing away in what her sister had laughingly called "the war room".

She looked at Hannah. Was she also being reminded?

"Coom on, Evelyn, we mun get a move on. Nah then, young man…" He led the way, they followed.

The next morning Hannah announced that she had "a bit o' business ter see to", which did not come as any great shock to her sister, for she knew full well that Hannah had some reason for coming to London. She supposed it would be to do with Ruth, probably another "posh" school that would turn her into a "refained" young lady so's she'd know how to behave when she was on the quayside gutting fish.

Oh, the money her sister must have spent on her education! And it wasn't as though she were her own child, for Hannah was only her aunt. But it was her money—and Owen must have left her well-provided for—and she thought again… of the Howarth fortune she was keeping well hidden. For when—if—the time came when one of the twins needed money for any reason, then it would be there. But that could be years hence. She must concentrate on now, as Hannah asked, "An what'll tha do wi' thissen till we 'ave us dinner?"

"Just go lookin' in shop windows—or I might tak' a walk."

"An' I thought this afternooin we could go see Nelson's Column."

"Why not? We dooan't want ter miss owt, fer I dooan't s'pose as we'll coom ter London ageean?"

Hannah looked thoughtful. "No, 'appen not."

It was a week of sight-seeing. Parliament, Eros, Portobello Market, Westminster Abbey, St. Paul's Cathedral, Buckingham Palace and the Changing of the Guard, and in a West End theatre a performance of Chu Chin Chow, the National and Tate Galleries, and as they meandered around the capital they stumbled upon the Alpine Galleries, and were amazed—for there was a exhibition by Laura and Harold Knight.

" 'Eee, Evelyn—just think, tha used ter model for 'er."

"Aye—fer pence."

"I'm sorry, Simon—but can you repeat that?" and her freckled face broke into a bemused grin, "for one moment I thought you said Lond-on."

He nodded. "That's reight. They'll be there another week at least, for aunt 'Annah seemed unsure as to when they' be arrivin' 'ome. Anyroad, shouldn't you still be in York?"

"Under normal circumstances, yes," his cousin replied, then went on to elaborate, "the exams finished earlier than expected, so now... well, I just wait till I hear one way or the other."

Simon, almost fearful of her reply asked, "an'... do yer really want ter go ter Cambridge?"

"Well, mum wants me to. What do you think?"

He stared at the tab rug in front of the hearth. "I'd... still, it's nowt ter do wi' me... but I'd rather yer wor in Steeas, an' then we could—"

"Go for walks down Ridge Lane, and look for fairies at Beck Meetings?"

"Aye, an' poke abaht in rock pools lookin' fer crabs."

"And run a tearoom," and she suddenly remembered their plans, "and poison lots of Germans."

"Oh Ruthie, stay in Steeas," and he put his arm round her, and wanted to kiss her properly, but knew he mustn't.

"Well, I'll be here for a week, certainly, you might be fed up of me by then," and she broke free, then said, "I hope mum left a key with someone in case of emergencies, for otherwise I'll have nowhere to stay."

"Well, yer can 'ave mam's room," he offered, "fer James is away fishin' somewhere up top o' Scotland, an' till the wanderers' return, I'm on mi own."

She considered. "We'll see."

"But anyroad," and he was not to be put off, "we could go ter 'cinema in Loftus. Loftus Empire! Sit on wooden planks, watch Pearl White an' listen ter 'piano."

"Now that," and Ruth Dacre jumped at his invitation, "is the best thing I've heard yet."

"Well?" and fearless, she held herself erect while waiting to hear her fate.

The consultant, so very familiar with this situation, gave the appearance of choosing his words carefully, even though he'd used them on many occasions, then went on to explain to the patient, "Mrs Danvers-Griffiths, when we have the results of the tests we have done today , then we can—"

"But is it serious?" she interrupted. "Am I goin' ter die?"

"Until we know the root cause, we can only speculate. Great strides are being made—radium treatment was unheard of twenty years ago, but

is achieving marvellous results these days—and even if surgery is necessary, we need to keep a positive outlook…"

"Aye, I can see that."

"It will seem a long week, but in seven days time—"

"I'll know if I need ter get mi affairs in order. Thank yer very much
fer seein' me'."

She was in no doubt as left the Harley Street consulting rooms. Their
diagnosis would be the same as the hospital in York. She'd been clutch-
ing at straws, hoping that fancy London doctors could have a magical
cure. Money did not buy everything. That was a popular misconception:
it could not guarantee her health or old age.

Her days were already numbered!

They half-walked, half-ran, holding hands and giggling like silly schoolgirls. Simon in a blue checked shirt and Sunday shoes, Ruth, her blonde
curls flowing over her shoulders before being suddenly caught in the
evening breeze and swirled above her head. Then, as they came over
Boulby cliffs and took the turn-off for Cowbar, Simon began showing-
off by doing cartwheels in the grass.

Oh, it was so wonderful being with his cousin!

In the cinema she'd held his hand, and he could smell the perfume
she was wearing. She'd seemed very grown up wearing something such as
that. It was a suggestion of heaven—it was Ruthie!

They came to the row of miners' cottages known to Staithes locals as
"tin-city" and as they began the steep descent down to the bridge the two
of them looked over the patched-up rooftops, but closer to them, the
steep ravine that cut the village in two. In the beck, and seeming far
below them, boats were tied on the wooden struts supporting the bridge.
They bobbed and rocked with the tide. Lazy, lethargic. The two of them
were suddenly silent, Simon regretful that he must soon say goodnight,
his cousin wishing he didn't have to.

They crossed the bridge then, turning into the street, Simon—now
holding her hand and feeling immensely proud and grown up—escorted
her up the street and toward Bank Top. He was sure she could hear his
heart beating, he thought it was going to burst. Outside her front door
she fumbled for her key, then said, "you can come in—for some supper."

He shook his head. "No Ruthie, that nooan a good idea."

"Well, a glass of lemonade then, or even—"

"Ruth, if I say 'yes' to you… well, you know what's going to 'appen,
don't you. Look, we're cousins."

"I thought… you wanted to."

" 'Course I bloody want to. You're all I think about. There could never be anyone else… but because I think so much about you I have to say—" and at that moment she took him in her arms and drew him closer. Breaking free of her kisses he managed, "we can't carry on like this aht 'ere. Somebody might see us."

"Well, come inside then."

"Ruthie, doy—please," but his cousin wanted, and was going to have, her wicked way with him.

The day before their holiday ended, Hannah again 'disappeared' for a morning, and returned subdued.

"Owt up wi' thee?" Evelyn wanted to know.

"No—I'm just… well, wantin' ter get back ter Steeas."

"But it's been a grand 'oliday. We've 'ad a lovely time."

"Aye, but all good things mun coom to an end," and Hannah Danvers-Griffiths felt hers was suddenly imminent. The tests had confirmed what she already knew.

She had cancer, it was the beginning of her end.

Chapter 19

Working in the mine was suddenly the most wonderful thing in the world, because as he walked home at the end of the day, Simon could pick bunches of wild flowers from the hedgerows, which he'd then either ceremoniously present to his cousin, or leave on her doorstep. He forgot his unkempt appearance, his dirty clothes and blackened face, for he was a prince dressed in fine silks paying court on the most beautiful girl in his kingdom. Then, upon leaving his gift of precious jewels, and with sudden renewed vigour he would run down the bank to Ring o' Bells, have a quick bite to eat, carry buckets of water to fill the tin bath, and not noticing the inconvenience of near cold water, would scrub his body till it shone. Then clean clothes, clean teeth (and again "borrowing" James' boots which were smarter than his) and he was ready.

He was indeed a happy young man—were it not for a secret fear that when—if—she were to go to Cambridge or the like… then she might meet someone else: some young man as bright as she was. And the two would… and that was unthinkable!

Or else, and this pleased him more, she'd forget this silly "education" and the two of them… well, he reasoned, they could get married. He was doing well at the pit, and his job was secure, not dependent on the weather or other uncertainties of fishing. The Grinkle pit was now linked up to the Whitby-Middlesbrough railway line, the ore no longer being transported by the narrow gauge that crossed Roxby Beck to nearby Port Mulgrave where it had been transported to Jarrow by barges towed by paddle steamers. And there was also an ironstone mine in nearby Loftus if Grinkle should for any reason need to lay men off.

He supposed he could earn enough to keep a wife and family, for if he and Ruth were married, then there'd certainly be little ones. Pretty daughters with ringlets and—and then he would stop his fanciful thoughts at the dreadful reality of what had—was happening between them.

That he was "in love" would not be seen as an excuse for his behaviour, for he'd been in love with her since he could remember. When she'd been a little girl and had smelled all soapy and clean and had been bundled into the big bed he'd shared with James. When they played games and shared secrets, swapped sweets and Christmas presents, stared into rock pools looking for baby crabs, or when aunt Hannah had invited him to stay for tea and the two of them had gorged themselves on chocolate cake, or even—and he suddenly thought about his aunt, and how she would react when she knew that "that" had happened.

There'd be hell to do when she arrived home from this London
holiday.

She wasn't the sort of person to cross, and he could just imagine…
and it was much safer—certainly more enjoyable to concentrate on now,
then a few days hence. Punishment would come soon enough—but first
came pleasure.

Her fingertip delicately traced the blue vein that seemed to run across his
shoulder and toward his chest, his body tensed under her touch as he
slowly stirred, then his hands gently stroked the head of curls as their lips
met. And now he must kiss her chin, her delicious neck, her breasts. His
tongue teased her nipples and as the two of them slid into a more comfortable position she could feel him inside her. His hands were still caressing, his hungry lips searching, and all the time he was murmuring
" 'Love you, Ruthie—I do love you, Ruthie," and his loving became
more ardent, their breathing laboured. But this lovemaking was no longer
gentle and refined—for they were in the throes of unashamed lust.

Much later, their passions spent but reluctant to leave her bed, Simon
stared at his own naked body, then at hers. His hand reached out, she
gently kissed it.

It was an interminably long hot summer, with the village swathed in sea-
frets that hung like tented nights causing Adam Dacre to wish that he'd
chosen some other occupation as he daily tended to his creels. Even the
sea itself seemed to be sweating, causing him to often lose his bearings as
he tried to look for his markers through the impenetrable mist. Fishing
was for young men, he told himself, and he was getting old, causing him
to envy the young lads in the village who would like water rats run naked
into the breakers or scramble over the rocks. It was a thing particular to
Staithes, he'd done it himself when he was their age, and, he supposed,
when these lads were grown men, then the next generation would do the
same.

Continuity, that was the main thing, and he'd so wished—but it wasn't
to be.

There would be no-one to carry on the Dacre name. He was the last
of that dynasty, and on realising this it made him almost afraid, for when
he died so would the Dacres.

The summer was also a traumatic time for his sister Hannah, who on the advice of the hospital consultant (and the "Harley Street" opinion, which confirmed the earlier diagnosis) was to undergo what in hushed tones was referred to as "major surgery"—it being an operation middle-aged women dreaded, and something men should know nothing about.

She gave an outward appearance of calm, but at night as she lay in bed was anything but. Things were starting to worry, torment her, but uppermost on her mind was the thought of Ruth being on her own if— and it was something she had to consider. If her days really were numbered and she had only months instead of years, then what would happen to her little girl?

She had made more than adequate financial arrangements , for Owen had left her the fortune most people dreamed about, and there was the house, and things like shares in companies, all of which was above her, but brought in an annual income without the need to go out to work. These things were all for Ruth, the solicitors had drawn up her will which she had signed and had been witnessed. She seemed more than friendly with Simon, but, Hannah told herself, when Ruth had finished her studies at university, then she surely want something better than a miner, or the education would have all been for nothing.

It was to free her from the drudgery of Staithes—for why be the bareback rider in the circus if you had the wherewithal to be the ringmaster?

"Me mam says tha needs cheerin' up, an' I mun tak' thee ter Whitby."

He wore an imbecilic grin, and hoped she'd realise he was purposely trying to make light of a serious situation in an effort to even fleetingly take away the worry his aunt's condition was having. "An' we mun end up at Botham's for afternoon tea," he continued, "an' 'ave potted meat sandwiches an' cream cakes, so there."

"Well..." and she pretended to seriously consider his proposition, "you'd better come in while I get ready, for if aunt Evelyn says—"

"Oh, she does," and he closed the door behind him, "an' it's wisest not ter argue wi' Steeas women—do as they say is t'best policy," then taking her in his arms he was suddenly gentle. " 'Ow are we, doy, reight fair?"

"I'm all right. And mum will be home... well, in a few days. She'll need looking after, but," and for one so young she seemed very grown up, "I imagine your mum will want to help, and I shall be here. We'll manage. The only thing is," and she pulled a face, "we'll not be able to do 'that'—if you know what I mean."

"Well then," and more than anxious to please, he offered, "what abaht… now? Affore we catch t'train," and his fingers curled a ringlet before he started nibbling her ear. "I love you," he whispered, "…an' look what's 'appenin' dahn 'ere," and he stroked the front of his trousers. "Yer do 'ave this effect on me, young woman."

"That's as may be. Look, let's catch that train, or else—"

"We'll save that till later, then?"

"Simon Howarth… if your mother knew—"

"Then all 'ell 'ud be let loose. I know. Uncle Adam'd 'ave me gelded," and the sudden thought of the wrath of his uncle calmed his amorous advances. "I'm sorry, doy. As yer say, we mun go an' get the afternoon train."

They held hands as they walked around the abbey, then from the top of the town's hundred-and-ninety-nine steps looked over the harbour and toward the open sea. Simon suddenly had a mental image of his brother, and could "smell" that fishy smell that was forever about his person. His clothes, his sweat, his half of their bed—something that the house was now free of, but would no doubt return when James re-appeared, and Simon, as he now thought about it realised that the earlier "closeness" between them was no more. Perhaps their becoming adults was the reason. They were grown up, and must make their own lives independent of their other half. James's life was the sea. His own future—and he hardly dared think about it, for it could be so very wonderful, was with his cousin Ruth.

Exams results and thoughts of Cambridge took second place in Ruth Dacre's life as a frail woman that had once been a tower of strength and the driving force behind the family returned to Staithes—to end her days, and James Howarth, his adventure and "initiation" into fishing proper, returned to his family.

He sported a beard and an unruly crop of hair, and away from the watchful eye of his mother (who must fuss round him like a mother hen) there was now a coarseness about him, in both his choice of words and his manner. Six months at sea had certainly made a mark—not least the long scar Simon noticed across his chest as the two of them undressed and climbed into nightshirts.

"Oh aye," he murmured as he saw his twin staring at the slash from an earlier fight he'd been in, "I 'ad a slight diff'rence of opinion wi' a feller thro t'Faroes early on."

"Tha took second prize?"

James shook his head. "No. 'Eee sort o'... 'fell overboard' if tha gets mi drift. Drowned! But accidents do 'appen at sea."

"I can imagine."

"But dooan't thee go blabbin' like a gurt bairn."

"Nowt ter do wi' me—an' I've better things ter do na' tell tales abaht thee—an' dooan't thee forget it." And the pleasantries over, the two brothers could get into a new routine of (at best) each one tolerating the other, but nothing more.

Yet if brotherly love seemed lacking, the relationship between uncle and "seafaring" nephew blossomed, being born of mutual respect and admiration, one for the other. As Adam Dacre listened to James' exploits he remembered his earlier fishing trip to Greenland—his own initiation with the sea proper, and James was able to help him re-live earlier triumphs and traumas. They would repair to the Cod & Lobster and consume more ale than was good for them. James would come out with filthy language as though it were everyday talk, and no longer shocked by his nephew's worse-than-swear-words Adam was becoming amused and quickly warming to the lad.

Sisters (and a daughter) were all very well, but there was something to be said for male company and "man's talk"—of which James Howarth was becoming such an expert.

Christmas came, but was anything but a time of celebrations. Hannah was defiantly clinging on to life, albeit much of it in bed, for she was now too weak to move. The earlier silver halo had spread to the rest of her hair, her sallow sunken cheekbones protruded, and there was an aura of death about the house. She saw the winter snowdrops, then rallied to admire the first daffodils before entering a long peaceful sleep from which she never recovered.

Even though expected, it was still something of a shock when it did happen, and now, feeling that she was at last able to "take control" after a lifetime of being in her sister's shadow, Evelyn, with her niece at her side began making arrangements for the biggest event in many Staithes folk's lives—their funeral!

Hannah had earlier intimated that "no expense wor ter be spared" and Evelyn saw it fitting that the hearse preceding the eight servers should be drawn by black horses with plumes, there would be black-edged funeral cards and wreaths of lilies and jasmine, white as death. It would be a morning burial, the whole village would turn out, she would wear her late sister's double silver fox furs, their heads hung down her back in sorrow—and perhaps a black veil.

The coffin would have silver handles and a pale blue satin shroud, and after the only to be expected port and funeral biscuits, pipes of tobacco (and cigars) outside the house, they would sing *In Heavenly Love Abiding*, the vicar would say a few words, then there would be the lifting and the cortège would slowly make its way to the cemetery.

She would walk with Adam, Ruth between James and Simon, then there would be more distant in-laws, friends, the villagers themselves— there would need to be food for afterwards

And something to drink and—and she began to suddenly imagine the wording in the will. Perhaps something like "and to my dear sister Evelyn I bequeath five thousand pounds, to my nephews and niece, one hundred pound each"—and add that the contents of the Howarth strongbox, and she really would want for nowt.

Who said funerals were sad occasions?

With all thoughts of "going to Cambridge" unrealised, and because she was, according to her aunt, "on 'er own, t'poor doy" it was decided that Ruth should move down into the village proper and live with her father. The villa at the top of the bank would be sold: the money (as was the Hannah Danvers-Griffiths fortune that she had inherited in its entirety) be placed in a trust fund.

She would, on reaching the stipulated age, be indeed a rich woman, but Ruth cared little for such things, the important thing to her now being to somehow "come to terms" with living with her father. A fisherman's cottage was not like the villa, for it was claustrophobic, the walls seemed to be closing in on her, nor was there any view should she care to look out of the windows. The air was stifling, and an ever present smell of crabs being boiled permeated the downstairs rooms, even her attic bedroom. From here she could just see the sea.

It was pewter.

It was depressing.

So was her life—for she had nothing to do, except clean, then have some sort of meal ready for her father at the end of his working day.

And Simon was so near, only a few doors away, but they had decided, while they were so very close to each other, there must be no "physical loving"—for no-one in the family must guess, or even suspect that there was anything between them.

He rested his oars as the coble bobbed merrily on the green pewter water. In the very far distance he could just see land. His lips tasted of salt, and as he licked them he imagined herrings cooked over the griddle and a pile of brown bread and butter. It was a good stand-by meal, something he could prepare in minutes, but now... well, with Ruth and her fancy cookery such simple things could only be remembered and savoured in the mind. Like blacklock pie, unless he were at Evelyn's and she'd made one—and there was also ling pie, and even he could make that—but not Ruth.

Daughters were not only a blessing, for they could also be—and it suddenly occurred to him—if he should have an "accident" (and drownings were not unusual on this stretch of coast and among this community) then... what would happen to his daughter?

She really would be all on her own. A young woman, well, not much more than a girl, and to have to face the world all on her own. It didn't— just didn't—bear thinking about. He often felt that he had let her down by not being a proper father to her, yet that was something over which he had no choice, but now he must make amends, and the seeds of a plan were beginning to form in his mind.

That evening, he thought long and hard, and over the ensuing weeks and months every time he put to sea the problem he had created for himself loomed up like some monster from the deep. Chapel anniversaries came and went, so did the annual Staithes Fair, then one autumn evening when he could bear it no longer he somewhat apprehensively called on his sister.

"Coom in, Adam, fer ah'm fair glad o' thee company terneet."

"On thee own, then?"

She nodded. "They're grown men nah—they coom an' go as they will."

"Then... we might be able ter... 'ave a private conversation without bein' interrupted?"

"Why lad, what's on thee mind?" and as he began to explain the reason for his visit, his sister could manage to no more than occasionally nod in agreement at his suggestions. It had not occurred to her... but suddenly seemed a more-than-interesting proposition he was laying on her table.

When he'd finished he turned to her. "Well, is it ter be?"

She paused for effect. "We mun... pick us time. Tha mun leeave that ter me—fer men can jump in wi' booath feet an' upset 'apple cart. But yes, Adam—I agree."

Chapter 20

It was many weeks later when James and his uncle (and this seemed to be coming a regular thing) were tending the lobster pots that Evelyn broke the news to her other son. He stared in utter disbelief as the stupid words came out of her mouth. What she was saying was impossible. It couldn't —just couldn't be!

It was wrong. Totally wrong!

"But mother, yer can't do that. Plan somebody else's life for 'em. Just who do you an' uncle Adam think yer are?" The cutlery and plate danced on the table as he slammed down his fist. "Just 'cos 'two o' yer 'ave been in Steeas since 'Ark landed that doesn't gi'e yer any right ter decide who's ter wed who."

"Yer uncle Adam—"

"Then damn an' bugger 'im—fer 'ee's no better na' you."

She stood defiant. "Ah sud smack thee across thee silly face—bray soom sense into thee. Adam's gi'en James a share in 'coble—an' James is goin' ter do 'reight thing an' marry an' care for 'is lass when owt ails 'im."

"But mam," he pleaded, "it's me an' Ruthie as loves one another. It's allus been that way, ever since we were bairns an' she'd stop neets an' yer'd shove us all in 'same bed. Yer know that. Yer know she can never love James, an' it's... well, even when she went ter York, we only looked for'ard ter been together at weekends—an' when there wor this talk abaht Cambridge, ah knew... after it all, then we'd get wed. We love one another."

" 'Ave yer done?" and she strove to compose herself, for this would need more delicate handling than even she had visualised. "Simon, lad," and she waved her hands as though trying to grasp the words out of the air, "love's all very well—but we mun live in 'real world. This is Steeas— an' weddin's is allus arranged between 'parents. Families an' in-laws inter-marry as tha well knows—"

"So why not me an' Ruthie? Besides, she could never love James... not after—"

"Stop there," she warned, "affore tha says summatt as tha'll later regret."

"But... if yer know... what I think yer might know—then James'll nooan want—"

"But 'ee'll nivver find out! For if tha should ever breathe so much as word..." and the look in her eyes said it all.

There was long brooding silence. "This 'marriage'll' coom ter nowt— an' I'll go nowhere near. Tha can explain that ter rest o' Steeas as best

way tha sees fit. An' even if shu weds me twin, it'll nooan stop us lovin'
one another. Neither you nor uncle Adam can do owt abaht that. Love's
stronger na' marriage."

"Anyroad," and she tried to steer her lovesick son to thoughts of his
own future, "there's other fish in t'sea. Mi' cousin Edith's lass, Vera.
Shu's nobbut seventeen, an' bonny as a picture."

"Shu's squint-eyed."

"Or there's Alice-May."

"But I love Ruthie—mother, can't ah get it through ter yer? We love
one another."

"But there's no room in Steeas fer 'love.' It's no good bein' mooin-
struck. Life's nooan allus fair. When ah wor young I wanted summatt as I
couldn't 'ave. Ah didn't want ter end up in a village shop weighin' aht
three penn'oth o' cough drops," and she got a sudden mental image of
Lizzie Howarth, and resolved there and then to be a much better mother-
in-law.

Simon looked near to tears as he asked, "and what does Ruth have to
say about bein' part of a business arrangement?"

"She knows nowt abaht it yet."

"Or James?"

"Ah... 'ad a word wi' Adam, an' we thought it best ter let you be 'first
ter know, so's yer'd nooan—"

"Upset 'apple cart?"

"Cause a lot o' unnecessary bother. Because this weddin's goin'
through, whether tha likes it or not. An' if tha feels tha needs ter keep
well away, then that's what tha mun do. But 'banns is ter be read first
Sunday o' next month. There's a cake ter see to, an' caterers, an' weddin'
outfits —an' wi' Ruth 'avin' no mother, it'll all fall on me ter organise."

"Well," he suddenly burst out, "tha'll 'ave no need ter tell 'er what ter
do on 'er weddin' night—for I've already—"

And he recoiled as the hand came across his face, and blood spurted
down his cheek.

"But... you can't marry 'im, Ruth," and Simon was no longer pleading,
for there was now something angry in his voice. "We allus said, that
when we grew up—"

"Yes. I know, but—"

"Well, nowt's changed, Ruthie. Look, yer'll soon be a wealthy woman,
an' then yer can do as yer want, an' not what they're plannin'."

"But it's all being arranged. My dad and your mum—"

"Need their 'eeads lookin' if they think for one moment as James can mak' thee 'appy. I doubt 'ee even knows owt abaht 'ow ter satisfy thee in bed—but there's more na' that ter a marriage. I tell thee Ruthie, we're made fer one another. Please, please say tha'll think carefully—dooan't go an' ruin thi life we gettin' tied dahn wi' James." He seemed near to tears, because for some reason she seemed not to be listening. She was already cutting him out of her life.

Adam Dacre was suddenly a happy man.

He felt he had at last done right by his daughter in securing her a sensible marriage. James Howarth would make a good husband, and would care for, and respect her, and in the fullness of time… but that was all in the future, for more immediate were thoughts of the wedding ceremony, and this dread he had about making a speech afterwards. It was the done thing, and he couldn't disappoint his daughter, but what could he—in front of a lot of folks, stand up and say? Most brides' fathers would have a wife on hand to prepare a sort of speech. Still, if Polly were alive, he doubted she have the faintest idea as to what he should say.

Talk of the wedding had naturally reminded him of his own wedding day. He'd been young, and had such dreams—that he and Polly would have lots of sons to carry on the Dacre name and genes into the next generation, that the two of them would grow old together surrounded by scores of grandchildren—but life had killed the dream.

Life in Staithes was hard—and it was cruel, and could end so very unexpectedly. A coble could go put to sea and, on the incoming tide, the boat-owner's body be washed ashore.

That was a constant danger, sudden storms could take any fisherman—and if he'd suffered that fate then his daughter—but that was not to be, for she would, by the end of the month have a husband to care for her. Not some silly intellectual all brain and no brawn (as he'd feared might have been the case if this silly university hadn't been stopped) but someone Staithes born and bred.

Oh, he was so looking forward to James being part of the family proper. He would become the son he'd never had but had always secretly hoped for. For the love and bonding between father and son was something special—a man's love for another man that was pure and unsullied. A daughter was… someone you cared for until another man took on that responsibility—but loving a son was for ever!

She wore a matching dress and coat of cream shantung silk, a blue hat with long feathers, a seed-pearl necklace, and to set off and compliment such an outfit, one of the late sister's furs.

Her shoes pinched, her neck looked decidedly scrawny as she took curling tongs to do last minute adjustments to the strands of hair refusing to behave themselves . Too much lipstick. It was making her look like a harbourside—but it was too late. Besides, it would wear off. She wanted a cup of tea but thought better of it—because her new stays didn't allow for cups of tea, eating, sitting down, breathing in—it was going to be quite an ordeal, the rest of the day—overshadowed (and although he'd threatened, she'd not believed him when he'd said he could not be best man as he'd not be attending the wedding) by Simon's sudden disappearance.

The daft lad—to walk out of the house at crack o' dawn, as if she hadn't enough to cope with. And what was James going to do? For—and she glanced at the mantle clock—the twins should now be on their way to church. The groom-to-be was upstairs fuming—Simon could be anywhere!

It was not a good omen for this marriage. She'd be glad when it was all out of the way.

Part III   1929

Vanity of vanities, saith the Preacher, vanity of vanities; all is vanity.
What profit hath a man of all his labour which he taketh under the sun?
One generation passeth away, and another generation cometh...

Ecclesiastes 1:2-4.

Chapter 21

Time does not always heal.

Wounds can fester, become angry and inflamed. Grievances, if left to brood can grow and consume, and a hurt and betrayal can, if unchecked, turn love to hate. And so it was with the twins who were now at war, one with the other. James had settled down to married life as best a man could with a wife who—well, perhaps there were some women who thought themselves brighter than their husbands, though in Staithes these delusions could usually be dealt with by just the one beating, and had it not been for his father (as he now called his uncle) then that problem could have been dealt with. But one day he'd see to it, if she continued.

There was also another "problem" which was lowering his standing in the bedroom department, for something that should be happening wasn't. He was man enough to "do what was expected" but with no results. She'd need to go see a doctor to find out what was wrong with her, then get it put right, or his mates would start laughing at him. Bloody wives, more bother than they were worth.

And there was also—and this caused him great annoyance, her stubborn refusal to transfer her wealth into his name. The man should be the provider and overseer of their assets, the wife be allocated (and hopefully be able to save from) a housekeeping allowance. She should not have funds at her own disposal that her husband was not able to draw on if the need arise. It made him feel untrustworthy, inadequate— and this linked to his inability to (so far) produce any sons—or even daughters, was not conducive to a happy married life.

Each morning Evelyn hoped, prayed that she'd hear word from Simon. Just a short letter telling her he was safe and well would suffice, but there was no such communication delivered by the postman. She'd stand at the door, waiting, but most days he'd go straight past Ring o' Bells, and with a resigned sigh she'd hope for something the following day.

He could be anywhere—anything could have happened to him.

He could be in Leeds, Manchester… have gone abroad—he could even be dead! For if he had no identification on him, then how would powers-that-be know to contact her if he really had come to a terrible end? To know for certain that he was no more—and she hardly dared think such a thing for fear of tempting fate—would be preferable to this uncertainty. It had been exactly the same all those years ago when David sulked and ran away.

Oh, the men in her life—and the trouble they caused.

But at least, her other lad appeared happy enough, though Ruth seemed quiet and subdued these days—still, with two men under her roof who got on so very well they often seemed to ignore her, it was hardly surprising that she said little. Evelyn must take her out for the day. Perhaps a trip so Scarborough, or they could go into Whitby and all at Botham's for afternoon tea.

Let the men fend for themselves for once, it wouldn't hurt 'em.

Seasons became months... months turned into years.

The sea provided a living (even though a somewhat precarious one at times) and in the bad years Adam would draw on the money left to him by his aunt many years previous. James, when things were bad, would demand that his wife support his drinking habit, but his words and threats went unheeded, for she knew that while her father was under their roof she was safe.

Newspapers carried stories of "a crash" on Wall Street, and the villagers imagined automobiles out of control and causing mayhem and chaos—by driving into stone walls!

As American business tycoons were becoming penniless because of the October 1929 Stock Market crash, causing panic-stricken brokers to sell millions of shares for whatever they could fetch, a "certain gentleman" was helping his employer profit from such a calamitous scenario. Like vultures feeding on carrion, J.R. Jerome Holdings and his number-one assistant were sucking the life blood of lesser companies—and the bright young man from England was also lining his own pockets. Fortunes were being made and lost by the minute, it was nerve-shattering and not for the faint-hearted, but Simon Howarth was driven on by some indefatigable force. He would work twenty-five hours a day, eight days a week, not needing to stop for food, or sleep—for he was like a machine. He now owned an apartment, a fast car, a wardrobe of immaculately tailored suits and silk shirts and had an inexhaustible supply of cocaine, bourbon and mistresses—and any and every depravity under the sun he had experienced. The genie was out of the bottle and, he had convinced himself, life was for living.

Life for him had another philosophy: eat or be eaten, and he looked around him at credit wiped out, factories closing, men without jobs, farmers without customers, as both agriculture and farming became depressed and industries such as coal and textiles suffering declining markets.

But he was, albeit temporarily, secure. Could enjoy the high life, even employ a coloured house-boy who was also a cook and with whom he enjoyed a certain rapport—sniff lines of white dust with society women before taking them to his bed, and as his life became more decadent he would even invite Georgie to join in—and turn the "lovemaking" session into an orgy. Georgie was well endowed, athletic and very agreeable—and the morning-after had the good sense to behave as though nothing untoward had happened.

A lot for knowing one's place: Georgie would only service the mistresses after his master had taken his pleasure!

The economic situation worsened, for in 1932, fifteen million Americans were out of work—and the Englishman who had made a fortune at the expense of others felt it was time to "move on" and he drifted round his new country, stopping as and where the mood took him. On the rare nights he was alone he would lie awake… remembering… wishing… and some day he knew it would happen.

There must come a time when, like fish returning to their breeding ground to spawn then die, he would (but not for those reasons) return to Staithes. And, he told himself, that was why he seemed incapable of forming any permanent relationship with the many women who drifted in and out of his life

And it happened!

He was in Boston, Massachusetts, and on 30th September, 1935, saw the premiere of the Gershwin musical *Porgy and Bess*. Each number had a message for him: *Summertime, and the Living is Easy*—well, the living was easy, for him, anyway. He was doing very well for himself. When he heard the number *I got plenty o' Nuttin* something struck a chord—because despite his wealth… he didn't have what he really wanted. He had "plenty of nothing", and later on in the show *There's a Boat Dat's Leavin' Soon For New York* convinced him… that the time had come.

Two months later he said farewell to Georgie his houseboy, and to the country that had given him so much and changed his fortunes, his way of thinking, his manner of speech, dress—his whole personality. A village yokel had left Staithes: a very different man would be returning.

Chapter 22

"A mucky sky scrawled over a mucky sea" was how Evelyn Howarth would have described the raw March morning as she made another journey to the beach to collect driftwood for her fire. Her shawl was wrapped round her, her shoulders ached from her earlier exertions and twinges of "rheumatics" which seemed to be the all-embracing name for winter aches and pains. And no use wasting money on fancy doctors saying this-and-that, dog-oil worked as well as anything and cost only pence—"fancy embrocations an' such like" could cost pounds, and that sort of money was better in her pocket than anyone else's.

She passed the slipway and the Cod & Lobster, and faced another buffeting blast as she reached the staithe and the bottom of Church Street. She stared out onto a lippy sea—it would be several hours before the boats returned, and she picked her way, being careful to avoid the long trails of bladder-wrack and flotsam that the waves had thrown up at high tide. Seaweed and pebbles, bits of old rope, even torn fishing net, and she could remember when she was only young her father had found a man's arm. The rest of him was never washed ashore, unless further along the coast.

Then there had been the wooden planks, part of the cargo from the ship that had foundered over Cowbar Steel, even cupboards and other bits of furniture were bouncing on the waves—and in more recent times there was the unexploded mine which had caused no end of trouble for some silly lads started throwing rocks at it.

A local in greatcoat and a scarf the size of a fishing net shuffled past. "Now then."

She returned his greeting, then, as always wondered afterwards as to what exactly "now then" meant—or even implied.

But it was just one of those expressions particular to Staithes.

If she were in this cold for much longer, she'd be using another expression—something much more explicit.

Now back at Ring o' Bells and beside a roaring fire, Evelyn sipped her mug of sweet tea as she tried to conjure up just one new way to cook the mainstay of her diet. Fish!

It could be boiled, steamed, fried, battered, turned into fishcakes, or baked in a pie. Eaten from its shell, sprinkled with salt and vinegar, served with any manner of sauces, and with any combination of vegetables—eaten standing up, eaten sitting down, swallowed in big gulps, or eaten in a "pickin an' pokin' " manner, and consumed for breakfast, lunch, tea or supper—but it was still fish.

She could remember once eating shark, and tuna, the steaks deep pink to brown, and not unlike animal meat in appearance—but certainly, in taste.

And, and this gave her hope, there would soon be spring lamb, and she licked her lips in appreciation when she thought of a leg roasting, spitting its fat all over the inside of her oven, and necessitating her throwing salt on the bottom shelf to stop the smell. She'd welcome it on a raw March morning, though. Lamb and new potatoes: that was a meal fit for a king, and the next time she went to the butchers she'd ask when there'd … and the sharp rap at her door caused her to stop her daydreaming.

"Aye, who is it?" she called out, as she began prizing herself from the rocking chair draped in antimacassars. The knocking was becoming more insistent. "Just thee wait a minute, see.—Ah'm coomin as fast as ah can," then, on opening the door she stared in near disbelief. For it couldn't be 'im, not after all these years—but it was, and she stood open mouthed staring at the smart overcoat and trousers with knife edge creases. He was wearing leather—real leather gloves and a smart trilby tilted at a rakish angle.

"Well, good morning, Mother—are you going to let me in or keep me at the door so's all the village can hear our conversation?"

She shook her head in disbelief. " Thoo Bugger! 'Doesn't look like thee, doesn't sound like thee—but tha's best coom in lad."

Now over the initial shock, which was quickly turning to anger, Evelyn Howarth turned again to face her son.

"By the 'ell—but tha's soom explainin' ter do. Where's tha been all these years, wi' nivver so much as a word lettin' me know tha wor all reight?"

"I've… been in America."

"Tha's been in America…? Well, that explains it all—ah dooan't think."

"I've also changed my nationality.   I'm now an American citizen."

"Dooan't talk daft, lad—tha 'proper Steeas'—fer tha wor born an' bred 'ere."

"I only returned a couple of weeks ago," he ignored her remark. "I had some business in London, and then I…"

"Thowt tha'd coom an' see thee mother? 'Ow very thoughtful."

"Mum, I've not come to cause trouble…"

"Oh, tha caused enough o' that when tha nigh on spoiled thi brother's weddin' wi' thee simple sulkin'. Ah'd all on ter 'old me 'eead up, ah wor that ashamed—an 'all Steeas talkin' abaht thee."

"Well, if they have such small minds," he dismissed village trivia, than suddenly asked, "are we going to have some tea? Are you going to invite me to sit down, or what?"

"Oh... sit thissen dahn."

"And you could ask 'what have you been getting up to in America?'— and I might even tell you."

The black iron kettle was placed over the fire. Evelyn rolled up her sleeves then took the date pasty from the cake tin. "It's either a slice o' this or biscuits."

"It doesn't matter, I'm not fussy."

"An tha can stop talkin' posh."

"I'm sorry—but I lost my accent years ago." He looked around the room. It was just as he'd remembered it. Pot dogs and brass candlesticks on the shelf above the fireplace, the creel draped with the eternal clothes drying, nets at the window to stop prying eyes and keep out any sunlight that dared to infiltrate the narrow alleyway. On the wall, the plaque "God is Love" and the set of copper-lustre jugs on top of the sideboard. Nothing had changed, except the woman who daily cared for these things. There were now fine lines around her eyes, her hair seemed sparse, her knuckles swollen from hard work. And there was also a sadness about her. She was getting old before her time—the price to pay for the austerity of this fishing village and the life she'd led.

He had scarcely brought his drink to his lips before, and as casually as discussing the weather, his mother asked, "an' what's made thee coom back ter Steeas, then?"

His reply, however, sent shivers down her spine, as he replied quite simply, "to claim my inheritance."

"Nay... if tha thinks there's ony brass coomin' ter thee—"

"I mean my cousin. Ruth and I were meant for each other. I realise she's married to James, but that's something we'll have to sort out. Ruth belongs to me—I shall stay in the neighbourhood as long as is necessary, but when I do leave, she's coming with me. But it must be of her own free will, for I wouldn't want a 'forced' mistress."

So casual and matter-of-fact did he sound that Evelyn Howarth was momentarily lost for words. Mother and son drank their tea in silence, one quietly confident as a poker player with a devilishly good hand, the other fearful as to what mischief he could be plotting. Finally, he spoke. "Very nice, the date pasty."

"It's all reight. Nowt special," and under his quizzical eye she started to fidget, then in the far corner of the room she saw a cobweb. She quickly turned to look in the opposite direction, hoping his glance would follow hers.

"And before you ask," and his voice brought her back to their unexpected reunion, "I've not come to stay, but to visit. I've bought a cottage in Runswick. It overlooks the sea, I have a cleaner woman comes in two mornings a week, and it came furnished but will do for the time being."

"…Well then?—"

"This is the address," and he made a show of taking a printed card from his wallet. "I shall expect you for afternoon tea one day next week. Shall we say… next Tuesday? And be sure to bring Ruth with you, for we have things to discuss. By the way, have they any young family?"

She shook her head. "No, they've nooa bairns."

He seemed relieved. "Then that says a lot for their marriage. Been wed over ten years, and nothing happening in that department."

"That's nowt ter do wi' me'—an' cert'nly nooan o' thi business. They're 'appy wi' one another, so ah'm beggin' thee, Simon, dooan't thee start causin' bother. Ruth's settled, let 'er be."

"Now if the two of you were to come… before lunch, say?" he ignored her pleading, "we could all three of us go in the car to… Scarborough?—or Saltburn?—even over the moors to Pickering and Thornton Dale. What do you say?"

"A car an' all! By gum, yer mun be made o' brass."

"I did well in America. As soon as I arrived back in England I contacted some London brokers, and they are to handle my investments. I don't need to go down the pit these days. In fact, I don't need to work again."

"…So tha's come ter crow?"

"No, mother. I've already told you why I'm here. Now," and he drained his cup, "can we make next Tuesday a definite 'yes'?"

She stood at the door and watched him descend the steps that led from High Barrass into the High Street… and began to wish that this day had never dawned.

Chapter 23

As Evelyn stared into her fire and began to ponder over the way her son has so calmly stated his intentions, she tried to convince herself that his threats were merely "talk" for if he had been serious then surely he would have kept such things to himself?

His feelings toward his cousin had been nothing more than childish fancies. It was time he settled down with some sensible wife—and, she had to admit, he now seemed a much better catch than James had been. Oh, lads!—they could cause their mothers no end of worry. If they were not hotheads and forever in fights, then they could be brooding and plotting any sort of mischief, just as Simon was doing.

Then another thought occurred to her. Should she warn James what devilment could be afoot—and should Ruth be made aware that Simon was now living in the next village, only minutes away, and that he was intending to—?"

She gave a stab at the near dying embers then threw another lump of driftwood over them.

Reluctantly, she knew she had to break the news to the rest of the family, for to keep silent might imply that something was amiss, but she would say as little as possible. Perhaps that Simon was now in the neighbourhood, and that he had invited her to his house, and then, the following Tuesday as she was about to leave she could, as if it were a spur-of-the-moment thing, invite Ruth to accompany her.

That way it would appear innocent and—not that she was going to be a party to any underhand business and have one twin rise up against the other—she would do as Simon had requested, thereby stop anything silly on his part, while Ruth would be able to tell her own version of her brother-in-laws exploits, and it would then seem all "family and friendly".

Besides, and Evelyn stopped her worrying, Ruth was no longer the girl that Simon remembered. She had passed that first flush of youth and innocence, for being married to a fisherman was a hard life: one's beauty quickly faded.

He seemed polite, if somewhat distant, and Evelyn felt that at any second something would either be said, or he might do something that would enforce his earlier boasting, and the afternoon would end in disaster.

But her son behaved like a perfect gentleman, and they found the Scarborough air from the open-topped car bracing and invigorating, the visit to the Rotunda Museum a pleasant diversion, though lunch at The

Royal seemed something of an ordeal as Evelyn worried that she might pick up the wrong knife or fork, and as part of the menu was in some fancy foreign language, that she might ask for something entirely different to what she was expecting. But Simon seemed to be familiar with the funny words (and even the way one pronounced them) as he gave their order to the waiter, then chose a wine to compliment the *Le Rognon Boeuf au Vin de Champagne.*

"Eee, it does sound posh—what is it?"

"Beef kidneys in Champagne sauce."

"Well, ah nivver did!"

Ruth seemed quiet throughout the meal, and Evelyn felt that perhaps… she was being less than fair to her son, for he was in no way saying or doing anything untoward. His earlier threats had been idle boasting, nothing more. Of that she felt sure.

And their trips here and there became a regular thing. Sometimes higher up the coast to Saltburn where they would walk round and admire the Italian Gardens before having tea at the town's famous Zetland Hotel—where the trains seemed to come into the hotel itself. Redcar was another favourite watering-hole, where, on clear days they could look across to Hartlepool. They went to Pickering then on to York, had a day at York races, picnics on the North York Moors which were taking on their carpet of heather, then as summer was turning to autumn Ruth no longer accompanied them, for something (which seemed to her husband "amaisin" after over ten years) happened.

She became pregnant.

She developed a liking for pickled onions with lots of marmalade spooned over, then mashed potatoes with treacle, and every morning was physically sick just at the though of the skeps of raw fish she had usually to help gut and clean.

Each day she would grow more round and fruitful, her walk becoming a sort of bouncy wobble, and the father-to-be was convinced she was carrying twins. He was a proud man, and in the Cod & Lobster with his cronies would boast of his love-making exploits, then he would rush home and with his father-in-law help wash the pots and pans, for "t'lass" needed to rest, it being now the job of the two men to care for her.

In a state of permanent embarrassment Ruth would, by day, parade her ungainly figure round the village, while at every opportunity she was regaled with tales from other mothers expounding on the pain and agony associated with giving birth to one's first child.

"Men? The' sud try bein' a woman at such a time," and the mother of five shook her head in commiseration. "An' there's folk in Steeas do still tell 'tale abaht that lass, a coomer-in as live up Cowbar... 'at 'ad a bairn wi' a reight big 'eead. Big as a set-pot—it ended in a circus—ooohhh, but she did 'ave a time deliverin' it," and she pulled her face in agony just at the thought of such a birth. "An' then it wor coomin yer could 'ere 'er skrikin' all over Steeas," then, her good new over, she gave an appraising look at the mother-to-be. "Tha carryin' it 'igh, ah'm thinkin'—could be twins."

"Mmm? 'Runs in families, so I'm told."

"Nah... thi 'usband's twin brother—ah thought ah saw 'im one day last week."

"He lives in Runswick, I believe."

The woman considered, then shook her head. "No, 'un—that wasn't where ah saw 'im."

Ruth swallowed. "Well... you know."

"No, not yet—but it'll coom ter me."

"Now then," and Ruth was glad her mother-in-law had come across the street and butted into their conversation.

"Now then, Evelyn," the woman greeted her in a similar fashion, then pointing to the bulge, pronounced, "Ah wor just sayin'—could be twins."

" 'Ist'ry repeatin' itssen."

"Shu looks all o' six month an' a breakfast gooan," Marion joked and, hand on her chin, took a step back as to view from a different angle. "But at least 'un, 'e'll nooan be troublin' thee, not until tha's dropped it. There'll be nooan o' that unnecessaryness when 'two o' yer get ter bed. Yer'll be able ter go streight ter sleep. Men? Huh—it's all they 'ave on their brain."

As they turned toward High Barrass, Ruth was suddenly quiet, and Evelyn, sensing that all was not well asked, "Nah they, doy—an' what's ter do."

"Oh, it was just something Marion said—I mean, she couldn't have, because—"

"Shu's nooan been tellin' that tale abaht 'bairn born wi' a reight big 'eead? Shu 'asn't a grain o' sense, tellin' that ter a woman in thy condition."

"...Yes, that was it." But she was thoughtful for the rest of the afternoon. Marion Tredgold couldn't possible have seen Simon Howarth anywhere other than Runswick. The fact that she never stirred out of the village Ruth chose to dismiss.

She must have made a mistake—yes, that was it.

It was a cruel November, and some days it never seemed to come light.

There were the frost-spangled Boulby cliffs, the pathway toward Cowbar was steep and slippery, and Ruth must content herself with a morning walk over the bridge then toward the lifeboat station, where she'd stand and look at the grey and great expanse of water, waves idly lapping the green slime-covered flat scaurs of rocks, and slowly and insidiously eroding the cliffs. She would look across the beach to the Cod & Lobster, which at high tide seemed to be on a rock stuck in the sea. There were tales that it had, on occasions been washed away, only to be re-built to stand until the next time. She could remember when the waves racing up the slipway had crashed against a building and had been flung into the pub doorway and bar, and had almost dragged the piano out with them. That was the time one of the locals who had an army of cats had managed to get them all upstairs into her bedroom, and they'd sat in the window, surveying the scene.

Beyond the "Cod" was the staithe, and the bottom of Church Street, and half way up was the narrow alleyway known as Dog Laup. Ruth stroked her protrusion, and knew better than to try to negotiate such an obstacle. High Barrass may well be dark and dismal—Dog Laup was ten times worse. To give birth at such a miserable time of the year must have a terrible effect on both mother and child, for the thoughts of a cold winter, and wet washing constantly draped over the creel and never getting dry—and nappies besides—oh no, it would be all too much.

The men in the household (who had almost overnight become experts on such matters) had calculated that the baby boy—or twins, as James was already boasting, would be born the end of April or early May, but she had other ideas.

Christmas was, he decided, a family time—assuming a man had "a family" and because this seemed something sadly lacking from his life, Simon Howarth chose to spend that festive period in London, but he would travel on the 15th which would gave him time to browse round the shops, but more important, meet with his broker.

The two men were in complete agreement. The outlook seemed gloomy. Political events in Europe made the threat of war seem far more likely, the market was in the doldrums, and there was a sense of foreboding. But if a man had the daring... ?

"I would advise you to hang onto your overseas assets—for the moment, but—"

"Let us 'play' with..." and Simon Howarth considered, swallowed, then wrote out a cheque.

"It's my Christmas present to myself, if you like. Now, with that sort of money, Granville, let's see what you can come up with that'll give me a not 'dramatic' but a sensible return. It's now Tuesday, I'll call on you again Friday morning."

"Leave it with me, Mr Howarth. Now, is there anything else I can do for you?"

He gave a laconic smile, and thought about his days in New York and nights of debauchery. "Er... I can't think of anything... but I can always phone you if necessary."

He spent the rest of the week shopping. It seemed strange, for there was a sense of unreal gayety. The capital was poised, waiting for something to happen. He visited Harrods, Fortnums, Saville Row, then there were visits the Tate and National Galleries, and the Theatre Royal for a performance of Ivor Novello's *Careless Rapture*, with Novello himself playing the speaking part of Michael, and Olive Gilbert in the role of Mme Simonetti.

It was a large-scale extravaganza with an on-stage earthquake, set in London and ending in China—and for just one moment he toyed with the idea moving to the Far East. Musicals seemed to have a profound effect on him, for it had been the performance of *Porgy and Bess* that had decided him to return to his roots. He tried again to concentrate, and he listened intently to: *Why is there ever Goodbye?* then: *Love made the song I sing to you*. And before he left the theatre, he booked a seat for the following evening.

Reminiscent of Christmas Days past, Evelyn had prepared a banquet.

There was the only-to-be expected goose from a local farmer, a joint of beef she just managed to get in the oven, and for later that day, she'd cooked a piece of pork. There were the usual vegetables and stuffings and sauces, the plum pudding she set alight when she brought it to the table and poured the wineglass of brandy over. There was a sweet white sauce laced with spirit, fruit cake, mince pies—even coffee, and she joined-in with the laughter of Christmas merrymaking, pulling crackers, eating chocolates, paring and nibbling segments of tangerines, then roast chestnuts, and even a glass of sherry wine.

James and Adam seemed more than contented. Ruth, who was beginning to complain of backache, moved in her by-now only-to-be-expected ungainly fashion. Struggling to lower herself into the rocking chair, struggling even more when she tried to prize herself out of it.

Her mother-in-law began to tackle the only-to-be-expected pile of washing-up such a feast had caused, and began to imagine the following Christmas when there would be another little life. Such a long time since there had been a baby about the place.

A new generation! Then she bit her lip as she thought…

There was only one thing missing this Christmas. Her other son.

Chapter 24

January was a cruel month for the fishermen, with the lifeboat more than once having to wrestle with the bad-tempered surging deep. Sheets of sleet relentlessly lashed the staithe, sou'-westered men looked on helpless as each wave raced up the High Street like the head of a bottle of good ale, then it would slurp and recede, taking anything and everything in its path. A family pet was dragged into the water and drowned, a mother shouting to her children above the roar of the waves, "Tak' that as a warnin'—tha could be 'next."

On such occasions the menfolk did the only thing possible, and repaired to the Cod & Lobster to commiserate, then as the beer loosened their tongues, they would try to out-do with their tales of walls of spume crashing against the cliffs, fishermen being dragged to their doom over Pot o' Steel, cobles smashed, bodies washed ashore, carelessly flung on the edge of the sands like discarded fishing nets.

Then on the occasional days when the men could put to sea, their catches were "rags" and often thrown back in disgust, and father and son-in-law, after securing their coble up the beck would, accompanied by much cursing and swearing from the younger man, be reduced to calling in the Black Lion to lift up their spirits (and also the Cod & Lobster) before returing to a woman who seemed to spend her day doing nothing —and taking her time doing that.

"It there nowt fer two 'ungry men?" for there'd be no sign of a meal, no smell of cooking or baking, just a heavily pregnant woman with a tear-stained face moving with the grace of an elephant. "Yer mam said she wor makin' backstones. 'Appen as she'll 'ave some spare."

"Bloody 'ell—is that 'best tha can do?"

"Coon on, James—we'll nooan be long cookin' bacon an' eggs," and the older man would try to keep the peace in what was rapidly becoming a fractious household.

"An' there's nooa bloody breead," and James on discovering an empty bread crock would storm out of the house in a temper. He'd be fuming. One of these days, he told himself—and she should think herself lucky that she was pregnant, he'd knock some sense into her.

February was grey and uneventful, and Evelyn, on her now weekly visits to Runswick began to envy her son's comfortable cottage which had something so lacking in Staithes—it had a lovely view! The windows looked onto the sea: from Ring o' Bells she could only look out on a dirty alleyway and fishermen's cottages opposite, as uninspiring as was her own.

But here, light came into the room—she could even see the gulls against the scurrying clouds, and the two of them sat drinking tea and eating seed cake that his "cleaner woman" had found time to make among her other duties.

What those were exactly his mother never bothered to ask, not wanting her expectations dashed. She was hoping whoever-she-was—and it was obvious from the way she was looking after the cottage that she could fettle, would be… a young widow woman who would know how to cater to a man's "needs" and help him forget who he couldn't have— or a farmer's daughter who would know how to cook, make butter and the like, and not be afraid of hard work. She must make enquiries as best she could. No use asking Simon outright, for he could tease when the mood took him, and this would be one such occasion. Nor was there ever any mention of Ruth—or James!

Two brothers, especially twins, at grievance with one another was bad, and they were equally to blame, for although James knew of her weekly visits he never once enquired as to Simon's health or spoke his name. It were as though he no longer existed.

He refilled her cup, then produced and opened a tin of fancy little almond biscuits.

"Try one. I bought them in London, from Fortnum's."

"Is it a posh shop, then?"

"Oh, you could call it that. If you like them I'll give you a tin to take home with you."

He seemed more "relaxed"—and reading signs (that were not there) Evelyn felt happy in the certain knowledge that soon—very soon, Simon would be introducing her to the new woman in his life.

On leaving, she gave a second glance round the cottage at Runswick. "Well, shu keeps 'spot neat an' tidy for thee."

His face took on a blank expression.

" 'Seed cake woman."

"Oh, yes. Er… will you be calling next week?"

"Oh aye—then tha can tell me… owt that's on thee mind as ah owt ter know abaht."

The following month dawned gentle, but was seen as a "bother breeder" for what was to come. Old crones read teacups and predicted calamities —there'd be "a reight ter do i' Steeas affore much longer" and one saw

"families at war, one wi' another" then old Louisa Tredgold, who practised her own particular black art of divination by throwing salt into the
fire and reading the pictures this conjured up, saw "a booat bein' dragged
under Pot o Steel an' all 'ands lost. Drooned!"

The month moved into its third week, with prophesies, as yet, unful-
filled.

Evelyn was on her way back from the shop with her few groceries. She
seemed to buy less and less as Simon was forever putting a tin of this-
and-that into her hand every Tuesday afternoon as she was about to
leave, or when they were out together he'd insist on calling at some high
class grocers where he'd buy all sorts of things for her. "Try this, mam,"
he'd say—and she did, and more often than not thoroughly enjoyed it. It
had been... picked walnuts last week, and it made fish taste entirely different, and there'd been the Mulligatawny soup, or what ever fancy name
it had been—then she saw her, frantically banging on the window, and
seconds later was beside a crying and thoroughly distressed daughter-in-
law.

"Nah then, doy, an' what's ter do?" but from the state of her, Evelyn
could see that her waters had already broken.

"It's the baby—I think it's on its way."

"Nay, not so sooin, surely," but the older woman could read the signs.
She was about to become a grandmother. She tried to collect her
thoughts, as Ruth gave a sharp cry.

"Let's get thee oopstairs, doy—an' then we can see what's what. Tak'
deep breaths—an' we mun let James know as—"

"No," she suddenly yelled. "I don't want him anywhere near."

"Eh?"

The young woman shook her tear-stained face, and knowing better
than to stand arguing, Evelyn steered and half pushed her up the steep
flight of stairs, pulled back the bedclothes, fluffed up the mattress and
pillows then helped the soon mother-to-be into a comfortable about-to-
give-birth position.

She gave another cry, and she tried hard to take deep breaths.

Evelyn was thinking as she was talking. " 'Appen as we sud send fer
'doctor thro 'Inderwell? Fer, if tha nigh on two month affore thee time
then there could be complications. We dooan't want little mite ter dee, do
we?"

"I'm not early," Ruth insisted.

"But James said—"

"It's not his baby—it's Simon's!"—and her mother-in-law reeled.

"I've not been going into Whitby every week, but calling at Runs-wick" and the jug and bowl fell from Evelyn's hands. It smashed as it hit the linoleum, quite literally shattering the silence, and Evelyn stared—at the broken pieces, then at the face sweating profusely, and this moment that seemed to be lasting for ever was suddenly broken by the slamming of a downstairs door.

Evelyn rushed to the window, to see her son James storming down the alleyway.

The late afternoon sky was mucky, with great waves and white water as far as the eye could see, all the fishing boats rocking and creaking on their moorings—except one!

There was a flash of lightning that seemed to cut the village in two, followed by a crack of thunder. Not a distant poor excuse for a rumble, but a clash of cymbals type, and there was a wind coming in from the sea, screaming up the High Street and whistling round Dog Loup. Fishermen secured their boats as they rocked and bounced in the now swelling beck, some for safety being tied to the struts of the bridge. There was a figure by the lifeboat station trying to take temporary shelter as he looked over the expanse of rolling waves, but he was disappointed.

"The silly young bugger," was all he could managed as two of the locals joined him, " 'ee sud 'ave more bloody sense."

"Coom on, Adam—there's nowt tha can do standin' aht ere."

He shook free of their hand on his shoulder—besides, a man in the house when a youngster was about to be born was just a hindrance. He'd be better repairing to the Cod, and keep calling home… just on the off-chance… that it might all be over, and all the "women's stuff" attended to, and then he and James—when the silly bugger got back ter Steeas, could go and look at the child together. Another sort of "man thing" and then they could return to the Cod and have a few drinks to wet the baby's head.

"Push again, doy—ah can see t'eead. It's coomin'. 'Old me 'and—an' yell aht if tha feels it'll 'elp."

"Just wait till I hands on Simon Howarth, I'll—" then there was another scream that should have shook all Staithes before the baby made its way into the world.

"It's a girl," And the mother gave a sigh—of joy and relief!

"Tha mun rest nah. Adam's gooan ter 'Inderwell—doctor's on 'is way—not as 'ee'll be able ter much nah, but we mun be sure. Better bein' safe na' sorry."

She could hear voices and went to investigate, to find the doctor, whom she led upstairs, then returned to have words with her brother.

"A little lass," she announced.

"An' it's getting worse aht there. Nivver seen such a bloody neet. There's gurt waves lollopin' oop 'beck—smashed two booats up already."

"An' what abaht thi coble. As that silly lad coom back yet?"

"They're goin' ter launch 'lifeboat—an' I'm goin' wi' 'em."

"Tha mun be careful, but ah mun stop wi' Ruth an 'babby—nooa good goin' dahn ter staithe, cos there's nowt ah can do."

She watched him leave, then, and feeling suddenly old, and as though there was worse to come, made a quick drink as she waited for the doctor to tell her all was well.

It was past midnight when two of her neighbours came to tell her the news. Their simple language made it sound so heroic: an act of selfless courage. But no matter how heartfelt their sadness—for among such close-knit fishing communities there is always sorrow at such times—it couldn't disguise what had happened, nor take away the hurt and loss which she and her daughter would feel months, years to come.

The lifeboat had managed to reach him. And then his coble had again been hit by the waves and, as he was stood up at the prow, he suddenly flung his arms open wide... and sacrificed himself to the surging waters. The lifeboat men had tried—tried desperately hard (but unsuccessfully)—to restrain Adam, who, on seeing what was happening had jumped into the waters in an effort to save him.

The lifeboat had had to abandon their rescue bid. Neither bodies had been recovered, but the search for them would continue at first light. The following morning there was a feeling of... such intense sadness in the village. Evelyn must choose the right moment to tell her daughter-in-law that she'd become a mother and a widow in the same evening, and that she herself had lost her son and her brother.

Life in Staithes could be past hard, past cruel.

It could be a living hell!

Simon—who seemed to be good at "organising" and was able to distance himself from what was happening—was taking care of the funeral arrangements; and the two women who were in a state of shock seemed to agree to whatever he suggested.

So many family funerals had Evelyn attended, but none would be so poignant or heart-rending as this one. She would need to draw deep on her well of courage. To lose one's son was something that only another mother who had experienced such a thing could understand and Evelyn lived from minute to minute as the day of the funerals drew nearer.

There'd be none of the flamboyance there was at Hannah's passing, for these two funerals were to be simple and heartfelt, with, so it would seem, the entire village attending—for the whole of Staithes was in mourning.

The recovered bodies were not pretty sights, and on Simon's suggestion, the coffins would be "screwed down" and the villagers remember them as they were, and not as the sea had mutilated them. He seemed completely detached from any family grief—he was doing a necessary job in a businesslike manner.

The day dawned, and as a mark of respect no boats went out, for the fishermen of Staithes must lay two of their own to rest. Simon arrived from Runswick early, for he was the mainstay of the day, it was his job to hold things together. He remained distant from the proceedings, an onlooker rather than a participant of this grief and sorrow, for he was simply in the village, not part of their mourning. The two coffins were outside the house of the dead as the villagers sang *For those in peril on the sea*, his mother and Ruth, with the baby in her arms, looking to each other for support and consolation, he himself simply "looking".

In the churchyard bunches of snowdrops were now dying and being superseded by clumps of wild daffodils, there was a mean wind whistling round the headstones, the day cold and damp in sympathy with the mourners stood at the sides of the open graves. Evelyn was reminded of Hannah's passing, she told herself she would be next, and she looked at Simon… and thought how different things could have been.

…If only!

And it would be after the funerals, and when mother and son were alone, that Evelyn must have words with him.

As with every Staithes passing, there arose speculation among the villagers as to "the will".

The legendary wealth of Bridie Dacre was again remembered and multiplied. Chamber pots full of sovereigns were calculated and these, it was reasoned, together with Capt Danvers-Griffiths's fortune, would make for a very rich widow. Surely enough money to buy happiness, for everything, according to Staithes, could be bought at a price.

Yet Ruth Dacre seemed completely unmoved as, with her mother-in-law, the two of them sat in silence in the solicitor's office as the last will and testament of Adam Dacre was read out to them. They emerged from a stuffy upstairs room to a bright May morning, and with baby Rachel in her arms, Evelyn led the way up Flowergate and to Botham's Café for some refreshment.

"We mun keep it in 'family—nooa good lettin' all Steeas know us business, though tha can tell Simon when 'ee calls this afternooin."

Ruth nodded, but was ready to agree to anything, becoming more and more withdrawn and in a world of her own, having a terrible burden to carry—for she "knew" why events had happened as they had, and although no fingers of accusation had been pointed at her, her husband's drowning was because of her infidelity. What had happened between her and Simon was to have been their secret. She had tried hard to resist him, but he was not the man she had earlier known. Nor could she reason with him—for the desire was still there.

And no longer was he the clumsy, inexperienced lover, for when he took her it was so unlike the quick fumblings of her husband who constantly smelled of fish and would hurriedly satisfy his own pleasure, giving no thought to hers, as Simon did. She would moan in ecstasy as he sought and stimulated her most intimate parts, and she would feel him constantly hard inside her, for his desire had seemed insatiable.

When she'd realised she was carrying his child, she had stopped her "trips to Whitby" as had been the excuse for her visiting his cottage in Runswick, but even then, he wouldn't be said nay, for he would walk along the cliff-path to Staithes, and seeing the fishing boats cast off, and knowing his brother was out of the way, would stealthily make his way to the cottage. That must have been when their neighbour Marion Tredgold had seen him. And if she had, then the rest of the village must have known what was happening.

Whispering, watching, waiting.

It would have gone through Staithes like a dose of flu, and the only ones who didn't catch even the slightest trace of this adultery were the Dacre family themselves, and even—especially now, she must give no clue as to her feelings for her late husband's twin. The past must remain in the past, yet every time she looked at Rachel she saw Simon, and the longing came flooding back.

But soon, she felt, would come her punishment. They would have to pay, the two of them, for the terrible wrong they had done.

Chapter 25

Life, though it seemed cruel in the midst of grief, had to go on. For now there was a new life—and the christening of baby Rachel Howarth had to be organised.

Evelyn must see to the arrangements, for Ruth was in a world of her own, not even capable of caring for the baby, who was "temporarily" with her grandmother. While Simon, like a king-in-waiting, must content himself with thoughts of what was to be, when Ruth was able to put away her mourning bonnet and they could begin their life together. Not once had he dared to ask, but yet when he saw Rachel, he felt he knew.

Spring gave way to summer, which was when Ruth began her walks across the bridge, then the steep climb up the bank to the cliffs above Pot o' Steel, where she'd search the horizon, looking for his coble—and would stand motionless staring into the distance. It was after one such walk that, several hours later, her body was discovered where she'd jumped, the waves washing away her sins.

She was at peace!

"I've 'ad enough—more na' enough—o' Steeas," and Evelyn, at fifty-two felt an old woman.

"What's ter become on us?" She asked the question without expecting an answer.

"I can't… begin to explain what I'm—"

"Ah'm nooan surprised. It all springs thro wantin' what tha couldn't 'ave—an' see where it's landed thee."

Her son was silent, for he could find no words in his defence. Finally he began, "if I could turn the clock back, mam—"

"Ter late fer that. But what we mun do next… is ter think abaht carin' fer that little girl o' thine—an' tha need well look shame-faced. Ruth told me who 'father wor when she started goin' into labour—an' ah think James wor lurkin' at 'bottom o' chamber steps an' 'ee 'eard 'er. That's why 'ee did what 'ee did."

Her son stared at her, not expecting such a revelation. "And you've known all this for… weeks?—Months, yet you've said nothing until now?"

"Ah thought yer'd get tergether, gi'en time, an' ah didn't want ter says owt as might muddy 'watter."

"So," and he took a deep breath, and looked again at the bundle asleep in her cot, "Rachel really is my daughter?"

"An' we mun do reight by 'er. Tha mun see a solicitor, an' legally
adopt er—an' we mun bring little mite up between us."

He wanted to burst into tears. He'd thought, hoped even, but not
until then was he sure.

Rachel Howarth was *his child!* Life was suddenly worth living.

"If… well, I know you said just now you'd had enough of Staithes—
do you want to come and stay at Runswick? Just for a few days, even?"

His mother considered, then looked at her grandchild. "Aye, we'd like
that, wouldn't we, Rachel."

A year passed, the "family" now firmly ensconced in the cottage at Runswick, and Simon felt a terrible wrench as he boarded the train. He had
business in London. There was the appointment with his broker, and also
a firm of solicitors who would have the necessary documents ready for
his signature. Solicitors did better out of families than did undertakers.

He saw a London somehow different from his last visit, for perhaps
the capital could sense the international tensions, and the realisation of
the possibility of war with Germany. There was a foreboding—yet an
almost unreal carnival gaiety among the audience at the Victoria Palace
for the performance of *Me And My Girl*, and again at the Drury Lane
Theatre for Ivor Novello's *The Dancing Years*, with Mary Ellis and Olive
Gilbert. A world away from fishing communities on the tip of the Yorkshire coast—as indeed, was London itself. He bought this and that.
Some clothes for his daughter, sweets and fancy chutneys, a smart-looking wireless from Harrods and some of their hand-made chocolates.

When he returned to his mother and daughter, Rachel had cut another
tooth, and according to his mother, would soon be "rompin' up an dahn,
all over 'spot."

It was a summer of father and daughter going to the beach or, with
his mother accompanying and fussing, rides in the car and any other
treats and outings. Yet these were shadowed by the threat that a war was
imminent. There was talk about Civil Defence measures, given that Tees-
side was a centre of industrial and commercial importance, and with its
heavy iron and steel industries a likely target should Hitler invade. But
much nearer home, the Skinningrove steelworks. Simon would look out
to sea, to an horizon dotted with ships on their way to the Tees. He'd
listen to news bulletins, read between the lines in the newspapers, then,
on a grim grey dawn of September 1st, 1939, motorized columns of German military troops roared into Poland, and the Second World War

began, Great Britain and France declaring war on Germany two days later, on Sunday, September 3rd.

Such news sent little shock or surprise to him, or the rest of the country, as Chamberlain's voice over the radio confirmed "This country is at war with Germany."

Mother and son stared at one another, then she said, "well, then, it's time we all moved."

"Eh?"

"Back ter 'bottom o' Steeas—it's safer na' 'ere," and having reached such an earth-shattering decision, Evelyn started gathering together what she considered to be essentials.

Gas masks had earlier been issued, and there was already talk of evacuating schoolchildren from Middlesbrough to the comparative safety of the countryside, England was suddenly gearing itself for another war. On the radio was a single "Home Service" programme started by the BBC, and German broadcasts to the United Kingdom were to be dominated by a William Joyce, an ex-member of the British Union of Fascists, though Evelyn found wireless "faffy" and something best avoided. She had more important things to concern herself with, like making sure there was plenty of tinned foods in her cupboards and a "cloutin' stick" handy. Should any Germans land in Staithes and come knocking on her door they'd get more than they bargained for.

Ration books were being delivered to every household, in the back of which the recipient was required to write their name and address, then inside the front cover the names of the retailers from whom they would obtain their allocated foodstuffs.

Simon made various trips to Scarborough and even York, returning with a car full of sacks of potatoes, another of turnips, bags of sugar and the like, and some currants and raisins. He'd done well, and he would scour the beach for wood for the fires, and even load the boot of the car with sacks of coal. They were preparing for a long siege, despite tales that "it would all be over by Christmas".

Then, one afternoon in October, the war seemed very real. A German aircraft thought to be on a reconnaissance flight to locate a battle cruiser believed to be in the Firth of Forth was spotted by a patrol some nine miles seaward of the nearby Whitby coastline, but after engaging in battle and suffering some 2,000 rounds from the patrol, the enemy aircraft ceased to return any fire. Two of the enemy had been killed, another wounded as the Heinkel glided low before smacking down in a cascade of spray some twenty miles east of Whitby.

The spitfires glided overhead to see two survivors scramble from the cockpit and slide down the fuselage and onto a wing that was already dipping below the heavy waves. Then they saw them release and inflate a small dingy.

It was two days later they were seen just north of Sandsend near the Whitby Middlesbrough Railway Line, and the fishermen in Staithes were amazed to hear that they were offered food and drink by the station-master's wife, before being taken to Whitby police station for a hot bath to thaw them out before being taken to hospital.

The following month another enemy plane crashed near Scarborough.

Christmas drew near, with no sign of the war being over.

"Thoo mucky little bugger," and she spoke for the rest of those huddled in the air-raid shelter at the top of Church Street to hear, as the Staithes fishwife pointed accusingly at one of the refugees from Hartle-pool that had been dumped on them. "Thoo mucky little bugger," she repeated, then went on to explain, "pissin' in a corner on soom news-paper. Nooa better 'ouse-trained na' puppies. "

"It's what we do at 'ome, Missis."

"Well, tha in Steeas nah," she reminded him, "if thas does that, tha'll mak' 'oose stink like a poke o' devils," then she shuffled her ample body to make room for the newcomers. "Now then."

Evelyn nodded, "Now then, Rhoda," and Rachel was deposited on her knee as Simon promised, "I'll collect you both later."

"An' what's ter do wi' Mannie then?" Rhoda enquired after the How-arths' new tenant.

"Oh, 'ee says 'war's upsettin' 'fish."

"Well," Rhoda sympathised, "yair can yer catch owt wi' a destroyer watchin' yer through binoculars."

"But they're on a constant lookout fer mines."

"Oh aye," another voice piped up, "there wor one balanced on a scaur o rock wheere 'tide 'ad left it. Waves lappin' rahnd it, excitin' it an' makin' it wobble."

"An' then there's minesweepers," Rhoda began a new rhetoric, "cuttin' floatin' buoys. Leeavin' 'fishin' gear adrift on 'sea bed—an' suddenly a bloody great explosion," and she threw her hands up in the air, "wi' all seea strewn wi' wood an' wreckage thro torpedoin' 'enemy ship. Eee, but it's a reight ter-do, this war."

She was thankful that Simon had had the sense and the wherewithal to stock the cupboards with provisions, for on 8th January the following year food rationing was introduced.

There was, for each person, a weekly allowance of twelve ounces of sugar, four ounces of bacon or ham, and the same amount of butter. Ration books that had been issued earlier were now to be used, and Evelyn imagined, if things carried on the way they were progressing, then other food stuffs would also be in short supply. From somewhere Simon had managed to procure a whole side of bacon, and this was hung in the attic, away from prying eyes, and there was always fish, even though meat seemed scarce—then as the year progressed that was also rationed, by price as opposed to weight.

But, the population must console itself, offal, poultry and game were not to be rationed, neither were meat pies or sausages, providing they were only "half meat", and Evelyn looked at "wartime recipes" that were being advocated, things like potato waffles, sweet potato pudding, potato pastry, potato stuffing—all very well, providing people had potatoes.

They flew over the forbidding greyness of the North Sea, occasionally masked by flurries of winter snow and low cloud, tracked by the radar station, and reported as "two unidentified aircraft at sixty miles, approaching at one thousand feet".

As the Hurricanes sped to intercept they received another message "Bandits off Whitby. Raiders attacking unarmed trawler," and the calm of the morning was split by the rattle of machine guns and a roar of low-flying aircraft resulting in a crippled Heinkel grazing the cliffs and flying dangerously low over the town, its smoking engines gradually sinking earthwards, and on the edge of the moors, and some two miles from Whitby the first enemy aircraft to crash on English soil during the Second World War was down

Two months later the RAF lost its first Spitfire to the guns of the Luftwaffe, the first British fighter to be shot down protecting the shores of England. A Spitfire of 41 Squadron.

War dragged on. Ted at the bottom of the village lost his hearing due to a mine exploding and was now deaf as a post, could only understand signs —and the ones he was making were anything but polite. The fishing boats, blatantly defying Hitler, tried to carry on as normal, but, as Evelyn asked herself on many occasions, what was "normal"?

With the Light Infantry in army barracks at the top of the bank guarding this particular stretch of coastline, a village of evacuees, the Skinningrove steelworks a target for enemy aircraft, the occasional German planes flying overhead, minesweepers out at sea, and now the latest thing, the Local Defence Volunteers. With no need for a medical examination, an upper age limit only vaguely enforced, and recruits having been asked to register at their local Police Station, Simon, despite being an American citizen, was one of the first to do so.

Some of them (the "lucky"? few) were given short Lee-Enfield rifles, standard issue from the First World War, the others paraded and patrolled with pickaxes, crowbars, axes or anything else they could improvise with. Several weeks after their formation they were issued with initialised armbands, with the promise of uniforms later, training was on a very freelance basis, and by the summer there was an official change to their name, they were to be known as the Home Guard.

Also during that summer came further reports of German aircraft crashing at nearby Whitby, and a particularly destructive attack on Middlesbrough, when on a brilliant moonlit night a single enemy plane dropped high explosive bombs over railway premises, demolishing the LNER Goods Master's Office and causing damage to Dorman Long's Britannia works. The bombs were heavy-calibre and damage was extensive. There were also air raids at the nearby Skinningrove steelworks, which illuminated the sky and could be heard and seen for miles.

Evelyn felt the war was getting nearer. She'd read about the London blitz—Staithes could be next.

Another night in the shelter, with Rachel in her arms and fast asleep, Evelyn, making herself comfortable as best she could, greeted the latest arrival with the customary "Now then."

"Aye—an' what's ter do?"

" 'Brought yer knittin' Edith—what is it yer on wi'?"

"It's a scarf fer Bert. 'Ee's 'ad quinsies."

"Ooohhh, that's bad," another voice piped up.

" 'Eee burst 'em wi' 'ot porridge! 'Eee feels better nah," then noticing the little lad who had crept in after her, Evelyn asked, "Nah then, an' who's this young man?"

"They call me Peter Watson, Missis."

"An' ah'm saddled reight, wi' that 'un," and stabbing her knitting as she spoke, the woman continued. "Dumped on us last week. Covered in impetigo, an' 'ungry as a 'unter an' yer get next ter nowt fer their board an' lodgin' –an' mucky little bugger pissed 'bed, first ncet. 'Course, Bert tanned 'is arse, mind yer."

"Missin' yer man an' dad, I'll bet," and Evelyn put out her hand towards him. "Coom 'ere, sit next ter me."

Suddenly, the sound of overhead aircraft made them freeze.

"They're aht in force terneet," someone commented, "there goes another, just above us," then they heard firing from the army barracks at the top of the bank. " 'Goin' further up 'coast. It's 'glare thro 'Ironworks, that's what they're aimin' for."

"Ah'm glad as ah dooan't live in Skinningrove."

Evelyn waited. It was a long night before the "all clear". With her charge still asleep she hurried back to Ring o' Bells, where she was able to have a mug of cocoa and a couple of hours well-earned rest.

The January of '41 saw further meat rationing, part of which was to be taken as corned beef, with dried fruits, rice, tapioca and the like on a "points" system, and the following month canned fruits, tomatoes and peas suffered a similar fate. Unappetising recipes such as lentil rissoles, butterbean cutlets or poached eggs on boiled turnip tops were advocated.

Mannie, Evelyn's tenant in what had been the "family home" and who now kept her supplied with fish as a perk-of-the-rent, hailed from Tyneside, and he and his wife were readily accepted into the community. She was generously proportioned, had a lovely accent, and was forever claiming that people in Staithes were better off than those in the big industrial towns. When things are tight communities pull together, and there was a certain "amusement" in congregating in the air-raid shelters at night, better than being stuck in front of the fire worrying your house might be the next to be hit.

In March high explosives fell on Chapel Bank at nearby Loftus, the Wesleyan Chapel looking a sorry sight and needing to be demolished. Then there were incendiary bombs in fields only a mile from the top of Cowbar, each time getting closer to Staithes. And Evelyn had another reason to worry—Simon enlisted and joined the RAF.

Condensed milk and cereals were next for the "points system", then in the summer, syrup and treacle. Cheese was rationed to one ounce per person per week, the next commodities to be "rationed" were jams and marmalade, and in August, even biscuits were to be rationed.

Fish, it seemed to Evelyn and the other women in the village, would soon become a breakfast, lunch, tea and supper thing. Heaven be praised for fish!

Chapter 26

Now thirty-nine years old, Simon Howarth, surrounded by young men half his age had to some of them become a father-figure, and was often called upon to give advice on matters of the heart, help write love letters, or even reassure a very innocent-seeming young lad that he had not caught anything through kissing some girl he'd met at a local hop.

There was a comradeship quite unlike anything he'd earlier known. Despite his age, he was one of the fellows, and because they looked up to him, any fears he had before a night raid he must keep to himself and when he woke that morning in January, 1943, the demons were again with him. He'd had a fretful night, the liquor he'd consumed before retiring had not blotted things out, but brought them to life. James, Ruth—would he ever come to terms with the part he had played in that tragedy?

No jury could convict him, but would God be forgiving?

He washed, dressed, then strolled to the mess for breakfast. The sun was lethargically spreading its fingers wide across the sky, tickling bits of white clouds which, like silly giggling schoolgirls, chased each other. A beautiful calm morning, were it not for the thought that this might be his last, for later that day his plane could be brought down, he could be kill-ed. He looked around him, The night frost was disappearing in wafts of steam, save for in the shadows, but the day was getting better by the minute. Then, half way through the morning came the words "Ops tonight. Briefing at 1800 hours." It was as he had expected—hoped—feared!

Trying hard to push the appointed time to the far recesses of his mind and dwell on the "now", this very moment of his life, he began mentally composing a letter to his daughter, for after two more days he'd have time off, and with some of the other lads would enjoy a couple of days in London when he'd call in one of the West End stores and buy her—oh—the whole bloody shopful if he could afford it. His mother wrote regularly keeping him informed of events in the village—not that that concerned him in the slightest, but he didn't have the heart to tell her—and such correspondence kept him up-to-date with the antics of Rachel. When this war was over, he'd never leave her side.

But more immediate was the mid-morning training flight across a peaceful and quiet sky, an afternoon of relaxation then a shower and another shave, and ten minutes of listening to Jammie who proudly showed him a white silk scarf his girl had sent him. He'd wear it when he was up there, and his hand rose from the edge of his bunk, to indicate his aircraft's smooth take-off. Another lad was reading his bible, and Simon considered… perhaps it did make the hell more bearable, having a faith?

The young man looked up at him, and Simon felt an intruder.

Then later that afternoon, he and the rest of the crew made their way to the main briefing room, a long low nissen-hut where tables and chairs faced a wall of maps, one showing Europe with shaded patches of the Hun defences and the night's target. The routes being marked by brightly coloured tapes, the targets themselves by even brighter coloured pins indicating the colours of the markers to be dropped. On a blackboard was a large drawing of the target, on another, the names of the skippers who are "on" together with times of take-off, bomb loads, and the like, and lastly, an indication of the weather and any low cloud to be expected.

The lads chatted, boisterous to hide any fears, then settled down as the briefing proper began

Simon glanced at his watch. 1800 hours exactly.

Briefing over, including matters such as the expected weather conditions, cloud heights, freezing levels, then the route itself, instructions for the target: If more than a certain amount of cloud below them, then primary flare droppers would revert to the role of "blind" markers. Come in at 15,000 ft, air speed 160 then release their first bundle 20 second later. It was not merely "precise" but exact and, the briefing over, the wireless operators, gunners and flight engineers began to drift away, leaving pilots, bomb-aimers and navigators to make the final arrangement to make the raid work, and Simon and the rest of the chaps headed for the mess and the "operational supper" which, for some reason had to be bacon and eggs, the portions greasy and generous.

"Never ever used to eat eggs," the young man sat opposite him stated, adding, "they do make me fart."

"You don't fart tonight if you're anywhere near me."

"Still," the lad went on, "think how lucky we all are. In civvy-street we'd only get one, two a month," he stuffed more bread into his mouth, and was temporarily quiet.

Simon sipped his coffee… and remembered his cottage at Runswick. When the war was over they could all go back there, and he'd have decorators from Whitby do inside and out, and Rachel could choose whatever colours she wanted for her room, and if he could rent a field, he'd buy her a pony, and a puppy.

But he must return to what was happening now, for very soon he would need to put on his flying boots and jacket—and the skipper gave his last-minute instructions—and an hour later he climbed into the aircraft, gave the thumbs-up sign to the skipper, then felt queasy in the pit of his stomach. He took deep breaths. In three hours he would be over the target—and the night's destruction could begin.

He looked again at his watch. In seven-and-a-half minutes they would be over Berlin. Again he told himself it was all a game. Nobody was going to get "hurt". No real casualties or fatalities, they'd all get up and walk away when it was over, the pilot would turn tail and head for England, and the following morning the night's bombing would all be forgotten.

If only life were so simple!

They would go in with the first wave, and if they were hit? Well, someone else would get a free run-in. In addition to the markers there were several tons of bombs on board. He turned the oxygen full on—the defences were suddenly waking up to what was about to happen to them. Beams from great searchlights were slicing through the blackness, coming together then dividing like dancers. Flashes of light were appearing on the starboard like fluorescent baubles from cascading Roman candles on bonfire night.

The skipper's voice came over. "Two minutes to go. Can you see anything?"

But there was no sign of the early flare-droppers, and as Simon began to have this "doubt" below them and to starboard were little balls of golden light. The first path-finder flares were down. Then more appeared, their light showing a river, a railway station, then the *Templehof*, the rest of the city spreading out to starboard. The aircraft swung round, before leveling out for its final bombing run, Simon could feel the adrenalin, then a sudden state of euphoria. Time and the world standing still, the target before them, and his thumb on the release mechanism. Little balls of light were still, almost defiantly, dancing far below them, and again the searchlights sprang to life. Then a little green worm appeared in the sky, and wiggled earthward, and there were crosses of light on the bombsight, and bright splashes as photographs were being taken, the dull lights being the "cookies", the quick spurts the guns firing and the 500-pounders bursting.

Then red markers were creeping up under the aircraft, and at a word from Simon were moved a little to the right, then with all his might he squeezed with his thumb, forcing the button down. The light from the bomb switch went off. "Bombs away!"—and he peered forward, to see them black and shiny in the glare of the searchlight. There arose angry red pools of smoke, white flashes, and again the dancing beams of light cutting the night sky. Red flak bursts, and a voice over the intercom telling them their new course, and the aeroplane rose sharply, dipping one wing toward the clouds of smoke that had been Berlin. Then they saw something burning in the sky before it blew up, the pieces falling to earth lit up from the arcs of light below.

The night's mission a success, they must now head for home, and at last across the German coast and back to base, where they circled at 4000 feet to await the code word to tell them there were no Hun night fighters who might have sneaked back with the returning bombers hoping to shoot them down as they came in to land. Below them was the flare-path with a double-row of lights, and minutes later Simon's plane was bumping along the runway.

"Are we all back?" was the question on every man's lips, and they were, except one that was still hovering overhead.

It was a quick wash, and back to the mess—for bacon and eggs!

A week later, enjoying a welcome 48 hour leave three airmen with their "daddy" were surveying the sights of a war-torn London. Everywhere was destruction or disruption, with whole streets demolished and a London transport which was at best erratic at worst non-existent. Most public buildings were closed, as were cafes, restaurants and places of entertainment save for the one that, like a magnet drew the lads in uniform, the Windmill, and after making much show of pretending to blindfold Alan, the nineteen-year-old and baby among them, the four men settled down for a show to be remembered.

Afterwards they found a bar that had (but, they reasoned, beggars could not be choosers) warm beer with a flat head to it, then one of them suggested that they return to the theatre for another two hours of heaven-in-the-nude.

They were out for pleasure, to briefly escape the hell of war, and in this were successful: even Simon Howarth was enjoying himself.

"Eee, Evelyn, doy—there's some women in Steeas look better in gas-masks than they do withaht 'em"—and Mannie, who was becoming quite a comedian, smiled at his own observation.

"Onybody in mind?"

"Well, ah'll bet there's one or two tha could mention, but tha can tell me later, fer ah'm up ter me eyes in it—ah'm fair throng."

Even though fishing and the like had been seriously affected, Mannie somehow or other kept busy, and he looked at the sack containing the still-alive crustaceans trying to escape, then recited, for the benefit of Rachel, "this little crab went to market, this little crab stayed in Stecas. This little crab went ter Skinningrove, an this little crab… went ter Saltburn." Then, looking at Evelyn he said sorrowfully "corn beef fritters! 'Missis says we need a change thro corned beef stew or corned beef pancakes. Bloody corned beef! Last week it wor corned beef rissoles, then corned beef wi' cabbage—I ask yer! Eee, when this war's over, hun, I'll 'ave a gurt side o' beef all ter mysel'," and licked his lips at the thought of such a luxury.

But it was common knowledge that Mannie and his family were living better than most, for the cooking smells emanating from the kitchen window were not simply "corned beef" dishes, as he led people to believe, nor was Florence the dreadful cook be jokingly described her. "My dear Florence is the only woman I know that can burn a pan o' watter," and he'd keep a straight face waiting for his audiences reaction—a rare one, was Mannie.

As Evelyn climbed the steep cliff path toward Runswick she also thought about when the war would be over and Simon would be home.

She'd have no need then to call at his cottage every few days to make sure that all was well, for he'd be there himself, and perhaps they'll all live together as before. She could remember—but she was being haunted by memories… of herself as a young woman being a model for Laura Johnson and some of the other group of painters. Paid a few pence for sitting still for a morning, and, she recalled, one of the artists, Rowland Henry Hill was still in the area, and she'd seen him only weeks ago, and he'd recognised her and spoken to her.

He was older, much older—but so was she.

No-one would want to paint her now, an old woman with a scrawny neck and more lines on her face then a railway station. Ooohh, time was cruel!

She sucked on a peppermint—no time to feel sorry for herself, she had far too much to do.

She turned the key, and once inside the cottage began her weekly ritual. She lit a fire, then washed the windows and scrubbed and donkey-stoned the front step, not that there were ever callers, except herself and occasionally the postman, and the outside looking presentable, Evelyn then concerned herself with her inside chores. A dust round, then her usual glance at the contents of the cupboards. Save for the odd tin of food even she was not desperate to try, they were bare. He'd have to stock up when he came home, that would be one of his first jobs, and she sighed as she remembered tins of peaches, the almond macaroons he bought in London, and the marzipan fruits in fancy boxes, and hand-made chocolates. Oh, a lifetime away, but the memory (and the taste) lingered.

Then she went up to his room to inspect his army of laundered shirts and fancy London suits—she'd have to keep his bed aired, because one never knew, he could suddenly be home on leave, or the bloody war could be over—now that would be a day for celebrations!

He'd be able to get to know Rachel properly, not as an "uncle" but as her father, for there were so many things he—the family—needed to put right.

But that would happen, it would all come right, given time.

She took a different route back to the village through the fields, then joined the road as top of the bank came into view, and the now familiar sight in and around the village, the band of volunteers known as the Home Guard. Vigilant in their defence of the stretch of coastline, also trained in first-aid, rescue work and incident control—they were becoming a force to reckoned with, and being comprised of, in the main, men from Staithes, guarding the village for the inhabitants of Staithes. It was their village, and they were going to defend it, and antics that had earlier been looked on in bewilderment were now regarded as commonplace, and no eyebrows were raised as they were seen on manoeuvres.

There were still reports of German atrocities and bombings, the latest at nearby Grinkle Park and also in Redcar where several houses had been demolished, and as Evelyn looked around her she told herself that if Hitler ever did reach Staithes he'd feel cheated and disappointed, and would ask himself what the war had been about.

Then, on a bright sunny morning with a calm sea and a clear horizon the telegram arrived—and she knew before she opened it what she was going to read, and it was as she had feared, dreaded—and she wished that the day had never dawned. After a successful bombing raid, and only minutes from safety, his and another Westland Lysander had been shot down. There were no survivors.

Her son was dead!

She stared at the telegram, and suddenly felt an old woman.

Death seemed easy—it was living that was difficult!

Seeing young men Simon's age going about their daily business, the cottage in Runswick full of now painful memories, or she would remember some seemingly innocent remark Simon had made about wanting his brother's wife—and her thoughts then turned to Rachel, who was now alone in the world save for her grandmother. She had never "known" her father, just an uncle Simon who was kind and generous, and bought and gave her anything she wanted.

Simon had planned, said he would tell her when she was old enough to understand... and Evelyn wondered if that day would dawn when her granddaughter would learn the truth.

But there were more pressing things to attend to, the necessary realities.

The cottage. And his clothes, books, personal effects, then there were his financial affairs, but she knew that here he had left nothing to chance, his daughter would one day be a rich young woman, being the last of the dynasty, and Evelyn told herself, she must now alter her own arrangements, there being no-one but her granddaughter to inherit the Lizzie Howarth fortune.

Then came the news the country was waiting for: the war was over!

At 3 pm, on 8th May, 1945, Winston Churchill addressed the nation, the radio broadcast a signal for the celebrations to begin. There was dancing in the streets and licensing laws were temporarily relaxed. Japan was still to be conquered, but the war in Europe would end at midnight—Staithes could get back to what it had been before the bloody war began!

Part IV 1951

MIRANDA.
O, wonder!
How many goodly creatures are there here!
How beauteous mankind is! O brave new world
That has such people in't!

The Tempest, Act V, scene 1.

Chapter 27

There was eventually a return to what was so-called "normal"—no more bombing, no more air-raid shelters, no more rationing, and for the fishermen of Staithes, their only battle was with the sea itself. News filtered through (but was of interest only to those who could remember the Staithes painters) that one of the group, Laura Johnson, or Dame Laura Knight as she was now known had been a War Artist for the Nuremberg War Trials, and with her husband Harold was still living in London in St John's Wood, wherever that was. On her earlier trip with Hannah, they'd never quite been able to find it—a wood in the middle of London didn't seem possible to her.

It seemed that the long-awaited happier times were coming, for there was a "Festival of Britain" then two years later London and the whole country was celebrating, for it was Coronation year. With street parties being held in every town and village, and the whole country being caught up in coronation euphoria, Staithes must also join in, there were decorated floats, and a fancy dress parade, with Mannie looking like Neptune waving a three pronged fork and surrounded by plump mermaid attendants. Mannie looked older—everybody was looking older!

Over the coming months Evelyn told herself yet again that there must be an "easier way" and with her granddaughter now ready to make her own mark on the world, she finally decided that it was time she also "made a move"—to one of the new houses being built at the top of the bank. There would be hot and cold running water, a bathroom, inside toilet—even a front garden, not that she wanted to grow anything—and she would become known not only as "proper Steeas" (having been born and bred in the village) but also, because to where she was to move to, a "Lane Ender".

Rachel, who was now (and another thing for her grandmother to boast about) a "State Registered Nurse" and working in a hospital in Scotland, was delighted when she heard of the intended move, and (because "reception" would be so much better at the top of the bank) bought "Gran" a television as a house-warming present, and so that they could keep in contact daily if need be: a black impressive-looking instrument with a plaited cord which was proudly displayed in the front window. Not every house in Staithes had a telephone: this was something to boast about!

But she was a "Lane Ender"—a world away from fishwives who spent summer afternoons sat outside their house knitting, or in the evenings would be lulled by the sound of the fishermen's choir as they practised in one of the chapels. A few hundred yards away, but a lifetime apart!

Chapter 28

Evelyn glanced at the clock, then mentally calculated. Phoning from Saltburn, she'd said "about twenty minutes" and that would be… well, any time now, and Evelyn suddenly remembered the taste of haggis, which was one of the things Rachel always brought with her. Haggis and oatcakes, for as she always joked "when in Rome"—but despite two years north of the border, Rachel Howarth was still Yorkshire.

Oh, she'd done well for herself, for though she was now a theatre sister, Rachel's greatest achievement, in the eyes of her grandmother was that she had broken free of the constraints of Staithes—she was a person in her own right. Her mother had tried with a fancy education, but had been held back by being forced into an arranged marriage. Yet among her generation, it was "marry into Steeas or become an old maid", but for Rachel… and then she saw the apple-green Austin A40 pull up outside her front window, and seconds later heard the greeting, "I'm home, Gran."

"Come in, doy."

"Ooohhh, that road was busy—lots of tourists about this time of year."

"Oh, aye. Now, we'll 'ave a cup o' tea, an' then yer can tell me all yer news."

They chatted, then unable to keep her secret any longer Rachel burst out, "Gran, I've met this young man…"

"—Fancy!"

"Oh, I do. I fancy him something awful," then she giggled and took a photo from her handbag, and handing it to her grandmother went on to explain, "he's called Marcus—he's a house-surgeon. He's not long been at the hospital, because he's only recently qualified, and all the girls are mad about him, and—"

"I can see why."

"Oh, isn't he lovely. And he's…" and she swallowed, "in Saltburn. Well, he will be later this afternoon, he's coming by train, I wanted to tell you all about him first, to see if it was all right…"

"Ter coom an stop wi' us? 'Course it's reight, doy. Yer see, it's nooan like Ring o' Bells—we've all 'mod cons' nah."

"Marcus's father is a doctor, in Chelmsford. He's not asked me to marry him yet… but…"

"Yer more na' 'acquaintances'?"

"Yes—but while he's staying here—"

210

"I'll put yer booath in 'back bedroom," and Evelyn look at the photograph again. Her granddaughter had chosen well.

"Next month, when Marcus gets paid… we're going to buy an engagement ring, if that's all right."

The old woman nodded in agreement.

"So," and feeling especially happy, Rachel suddenly suggested, "shall we go down into the village? If walking down the bank's difficult, we could go in car."

"No, let's walk, doy—for ah want all Steeas ter see thee… an' tha' mun show Marcus off when 'ee arrives."

As the two of them picked their way carefully along the cliff path toward High Barrass, Evelyn was again haunted by ghosts from her past. Her two brothers, ringlets and rosy cheeked Polly, Old Rall and her crony Sair-Anne, the fishwives arguing, their strong, silent men, the auctioneer on the quayside selling their catch, the woman in Boathouse Yard who kept a monkey, and the artists who some sixty years previously had descended on the village and had immortalised it on canvas.

They'd walked down High Barrass steps and were standing on the Staithe, then they meandered along the sand as Rachel began leading her toward Penny Nab. Suddenly, she stopped. "Oohh look, Gran—little baby crabs," and she paused staring into the rock pool, and watched them scurry and bury themselves among the trails of seaweed. "Magic," she pronounced it.

"Oh aye," her grandmother agreed, "fer 'ere' s the power o' magic power. The Staithes group tried ter capture it on their canvases, but it's still 'ere."

Evelyn looked around her, a voice from the past was being carried on the wind. "One an' thrup'nce? Who'll gi'e me one an' thrup'nce? There was Hannah, her father, one of the locals with a concertina, her two lads squabbling over a bag of humbugs—and Old Rall looking on, nodding her head and pronouncing her usual, "Nea, nea."

Staithes as it used to be.

"One an' thrup'nce?"—such memories were priceless!